Franko Blade of the Shattered Star

Matthew Linton

Matthew Linton

Book Cover by Jeff Dehut

To my endlessly patient wife, Sheila. Thank you for everything you do.

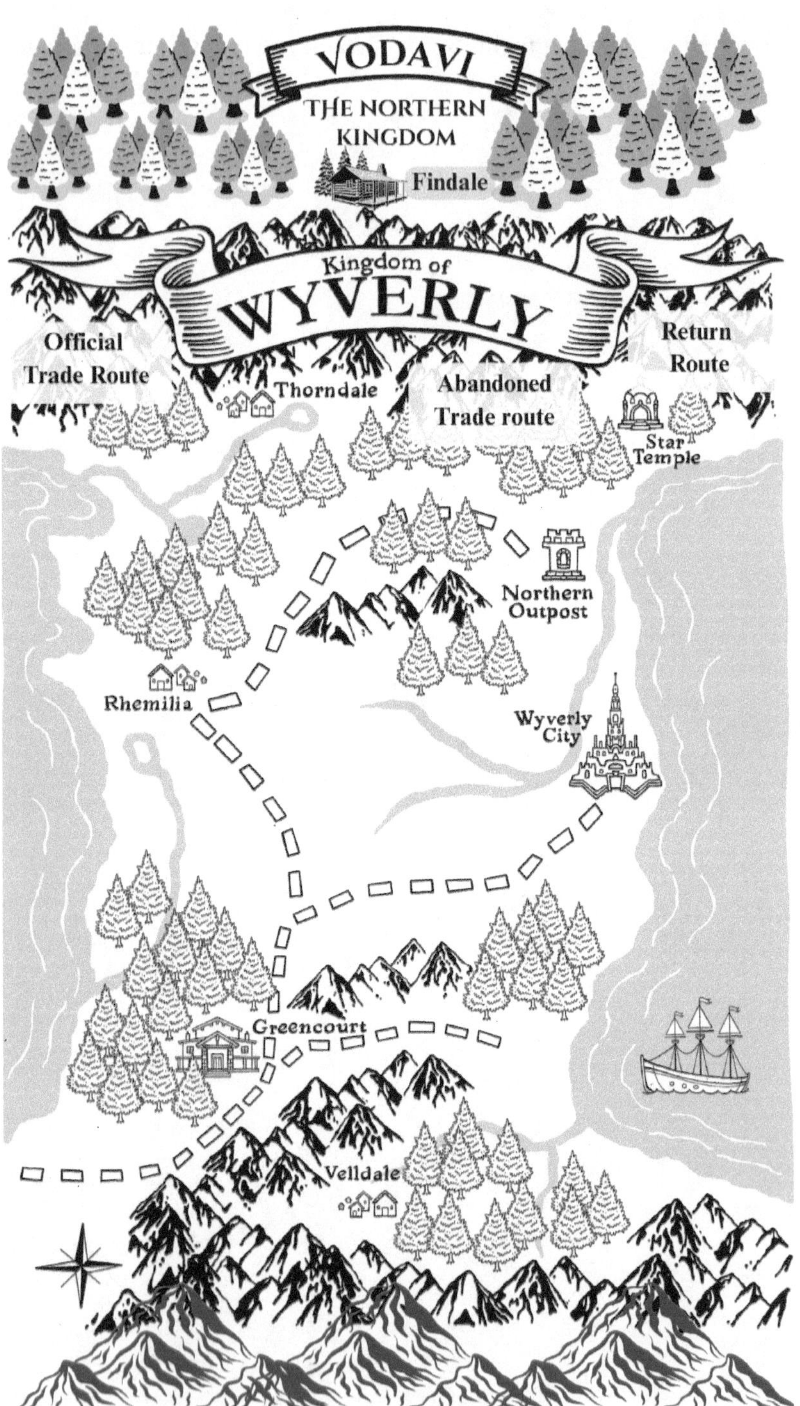
VODAVI
THE NORTHERN KINGDOM
Findale
Kingdom of
WYVERLY
Official Trade Route
Return Route
Thorndale
Abandoned Trade route
Star Temple
Northern Outpost
Rhemilia
Wyverly City
Greencourt
Velldale

Contents

He's Out Here

"We've been searching for three days, soldier," Captain Aldo said with a tinge of irritation in his voice. "Are you sure he's out here, Gwendolyn?"

"I'm positive, and it's just Gwen now, Captain," she replied, still looking off into the distance, clutching her cloak to keep it wrapped over her body. "And I'm not a soldier anymore."

It was a cold and rainy afternoon in the northern forest. Gwen had been working with Captain Aldo and the others to track Franko down. She wouldn't tell anybody why it was exactly that she felt the need to do so, but either way, Franko was a highly respected and valuable member of the Wyverly Guard, and they wanted him back.

"It just seems like we would have found something by now, at least some trace of him somewhere out here," Aldo replied, shaking his head in frustration.

Gwen finally turned towards him, her jaw tightened. "He's—out here," she said adamantly.

"What makes you so sure of this?" he asked, sternly. "He could have run off with that woman to stars' know where. You said so yourself, remember? We're on the border of Vodavi; we've got to be careful. Relations with the Northern Kingdom are better than they were, but still not—"

"I told you, he's out here!" she cut him off sharply.

Captain Aldo sighed and ran his fingers through his hair. "Okay, I guess we'll just keep looking," he replied in resignation as he turned to walk back toward camp to join the others.

Gwen closed her eyes and exhaled sharply. She was beginning to lose her patience; they all were. *Franko,* she thought to herself, *where in stars' light are you? I know you're here. It's time to come home. You... are coming with me.*

Unbeknownst to them, a hooded figure stood watching from the treetops.

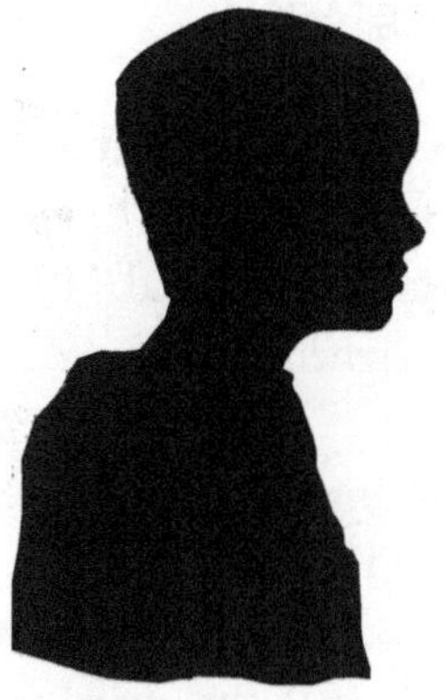

Chapter 1

Closest Thing to Home

"The stars are smiling upon us today, Franko!" Ringo hollered excitedly as he approached his young son, a sack full of goodies in hand.

"Father!" the boy exclaimed, his face beaming. "What happened? What did you get?"

"Well, son, all those lead sticks you helped me get have just turned quite the profit," Ringo remarked, wiggling his eyebrows with a coy smirk on his face as he set the sack down in front of his son. "All the way out here in Greencourt, they don't have easy access to lead like they do at the Wyverly Capital. So they pay, and they pay good!"

"That's great, Father!" the boy giggled with excitement. "So, what's in the bag?"

"I think you'll need to open up and find that out for yourself, Franko," Ringo replied, trying but failing to hold back a smile.

Franko peeked in the sack to find a bag of hard candy and a wooden play sword as long as his arm. "Father!" he yelled, unable to contain his excitement. "Berry candy and a sword!" the boy said with his eyes wide open, his jaw practically hitting the ground. "I haven't had sweets like this in so long! Not since my eighth birthday. And this sword, it looks brand new!"

"It *is* brand new, Franko," Ringo chuckled. "Think of this as a little reward for helping your dear old dad out so much."

The boy quickly popped a berry candy in his mouth, the sweetness overpowering his taste buds. He took the sword and tucked it in his belt before looking through the rest of the sack. It was amazing; they hadn't had a payday like this in ages: a couple of new changes of clothes for both him and his father, some cured meat, a couple of canteens, and what appeared to be an old, tarnished, broken sword.

Franko held the sword up and looked at it, a puzzled expression on his face. "What's this doing here? Is this for me too?"

Ringo's countenance dropped at the sight, his smile fading into a frown. "Uhh... no, son... that's... that's for me," he said somberly as he reached for the broken sword and looked at it, a melancholy expression upon his face.

"Is everything okay, Father?" the boy asked, concerned.

Ringo let out a weary sigh and stroked his short beard thoughtfully. "Yes, son. I'm fine," he replied softly as he set the sword down gently in the front seat of the wagon.

"Why do you have that sword, Father? What good is a broken blade?"

Ringo lifted his ten-year-old son and set him down on the wagon's tailgate. "Franko," his father said gently, placing his hands on the boy's shoulders. "I think it may be time to tell you about our family. About our past and what happened to your mother."

The boy looked intently at his father, "Mother? You said she got sick and died when I was a baby."

"Yes, son. I know that's what I told you. But it's not exactly the truth."

"Wha... what's the truth, then?" the boy asked, dread welling up in his eyes.

"Do you remember me telling you about the Garelian rebels, Franko?"

"Yes," the boy nodded. "They were bad people who worshipped a demon, right?"

"That's right, Franko," his father nodded. "There's an old fairytale in the land that says a Demon King named Garel once terrorized the kingdom of Wyverly. The legend says he was defeated several thousand years ago."

"Yes, I've heard all this. The Star Sage sealed him away, but there's people out there now that worship him," the boy added.

"There are, son. They call themselves the Garelians, they think he was really a god, and the kingdom lied and said he was evil," Ringo sighed as he shook his head. "They believe that he'll come back someday, and they want to be there to greet him when he does. They think he'll honor them as loyal followers and rule the land with him."

"But that's just a fairytale, right Father?" the boy asked, his eyebrows furrowed. "It's not real, right?"

"No, son. But they still believe in it. They're dangerous, that's why the kingdom banned Garelians ages ago. We're only allowed to worship the stars. But some Garelians still exist."

"Oh," Franko responded, taken aback by his father's words. "So... what does this have to do with Mother?"

"Franko," his father said, looking intently into the boy's eyes. "I told you that your mother got sick. But that's not exactly the truth." Ringo paused and clenched his eyes shut, fighting back tears. "When you were still a baby, she left to visit some family, and she was found dead shortly thereafter. I believe the Garelians were behind it."

Franko's heart sank into his gut. "The Garelians? Why?" he asked desperately.

Ringo bit his lip, bitterness twisting his face. "It's hard to explain, son. It's just me and you now."

This revelation paralyzed Franko. He had always thought his mother died of a sickness, but it turns out she had been murdered. Tears streamed down the boy's face. "I don't understand, Father."

Ringo began to sob the words out softly. "It's just best not to think of it, Franko. It's a very painful thing for me to say. I just felt you should know."

The boy's lip began to quiver. Ringo pulled the boy into his embrace. "I'm sorry, son. Please know that you will always have me. I will love you always, Franko," he said through his tears, offering what comfort he could to his heartbroken young son.

The boy rubbed the tears from his face, his heart lifting slightly as he found some relief in his father's comforting words. "Does what you just told me have something to do with that broken sword, Father?" asked the boy as he sniffled.

"It does, Franko," his father answered in a low voice, wishing his son had never seen the sword. "That sword was broken in a battle we fought with the man who I believe killed your mother. He and some other Garelians had attacked us once when we went out traveling, not long before you were born. During the battle, the sword was broken by a man who fought with a large axe, his name is Lace. He considers himself the high priest of the Garelians and is an extremely dangerous man."

The name pierced Franko's ears when he heard it, *Lace*. "Is that man the one who killed mother?"

"Yes, Franko. I'm almost certain of it," he replied softly, pulling a piece of parchment out of his satchel. "I stayed in Greencourt for a time after you were born with the hope that she would soon come back. But after a short while, I was given this letter by a courier for the kingdom. I think you're old enough to read this yourself."

The young boy's heart began to race as he opened the letter. It was from the Wyverly Guard, addressed to his father.

To Ringo the merchant. Last known location, Greencourt.

It is with the Royal Guard's deepest regret that we inform you that a Wyverly patrol had located a mortally wounded woman along the northern path of the kingdom. We did all we could to treat her injuries and take her to the nearest town. But sadly, she succumbed to her injuries and passed away during transport. She had stated before she passed that she was the wife of a traveling merchant known as

Ringo, who was last known to be staying in Greencourt. She requested that a message be sent to you to make you aware of her passing. Sadly, we were unable to get any information or description of her attacker.

You have our sincerest condolences. May the stars grant you peace during this trying time.

Office of the Wyverly Guard

Franko began to sob, and his father embraced him. “I’m sorry that you had to find out like this, Franko. I know she loved you dearly,” he assured the boy.

"I sold that sword for a few coppers shortly after. It wasn't worth much, but I figured a metal worker might have some use for it. You see, son, your mother and I lived here in Greencourt for a little while. You were born in this town, Franko."

The boy's eyes widened, and he wiped the tears from his cheeks with his sleeve. “Really?" he asked. "You mean, this is kind of like our home?"

Being traveling merchants, Ringo and his son were on the road constantly. They never had a real home and spent most nights sleeping under the stars. Though Franko wasn't one to complain, he couldn't help but long for a place to call home.

"You could say that, Franko," his father replied, life returning to his eyes as the conversation returned to a more pleasant topic. "This is the closest thing we've ever had to a home, anyway."

“I tell you what, son. Would it cheer you up if we walked around town for a bit? Maybe I can get you a few more pieces of berry candy,” Ringo said as he tilted his head with raised eyebrows.

"Can we, Father?" he asked, his eyes now beaming with excitement and longing.

"Of course, son," Ringo said as he tousled the boy's hair and set him back on the ground. "Some of the folks here still remember me. It's not every day a baby is delivered at the town bed-and-breakfast, ya know."

Ringo put his arm around his son's shoulders, and they walked into Greencourt, the closest thing Franko could call home.

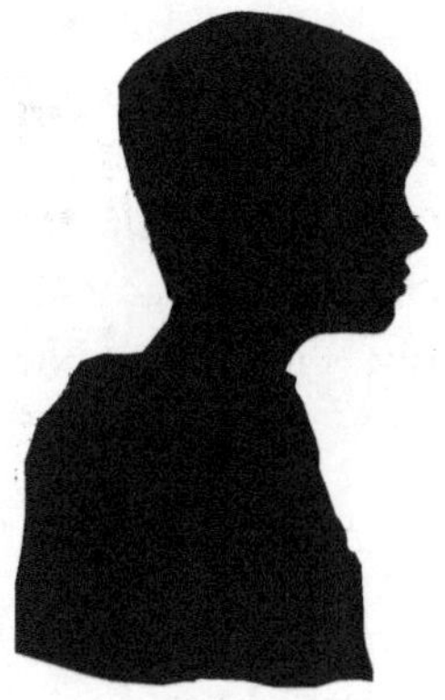

Chapter 2

The Broken

As Ringo and his son made their way through Greencourt, he showed him the bed-and-breakfast where he had been born ten years earlier. Mr. and Mrs. Chambers had taken it over just before Franko's birth. They were thrilled to see the boy return for a visit and to see how he had grown into a handsome young lad. While they were still making their way through town, young Franko spotted some children kicking a ball around a field off in the distance.

He looked to his father, who was busy talking to some townsfolk. "Father, I'm going to go see what those children are doing."

Ringo pulled himself away from the conversation just long enough to give his son a nod of approval. Franko nervously approached the group of kids. He hadn't often played with children his age because he and his father were always on the move, never staying in one place for long. As he approached, his eyes met an adorable young girl with light brown hair tied in pigtails who appeared to be about the same age as him. She met his gaze and smiled politely. The girl walked toward Franko, noticing he was watching them from a safe distance.

"Hey there. I don't think I've ever seen you around here before," she said warmly. "My name's Gwendolyn, what's your name?"

The boy swallowed nervously, "I'm Franko. Nice to meet you, Gwendolyn," he replied, doing his best to remember the good manners his father had drilled into him.

"Franko? That's a cute name, I like it."

A smile crossed Franko's face. "Thank you. I like your name, too, Gwendolyn. It's a very pretty name," he said softly as he found himself mesmerized by her bright blue eyes. She was quite possibly the most beautiful girl he had ever seen in his entire ten years of living.

Gwendolyn let out a quick giggle. "Thank you. Would you like to join us in a game?"

He looked nervously at the field and the other children playing, then back at Gwendolyn. "I would be happy to. But I haven't played many games. I don't really know the rules."

Gwendolyn covered her mouth to stifle a giggle. "You've never played rushball, Franko? I think you may be the first boy I've ever met who's never played before."

Franko's face flushed with embarrassment, and he looked down and anxiously rubbed the back of his neck. "I'm sorry. We are always traveling, I don't ever get to do things like this."

Gwendolyn giggled again. "You're silly. I'm just teasing, Franko," she held her hand out for him to grab. "Come with me, we'll show you how to play. We just split into teams and try to kick the ball into the other team's goal. That's pretty much it."

Franko's heart raced as he hesitantly grabbed her hand. He had never held a girl's hand before; it felt soft and warm—comforting. He arrived on the makeshift pitch and became anxiously aware of all the other kids looking at him. He tried to act as if he hadn't noticed and jumped in with Gwendolyn and the rest to play.

As much as he would have liked to say that things went well, they sadly did not. Franko didn't understand things like ball control or passing, so every time the ball came close, he would kick it as hard as he could—much to his teammates' dismay. To nobody's surprise, Franko and his team lost badly.

Among other things, he didn't understand the concept of keeping score or winning and losing; he was just glad he got to play with Gwendolyn. His teammates lost their patience quickly and left after the game, without even saying goodbye. All of them, that is, except for Bruno.

"Thanks a lot, *new kid*," Bruno snarled as he approached. He was about a head taller than Franko and likely a couple of years older.

"Sorry, I didn't know the rules," Franko said cautiously. "I'll do better next time."

"There won't be a *next time*," Bruno snapped back.

"Cut it out, Bruno," Gwendolyn interjected. "I told him he could play, and we would help him out. I guess I should have warned him about you," she said with a bite to her voice.

"Well, maybe *you* should have told *us* about *him* instead," he remarked as he scrunched his fat nose at her. "I guess you didn't need to, though. I saw his dad at the shop earlier; he bought some useless piece of junk from Father's scrap pile," he said as he directed his gaze back to Franko. "Father talked to his dad for a while. Talked about his family and how this kid was born here. Like that makes him one of us," he huffed.

Franko tensed up; he was prepared to defend his father's honor if this brat said anything bad about him. "What are you talking about, Bruno?" he asked, his jaw clenched.

"From what I heard, it sounds like your dad bought a useless, broken blade. Figures," he said derisively. "A broken blade for a broken man with a broken family and a broken boy."

Franko didn't hesitate and punched the boy square in his nose. "Don't talk about my Father that way!" he snapped.

Bruno grabbed his nose, eyes watering and filled with rage. "You little—" he was about to charge Franko when he stopped in his tracks and caught Gwendolyn's furious glare. He then realized he had messed up badly.

"What did you just say about a *broken family*, Bruno?" she hissed, eyes full of rage.

Bruno held up his hands defensively, "Oh, no. Gwendolyn, I... I didn't mean it like—"

His plea for peace was interrupted by another punch right in the nose. But this time, it was an enraged Gwendolyn who delivered it.

Bruno fell back, crying. He looked pleadingly at Gwendolyn, then ran home, screaming. "I'm telling Mother!"

Gwendolyn turned back to Franko, "I'm sorry about that," she said warmly. "Bruno's my big brother, he's not a bad kid once you get to know him."

Franko still stood frozen at the sight of Gwendolyn punching Bruno right in the face. "Umm... I guess I'll just have to take your word for it," he said cautiously.

"Good," she replied with a proud smile. "Well, it was nice meeting you, Franko. How long will you be in Greencourt for?"

"I'm not sure, really, a day or two maybe. We usually don't stay anywhere long, unless there's some work for us to do."

"What kind of work does your father do, Franko?" she asked as she picked up the leather ball.

Franko hesitated. *What do we do, exactly?* he asked himself. "Whatever we have to. We do everything."

Gwendolyn looked at him skeptically. "Okay, well, here," she said as she tossed the ball to him. "Maybe you can put *getting better at rushball* on your list of *everything*," she replied with a playful smile. "We're going to play again tomorrow, and this time, I don't want to lose."

"Okay," Franko said, his cheeks flushed again. "I'll make sure to practice some this evening," he said as he examined the ball. "I hope we can be on the same team again."

"Only if you show me that you've been practicing," she responded as she walked away, her pigtails bouncing on her shoulders.

Gwendolyn, he thought to himself. *She's so pretty... I have to learn how to play this game.*

Franko made his way to the woods nearby, on the outskirts of town. He still had the ball that Gwendolyn had tossed at him. He started practicing his kicks, dribbling, and passing as best he could, into the evening. He pretended some trees were his teammates and others his opponents, kicking the ball back and forth and weaving between them.

He used two trees spaced several feet apart as a pretend goal. He didn't stop until his aim was nearly perfect. By the time the sun had set, he was far from an expert, but had a much better handle on rushball than he had earlier that day. He was drenched in sweat, but could successfully aim and target a pinecone and kick it off a tree more often than not. It was growing dark, and with his spirits high, Franko decided it was time to return to his father.

He headed to the bed-and-breakfast to meet his father. Upon entering the room, he saw him sitting in a chair with the broken sword in his lap. He looked to be in deep thought as he stared out the window into the moonlight.

"What have you been up to, son?" he said, his voice sounding stoic.

Franko's eyes darted around the room nervously; he couldn't tell if his father was upset or sad. "I was just playing with some new friends I made, that's all."

Ringo nodded slowly. "*Friends*," he said with a bitter chuckle. "They can be little more than a liability if you aren't careful," he added, a tinge of bitterness in his voice. “I heard someone saying that you punched another boy today after he taunted you. I thought I taught you not to let words drive you to violence, Franko.”

“I'm sorry, Father,” the boy remarked sheepishly as he looked down in embarrassment. “I'll do better.”

“I know you will, son,” Ringo replied gently, still gazing out the window beside him.

Franko couldn't help but notice how his father had been acting differently ever since he got that sword back. The boy was nervous about bringing it up, but he couldn't squelch his curiosity. "Father," he asked pensively, "why did you get that sword back?"

Ringo straightened up in his chair and slowly shifted his gaze toward Franko. "I don't know, son. I don't think I have a good answer for that. Like I said, after I escaped those men who attacked your mother and me, I came back here to Greencourt. I decided to sell it for some copper to buy a little bit of food." He closed his eyes and inhaled sharply. "When we came back by earlier today, I stopped by the shop I sold it to all those years ago. I saw that the shopkeeper still had it in his scrap pile. I couldn't bear to see it that way, all rusted and tarnished, discarded like trash. So I bought it back. I don't know if that makes sense or not, but that's what I did," he said with an edge to his voice. "It's broken, but it still means something to me."

Franko recalled the words Bruno had said to him in anger earlier that day: *A broken blade for a broken man with a broken family and a broken boy.*

"Father," the boy asked hesitantly, "what does it mean if a *person* is broken?"

Ringo's eyebrows furrowed as he looked at his son, a mixture of irritation and confusion on his face. "The same thing it means if anything else is broken, Franko. It's of no use to the world. Trash." He sighed and held the broken blade across his hands. "A man is a blade, son. When it's sharp, the world respects it. But when it breaks, the world discards it. The world is cruel to a broken blade. We, Franko, are *broken*."

***

As Franko lay in bed that night, he thought back on the eventful day. The embarrassing game of rushball, the confrontation with Bruno... and Gwendolyn. *I practiced for hours. I wonder if I'll be able to impress her?* He asked himself. *Will she notice? Does she like me? Will she want to be my friend?*

Then the still silence of the small country town evening seemed suddenly deafening. His mind shifted as he began to recall what his father had told him earlier that day, before rushball, before Gwendolyn. What he had said about his mother's death and the words in that letter. *They found her on the side of the road... she died during transport.*

"Mother..." he whispered as a tear rolled down his cheek. "I wonder what kind of person you were. What were you like? What did you look like? I bet you were as kind as you were beautiful. Father won't tell me anything about you. He hasn't even told me your name. He gets so unsettled whenever you're brought up, and nothing unsettles him."

The boy turned restlessly from one side to another, trying to choke back his tears. "You must have been so scared back then... so lonely... Is that how you felt when you died? Were you alone? Were you in pain? I'm so sorry. I wish I could have been there with you. That at the very least I could have been by your side to hold your hand. To tell you that I love you. I'm sorry you died alone, Mother. It makes me so sad for you. I'm... so... sorry," he mumbled, the words dribbling out of his mouth as he gave in to sleep.

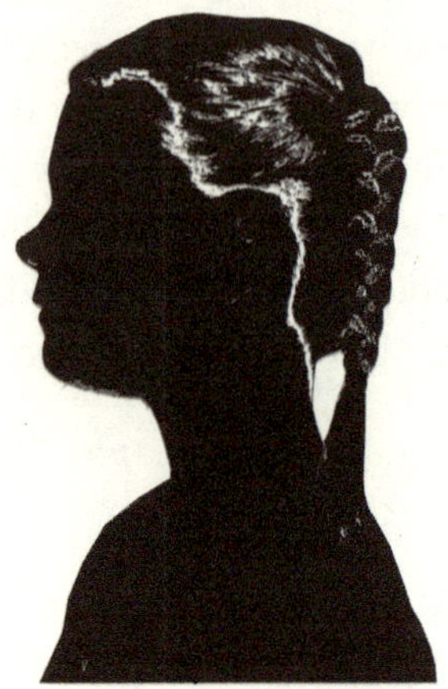

Chapter 3

One Thing I Can Do

Franko got up early the next day and spent the morning helping his father with some chores. The two didn't say much to each other. He felt that his father was almost intentionally avoiding eye contact with him. *Father, you were acting so strange yesterday. I hope you feel better.*

Once he was done helping with the chores, Franko went to see if he could find Gwendolyn and the others. He felt far more prepared than he had yesterday.

It didn't take long before the children all congregated on the field again. Franko stood nearby, slightly anxious about his lingering embarrassment from the day before, but confident that he had gotten much better.

He saw Bruno standing with some boys at the other end; like Ringo, he was avoiding eye contact with him. *I'm pretty sure I know why*, he thought with a smirk.

As they began to pick teams, nobody wanted to choose Franko, as he suspected. He still stood confidently, and when Gwendolyn looked his way, he raised his eyebrows and gave her a knowing nod.

She smiled and nodded back. "I'll take the new boy again," she said, to her teammates' dismay.

As the game started, it was clear that Franko's hours of practice the evening before had paid off. He wasn't the best player on the field, but he could more than keep up, even dribbling the ball around Bruno, causing the big oaf to fall flat on his face at one point.

"I can tell you practiced, Franko," Gwendolyn said between breaths as she was running beside him down the field.

"I told you I would," he replied as he passed the ball to another boy. He then turned his attention to her. "If we win, you need to show me what else you do around here for fun."

"I would like that," she replied with a big smile. "But *only* if we win," she added playfully.

Just then, the boy passed the ball back to Franko. He dribbled down the field, avoiding the defenders, and kicked it between the goal markers. Game over.

As his teammates congratulated him, Franko saw Bruno with a pouty look on his face as he walked off with his friends.

"I guess that punch in the nose didn't change his attitude that much, did it?" Franko asked, smirking as the losers left.

"He's not that bad," Gwendolyn remarked. "I told you, he's nice once you get to know him. I think he'll come around. He's just embarrassed right now."

"Over losing or getting beat up by his sister?" Franko chuckled.

"Both, I'm sure," she giggled. "I'm sorry you saw that. I'm not the type of girl who just goes around punching people." She paused for a moment and reached for his hand again. "Well, we made a deal, didn't we?" she asked. "C'mon, let me show you around a little. I can show you the woods we like to play in."

As the two of them walked through the woods on the outskirts of town, Franko couldn't help but wonder what it was about Bruno's comment the day before that upset her so much. *Was it just to defend me? Was it about something else? Why did Bruno's words trigger that fire inside of her?*

"Gwendolyn, can I ask you something?" Franko said as he stepped over a small puddle.

"Is this still about what happened yesterday with Bruno?" she replied, anticipating the motive behind his question.

Franko paused for a moment. "I was just wondering why that upset you so much, that's all. You couldn't have been upset just because it made me mad." He looked over to Gwendolyn, whose face was downcast. "I mean, you don't need to tell me if you don't want," he said to assure her.

Gwendolyn sighed and gave him a quick nod. "It's okay. Bruno is a good brother, and his parents are good people. He just needs to learn when to shut up," she said with a wry smirk as she poked Franko in the side with her elbow and ran ahead of him.

"Where are you going?" Franko hollered with a chuckle as she sped on ahead.

"To the lake that we swim and fish in," she yelled over her shoulder, and kept running.

He finally caught up to her when they came to a small lake in the middle of the woods. Gwendolyn was standing on a large rock on the bank, waiting for him with a playful smile on her face.

He went and stood next to her as they stared out at the lake together for some time before Gwendolyn spoke up. "Franko," she said softly as her gaze met his. "Have you at least skipped rocks before?" she asked as she knelt to grab a smooth, flat stone nearby.

"That's one thing I can do!" he chuckled as he grabbed a stone himself.

"Good," she replied. "Let's see who can skip the most times. The winner gets to ask the loser a question."

"Sure. You can go first," remembering the manners Ringo had taught him: *ladies first, always.*

She threw her stone and, much to his surprise, managed to get four skips before sinking in the lake.

"You're really good at this, Gwendolyn," Franko remarked in amazement. He tossed his stone and only managed three skips.

"I win!" she declared. "So Franko, tell me about your family. Is it just you and your father?"

Franko swallowed nervously at her request. "It's just me and Father now. I don't really have much to say about my family," he replied uncomfortably.

"Well, can you tell me what brought you to Greencourt? Bruno said something about how you were born here. Why did you leave, and why did you come back?"

"I thought it was just supposed to be one question," he retorted playfully.

"Fair enough," she replied, tossing another stone. Only three skips this time.

Franko took his turn. Four skips.

"I win!" he said, pumping his fist in excitement.

"Fine," she sighed. "Go ahead."

"You said Bruno is your brother. How come you said *his parents* earlier when you were talking about them?"

Gwendolyn paused for a moment, she drew a deep breath, "I said Bruno was my brother, but he's not my *real* brother, he's my cousin. My aunt and uncle, Bruno's parents, adopted me a few years ago. My parents both died, and I was about to be sent off to an orphanage, but they took me in."

"I'm sorry. I'm glad you were able to stay in Greencourt, though," he replied. "What's your favorite thing to do?"

"One question, Franko," she answered, throwing another stone. Five skips.

"Five!" he gasped in disbelief. "I'll never beat that." He threw as hard as he could. Three skips.

"Where's your mother, Franko?" Gwendolyn asked, a smug smirk crossing her face.

"She died when I was a baby," he told her as he stared down at the lake water. "Father said some bad people killed her."

Gwendolyn's smirk instantly faded. "I'm sorry. Guess we've both lost someone." She threw again, skipping four times.

Franko took his turn, skipping only three again. "Go ahead," he said, hanging his head in resignation.

"What kind of stuff do you and your father do everyday?"

"Whatever we have to," he replied shortly.

Gwendolyn stiffened up. "That's not an answer, Franko. You know what I mean."

Franko groaned at Gwendolyn's persistence. He knew enough to know that he and his father were poor compared to most people, and was embarrassed to say it. "We travel across the kingdom, sometimes farther. We take whatever work we can get, we buy or trade stuff in one place and then try to sell it in another for a profit." He looked at her apprehensively, expecting her to look at him with the contempt people often have for the poor, or even worse, with pity.

"Oh, so you're merchants," she replied, eyebrows raised, as if she made some sort of clever connection.

Franko felt his body relax at her response. *She doesn't see me as just some poor boy*, he thought to himself. "Yes, that's sort of what we do."

"My turn," she said, skipping another stone. Four skips again.

Ugh, she's good. I'll never win again. He took his turn, five skips.

This time, it was Franko who wore a victorious smirk across his face. "So I was asking, what's your favorite thing to do?"

Gwendolyn swayed back and forth for a bit, looking up thoughtfully. "I like lots of things: picking flowers, swimming, rushball, singing..." Her voice trailed off as she tried to think of other things.

"You like singing?" he asked. "What kind of songs do you like to sing?"

"Remember the rules, Franko," she taunted, throwing another stone.

Five skips, again! Franko tossed his stone in frustration. Two skips. He hung his head and crossed his arms. "This isn't fun anymore," he pouted.

"You're only saying that because you're losing," Gwendolyn chided playfully. "My turn again. Bruno said earlier that you were born in Greencourt. I wanna know why you don't still live here. Where do you live?"

Franko's gut began to tie in knots. "We don't *live* anywhere. I told you, we travel. We spend most of our nights outside, sleeping under the stars. I like it that way," he replied with a bite in his voice.

"Oh," she replied. "So you're homeless?"

Homeless, the word cut through him like a blade. "No!" he snapped. "I'm not playing this stupid game anymore. I'm leaving." He turned sharply and stomped away.

"Franko, wait!" she hollered as she chased after him. "I'm sorry. I didn't mean it like that."

"It's okay, Gwendolyn," he replied, not bothering to look back at her as he kept walking. "It's getting late and Father's probably worried."

"Are you just going to let me walk home by myself?" she asked as she finally caught up to him.

"I think Father, and I just need to go after today," Franko said tersely.

"Franko, stop!" she shouted as she grabbed his arm. "I didn't mean anything by it. I'm sorry I made you angry. I like you, Franko. Please don't stay mad at me."

His expression softened slightly at Gwendolyn's plea. "I told you, Gwendolyn. It's okay. I just don't think we belong in a place like this."

"What's wrong with Greencourt, Franko?"

"Nothing. I just don't think we belong here," he replied. "Father and I, it's just been the two of us my whole life. I told you—We travel, we sleep under the stars, and I like it that way."

She held a playfully pouty look on her face, in hopes of cheering him up. "So you aren't still mad at me?" she asked as she batted her eyes.

"No," Franko chuckled. "I like you too, Gwendolyn. But we really do need to get ready to leave in the morning. But first," he added. "I'll walk you home."

"Good!" she replied excitedly as she skipped beside him.

Once they got to Gwendolyn's house, she stopped and turned toward him with her pinky raised.

"What are you doing?" Franko said with a confused giggle.

"Let's make a promise," she adamantly replied.

Franko blinked in bewilderment. "A promise? For what?"

"That we'll meet again," she said with an expectant expression on her face.

He wrapped his pinky around hers. "A promise that we'll meet again," he said with a confident nod. "I would like that."

The two parted ways, and Franko's heart leapt as he went to meet up with his father to help with the evening chores.

Chapter 4

Where There's Conflict, There's Opportunity

The next morning, they loaded the wagon up and bade farewell to the friendly townsfolk of Greencourt. Franko was hoping he would see them again, but feared that may never happen. But then he remembered the promise he had made to Gwendolyn. He would have to come back again; there was no question about it.

Ringo walked up to his son as the boy finished loading the wagon and slapped him playfully on the shoulder. "Good job getting that wagon sorted so quickly, Franko," he said with his cheery demeanor having returned. He looked around, then trained his focus on his son. "Son," he said in a voice so soft it was almost a whisper. "I'm sorry for the way I've been acting lately. I was just not myself. I hadn't been to this place since... since everything happened. It just messed with my head. We aren't broken, Franko. Do you understand?"

The boy nodded to appease his father, but deep down, he wondered if they, in fact, were broken. Without a home, without a mother, and without any plans beyond what the next day may bring.

"And there's something else I wanted to give you," Ringo added as he took off his necklace with a large star pendant on it. "Here, this belongs to you now," he said, putting it around his son's neck.

"Really?!" Franko asked, unable to hold back his excitement.

"Really," Ringo replied. "I won it in a card game many years ago. I think it's time to pass some of that good fortune on to the next generation."

Franko held the pendant in front of him, admiring the intricately designed gold and silver-colored star fastened to a thick, silvery base. "I love it, Father. Thank you."

"You are very welcome, son," Ringo replied as he tousled the boy's hair.

"Franko!" shouted a young female voice from the distance. The boy's eyes lit up as he saw Gwendolyn approaching. She was coming to say goodbye, just as she had said she would. But it appeared someone was with her—Bruno.

Franko smiled at Gwendolyn, then cast a hostile glare at Bruno, whose face was downcast. "I'm glad you stopped by, Gwendolyn," he said as the two embraced.

Bruno approached Franko sheepishly, looking down at the ground with his arms crossed. "Franko," he said softly, "I just wanted to tell you that I'm really sorry for the mean stuff I said. Please forgive me."

Franko nodded at the humbled boy. "Thank you, Bruno. I forgive you," he said as he patted the big oaf on the shoulder.

"Well, I'm glad that's out of the way," Gwendolyn said, her face practically glowing. "And Franko, don't forget our promise, you'll come back to see me again, right?"

He chuckled and nodded his head, "Of course. How could I forget a promise?"

“So where are you going to next?” she asked, leaning her head toward him in curiosity.

“Father had mentioned something about going to Vodavi,” he replied.

“Vodavi! The Northern Kingdom?” she said as she drew her head back in shock. “Aren’t they Wyverly’s enemy?”

“I guess,” Franko shrugged. “That doesn’t mean much to us. We go where Father thinks we have the best chance of finding good work. He said something about Vodavi cedar the other day.”

“How will you get there? I hear they've practically stopped all trade through the main route,” Bruno interjected.

“I don’t know,” Franko responded. “Father handles that stuff.”

“You’re not going through the forests, I hope. There’s Forest Folk out there.” Gwendolyn added, her hands clutched in front of her in concern. “I hear they attack merchants like you and your father.”

“They’re not like that,” Franko said matter-of-factly, shaking his head. “They do steal, but they usually aren’t violent. Father and I have run into them before. Nothing we can’t handle.”

"Is it true that Forest Folk can't talk?" Bruno asked.

"Not much, they just kind of talk with growls and whistles," Franko answered. "Father says that they're like *feral humans*. Whatever that means."

“Some travelers have also mentioned that deep in the forests, there’s a demon that lives there. Kind of like a forest guardian,” Bruno said ominously.

“Cut it out, Bruno,” Gwendolyn said with an exhausted sigh.

“It’s true, Gwendolyn. I know you’ve heard about it before, haven’t you, Franko?”

“I have,” he remarked, nodding his head in resignation. “But Father says he doesn’t believe in that stuff. Probably just another fairytale.”

“Told ya, Bruno,” Gwendolyn said tauntingly as she stuck her tongue out at him. “Now, quit trying to scare him. It’s not funny.”

“I’m just saying what I’ve heard,” Bruno replied defensively. “They’ve said there’s a demon deep in the forest. It stalks its human prey, then attacks, biting them in the neck and sucking their blood out.”

Franko and Gwendolyn both exchanged a look and chuckled. “Yes, I've heard that too, along with all kinds of other things,” he responded. “Father says that all just sounds like something out of a storybook.”

“I’m just saying that I don’t think you should go through the forest, Franko,” Bruno concluded. “Gwendolyn would be really upset if something happened to you.”

"Shut up, Bruno!" Gwendolyn grunted through her clenched teeth as she pinched him.

"Ouch! What did you do that for?" he said as he rubbed his hurting side.

“Whatever is out there, Father and I can handle it,” Franko interrupted. “For now, I just need to help him get ready.”

He turned toward Gwendolyn. “Gwendolyn, I’m going to keep my promise and come visit again. Maybe I’ll get even better at rushball by then,” he added with a smile. “Just promise me you won’t forget about our friendship. I wish there were some way we could still talk.”

Gwendolyn tucked in her lips and raised her eyebrows. "There is another thing we could do. But I know since you're always on the road, it might not be possible."

Franko tilted his head in confusion as to what she could be implying. "What would that be?"

"You could write me a letter, if you have the chance. I'd write you back, but I wouldn't know where to send it."

"A letter?" Franko was taken aback. "I've never written one before. But sure, I don't mind writing you letters."

"Perfect!" she said as she and Franko exchanged one last hug, followed by a cautious, yet sincere handshake with Bruno before the siblings left to go about their day.

"Are those your new friends?" Ringo asked his son teasingly as he approached. "You didn't mention anything about a girl."

"Oh, I, uh... guess I didn't think it was that important," Franko said, rubbing the back of his neck as he blushed.

"It's alright, son. You're only human," his father replied with a chuckle as he shook his head. "Let's hit the road, Franko. There's word spreading of a potential conflict between Wyverly and the northern kingdom of Vodavi. And, as you know, where there's conflict, there's opportunity."

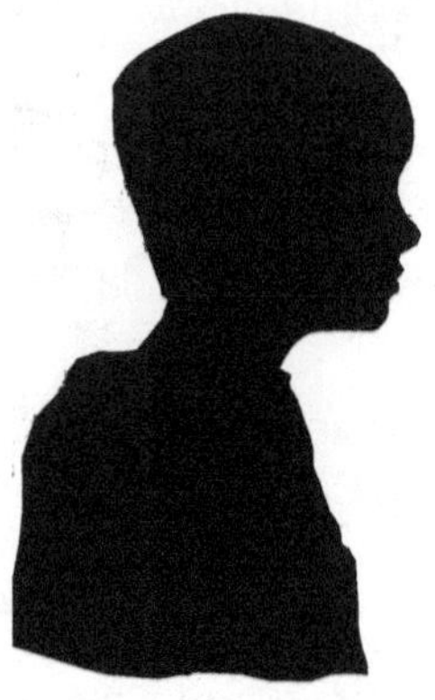

Chapter 5

Footprints

It had been several days since Franko and his father had left Greencourt. Ringo had planned to go to the northern kingdom of Vodavi, but the official trade routes were well guarded, and travel was heavily restricted. He had decided to take an old route through the northern woods, one he knew was seldom traveled anymore.

As they approached the northern forests of Wyverly, Ringo made sure that most of the coin they had, along with Franko's star pendant, the broken sword, and the toy wooden sword, were hidden away in a small compartment under the front seat of the wagon. Forest Folk were known to stalk the edges of the forest in hopes of stealing from merchants and travelers.

I think this is where they say the Forest Demon lives, Franko thought to himself. He dared not mention it to his father, who always referred to such talk as superstitious nonsense. As much as he tried to push those unsettling thoughts about the Forest Demon away from him, he couldn't help but feel the butterflies in his stomach as they slowly made their way through the northern woods. Every rustle of leaves heard off in the distance, every twig snapping, all made the boy feel on edge. However, Ringo's concerns were only on the menace of the Forest Folk.

"Well, son. This seems as good a place as any," Ringo remarked as he looked around the forest surrounding them.

"Here?" Franko asked, a confused expression on his face. "Aren't you worried about the Forest Folk?"

"Nah," his father replied dismissively as he scanned his surroundings. "I feel like they would have shown themselves by now. We're as safe here as we'd be anywhere."

They weren't too far from the edge of the Wyverly side of the forest, which made Franko feel slightly more comfortable. *Everyone says the demon lives deeper in the woods. I hope it doesn't know we're here.*

They set up camp and lay down for the evening shortly after. The boy huddled close to his father.

Ringo turned to his son, who usually wasn't one to snuggle. "You're worried about the demon everyone says lives in these woods, aren't you?" he asked playfully.

Franko shrank back at the question. "No," he said sheepishly.

Ringo sat up and let out an exhausted sigh as he smiled at his son. "I can tell when something's got your breeches tied up, son. I tell you what, I'll stay up until I hear you start to snore, then I'll know you're asleep. Will that make you feel a little better?"

Franko paused for a moment, then nodded quickly. He always had a hard time hiding things from his father.

"Alright, Franko. I'm glad we got that out of the way. You try to get some sleep, I'll be watching over you," he said reassuringly as he tousled the boy's hair. "You know, son. I don't believe in that stuff. Spirits and demons. It's all just a fairytale to scare kids."

"I know, Father. I'm sorry," Franko replied, ashamed that his father found him out.

Ringo chuckled and patted his son on his shoulder. "It's okay, son. You don't need to apologize for anything. We all get scared sometimes."

Now feeling better that his father was going to be watching over him, Franko closed his eyes and slept soundly.

***

As the sun began to rise, Franko awoke to find his father still asleep. He got up to look to see if there were any berries nearby to snack on, only to notice something that froze him in his tracks.

He noticed the footprints encircling their camp. The closest ones were just mere inches from where the boy had been lying.

"Footprints!" the boy gasped.

"Father! Wake up!" he shouted frantically. "Someone's been here!"

Ringo stirred himself awake and slowly came to. "Are you sure, Franko?" he said, rubbing the sleep from his eyes.

"Yes, I'm sure! Look!" the boy exclaimed as he directed his father's attention to the footprints that were all around where they had slept.

"Stars be damned!" Ringo grunted. "Stay close, got it?"

Ringo inspected the footprints and then went through all their belongings. "Whoever it was, it doesn't look like they stole anything," he remarked as he packed everything back up. "Also, those footprints are pretty small. I wonder if it was a child or a young woman of the Forest Folk. Maybe we didn't have anything they needed. Being poor has its perks sometimes, Franko," Ringo said with a wink as he patted his son on the shoulder.

"Why don't you go out and see if you find any nuts and berries for us to munch on while I load up?" Ringo said as he combed his fingers through his son's hair and straightened the boy's shirt. "Or better yet, if you can get your hands on a rabbit or squirrel. Holler if you see the Forest Demon, Franko," he added with a wry smirk.

"I will, Father," Franko replied with a snicker, shaking his head. *Meat*, he thought longingly, *we haven't had meat in days. Hopefully, I can catch something.*

Franko ventured out into the forest to search for some food, feeling braver now that there appeared to be little more concern than some harmless Forest Folk lurking about, who evidently had little interest in their belongings.

He managed to get a handful of pecans and berries that he placed in his satchel, but it was a real meal he was after. Further and further out he searched. *This is too far from camp*, he thought, *if I don't spot something soon, I'll need to head back. Father will get worried.*

"No critters to eat, but it's better than nothing," he said with a sigh.

With enough nuts and berries to hold them over, Franko headed back to camp—a figure cloaked in gray watching him from the treetops.

***

The rest of their day was largely uneventful. The two slowly made their way along the overgrown, seldom-used path. They were now deep within the northern forests of Wyverly.

"Father, it's so silent this far into the forest," Franko said, his voice uneasy.

"Yesterday you were jumpy over the slightest noise, and today you're unsettled because there isn't enough noise," Ringo said with a chuckle as he wiped the sweat from his brow. "I can't keep up with what scares you anymore, Franko."

Once late afternoon had arrived, Ringo decided to set up camp again for the evening, not far from a stream.

"Why don't you go grab some dry sticks, and I'll go catch some fish. I'll be back in about an hour," he told the boy.

Franko did as his father asked, and the two met back at the campsite sometime later. "Father, why aren't you more worried about what might be out here?" he asked as they sat around the fire, eating the fish his father had caught.

"I already told you, Franko," Ringo replied with a mouthful of fish. "Forest Folk are about all that's out this way, and they're just a nuisance. Besides," he added. "You saw what happened yesterday. They snooped around when we were sleeping and didn't see anything worth taking. I doubt they'll bother us again. We haven't seen any signs of 'em since."

The boy nodded thoughtfully as he swallowed the last bite of fish for the evening. *I guess Father's right, I'm getting worked up over nothing.*

The two lay down for the evening, falling asleep soundly under the stars.

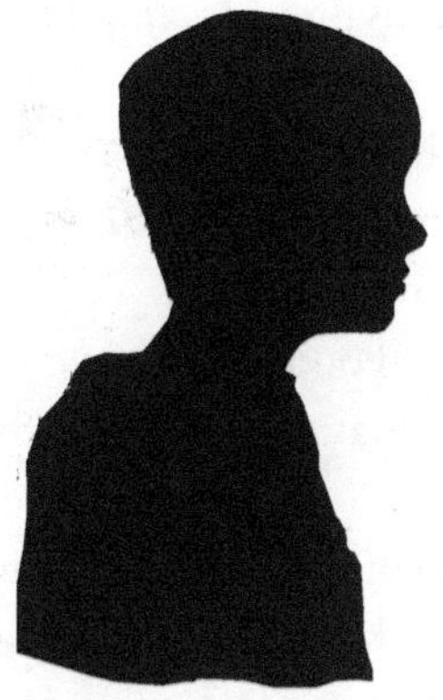

Chapter 6

Just a Bad Dream

The following morning, Franko was startled awake at the crack of dawn by the sound of rustling leaves not far from his head. He shot up and studied his surroundings.

What was that? he asked himself as he shook his head to wake himself up. He looked to see his father still asleep.

Then, he heard it again. But this time, he saw movement. Some tiny critter was scurrying about in the leaves not far from camp.

I won't wake Father for this. It looks like I'm gonna get us some squirrel for breakfast, he thought with a sly grin.

He went to his father's sack, hanging on the side of the wagon, and grabbed the broken sword. *Just in case there's some Forest Folk snooping around again.* And off Franko went to catch a forest critter.

He saw the movement again, something small dashing through the dead leaves, and sprinted after his prey, straying further and further from camp.

That's odd, he thought as he noticed how strangely the creature was moving, in straight, jerky lines rather than running in different directions or climbing a tree to escape.

"Either way," he remarked. "Food is food, even if it's stupid. I've got you now!" he said with determination as he leapt and grabbed the critter by its tail.

Franko stood up and pulled out his blade to slaughter the animal, but once he began to study his catch, a puzzled expression crossed his face. It wasn't a live squirrel at all. It was just the skin of a squirrel with a thin string tied to it.

"What in stars' light is—aaah!"

He never saw it coming. He was slammed down hard, face-first on the ground, knocking the air out of his lungs. The blade fell out of his grip from the impact, landing several paces away.

Someone or something was crouched on top of him, with their feet pressing against his back, pinning him to the ground.

"Looky look, I've got a fish on my hook," it said in a low and raspy feminine voice as she took her finger and hooked the inside of the boy's cheek. "Like a trout chasing a worm. When you catch him, he will squirm."

Oh no, it's the Forest Demon! Franko thought, his mind panicking. He gasped desperately for air, thrashing his arms and legs at the dead leaves on the forest floor to try and break free, but to no avail.

The menacing creature then grabbed Franko's head and turned it to the side before pinning it to the ground. "Food is food, even if it's stupid," she rasped as she pulled his collar back with her other hand, exposing his neck.

"Yes, yes, this will do," she said in a ravenous tone. "Now stop flailing around, it makes a mess."

Franko could barely see who his attacker was through the corner of his eye, the dim light of the sun just beginning to rise doing little to help. All he could make out was that it was some sort of figure in a dark gray cloak with its hood up, making it impossible to see any of its features.

Bruno was right, she's gonna bite me and suck out my blood!

His eyes were wide in terror as he watched her leaning towards him, making some sort of hissing sound as her hooded face neared his. Only for her to suddenly stop.

She cocked her head one way and then another, as if she was listening to something. "What? Are you certain? Him?" she asked in an exasperated tone. "Why him?"

Who in stars' name is she talking to? Franko thought.

She let out a frustrated growl. "Very well," she said grudgingly.

The mysterious figure released his collar from her grip, but kept her hand against his head to keep him from moving. She leaned her face toward his ear.

"This is your lucky day, child. The trees have put you under their protection," she whispered, a resentful bite in her voice. "Though real this may seem, it is just a bad dream," she added as she placed a cloth over his mouth and nose.

The rag smelled of an earthy, herbal scent that overwhelmed his senses. He quickly became light-headed and passed out.

***

"Father!" Franko hollered, and he woke up, his arms flailing and his breathing heavy. "Father!"

"What now, Franko?" Ringo replied, a tinge of irritation in his voice. He was standing by the wagon, using his finger to brush his teeth with crushed herbs.

Franko looked around to see that he was still in his sleep sack at the campsite. By the looks of it, the sun had come up some time ago. "Father, it was the Forest Demon. She attacked me in the woods earlier this morning!"

Ringo heaved a weary sigh and sagged his shoulders. "Really, son?" he asked skeptically. "You were dead asleep when I woke up."

The boy looked around in disbelief. "It—it was real. I swear!"

"Sounds like a bad dream, Franko," Ringo replied as he turned around and continued brushing his teeth.

"It was real. It felt so real," he said as he stood up, rubbing the sleep from his eyes.

Then, a realization had struck him. "The sword!" he said as he ran to the wagon. "I took the sword with me, and it was knocked out of my hand when she jumped me."

"She?" Ringo asked as he shot a sideways glance toward his son. "And what's this about my sword? Did you take it without asking?"

Franko ignored his father's remarks and dug through the sack, only to see the sword still lying in there. "It's still here," he said in disbelief.

"It better be," Ringo said sternly as he reached and snatched the sack out of his son's grasp.

"But I swear it was real," Franko said, rubbing his hands through his hair as he tried to process everything.

"Franko, you got all worked up over those star-forsaken demon stories and had a nightmare," Ringo remarked as he put his shirt on and combed his hair with his fingers. "And don't go around taking that sword without asking first. In real life or in your dreams," he added dryly.

The young boy leaned up against the wagon, his mind racing. "I don't believe it," he whispered.

"If we see that demon, I'll make sure to thank her for the courtesy of returning you to your sleep sack and putting my sword back just as I left it," he said with a smirk as he walked up to his son.

"Don't get too worked up, son. I'm sure it won't be the last time a lady leaves you high and dry," he added with a snicker as he slapped the boy on the shoulder. "C'mon, let's get ready to move."

Franko nodded and helped his father pack the wagon. *These woods are messing with my head*, he thought as he stared off into the distance.

The two began their journey for the day, unaware that a lock of Franko's hair had been cut from the back of his head.

Not far from them, a figure cloaked in gray was perched upon a tree branch up high, watching their every move.

"Franko..." she whispered with a mischievous smile as she rubbed the lock of his hair between her fingers. "Welcome to my forest... I do hope you find your visit to be... a *memorable* one."

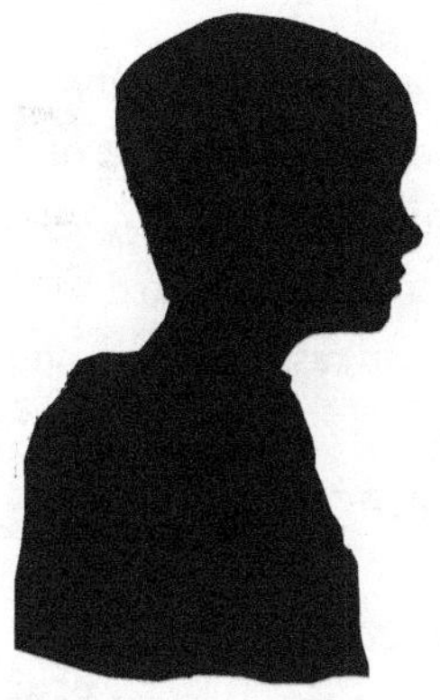

Chapter 7

Two Squirrels

As evening approached, Ringo decided to set up camp after a long day of travel. "I'm going to gather some firewood. You can come with me if you're worried you'll run into that scary woman you dreamt about," he teased.

"I'm not worried, Father," Franko replied flatly. "It was just a nightmare, like you said. I was only a little freaked out at first because it felt real."

"Don't take it too hard, son," Ringo replied with a pouty look on his face. "For what it's worth, I think you're a real catch. Her loss, Franko," he added as he tried but failed to keep a straight face.

"I think I'll just go foraging for some nuts and berries again, Father," Franko huffed as he turned to stomp away, eager not to have to endure his father's ribbings any longer.

"Oh, don't be mad at your old man, son," Ringo hollered. "She'll come back for you, they *always* do."

Ugh, Father, he groaned. *You're too much sometimes.*

As Franko kept walking, he heard the creak of a high tree branch and saw a pinecone fall to the ground.

"Go away, squirrel," he shouted up toward the forest canopy.

"Frankooooo," a feminine and raspy voice echoed through the woods, tauntingly. "Frankooooo."

That voice! he thought as he began to look around frantically. "Who—who's there?"

There was no response. Franko then heard a soft thud behind him and turned around to see two dead squirrels lying on the ground. He looked upon them, almost too scared to move.

"Are these... for me?" he asked.

No response again.

Franko quickly grabbed the squirrels and sprinted back toward camp. A gray cloaked figure sat perched upon a tree branch up high, watching him.

He returned to the campsite and met his father, with a panicked expression on his face.

"Franko, what happened?" Ringo asked when he noticed his son's expression and saw him gasping for air.

"There... there was someone out there," he said between breaths.

Ringo looked at him skeptically. "Are you sure? Franko, are you playing a joke, trying to get back at me? Look, I'm sorry if I went too far earlier—"

He stopped himself when he saw the earnest look in his son's eyes. "Son, what exactly happened?"

Franko told him about the bizarre encounter. About the voice coming from the forest canopy, then about the squirrels dropping to the ground close by.

Ringo grabbed the squirrels and inspected them. "Looks like these were slaughtered and gutted with a sharp blade," he said thoughtfully as he looked them over with care. "Sounds like Forest Folk mischief, son."

"You really think this was just the Forest Folk?" Franko asked incredulously.

"That's the most likely answer," Ringo replied as he scanned their surroundings. "Like I said, they're more of a nuisance than anything else, but some of them are decent folks. By the looks of it, these are safe to eat. They have been known to help travelers in the past."

Franko leaned his hand against a nearby tree, trying to catch his breath. "If you say so, Father."

"Franko," Ringo remarked softly. "I think from now on, we need to stay close. No more splitting up. Just to stay on the safe side."

Chapter 8

The Forest Demon

Franko and Ringo left shortly after breakfast to continue their journey through the northern forest toward Vodavi. His father had spoken little to him since the events of the evening before. *I wonder if Father feels bad about teasing me so much,* he thought.

As the two were doing their best to make their way through the rough terrain over the course of the afternoon, they found themselves surrounded. There appeared to be at least two dozen of them—gaunt and disheveled-looking men and women wearing rags and tattered clothing.

Forest Folk, Franko realized. Even though he knew he and his father were considered poor on a good day, he couldn't help feeling a little sorry for the feral humans who lived in the woods.

"Let me handle this, son," Ringo whispered to Franko as he dismounted. They had encountered Forest Folk before; the altercations never resorted to violence, but Ringo still made sure to watch how he spoke to them.

"Ah, here to help a couple weary travelers, I see," Ringo said with his arms raised to his sides, a pretentious smile across his face. He was assuming they couldn't understand what he was saying, as most could speak and understand little of the common tongue. "Was that you who gave my son those squirrels? If it was, thank you. Because I must say, they were delicious!"

"Save it, merchant. Show us what you've got," barked a young man wearing a blue bandana as he stepped forward.

Ringo's face jolted in surprise at the sight of a fluent-speaking member of their pack. "You... can talk pretty good there, young man," he said pensively.

"Yeah, we're full of surprises," the young man said sarcastically. "Now step away, and tell your kid to get down."

Ringo stood with his arms still held up and turned toward Franko. "It's okay, son. You can get down. They won't hurt us," he said calmly with a nod.

After Franko stepped down, the young man and his feral comrades sifted through their belongings, whistling and growling at each other to communicate. "This is all you've got?" the young man in the bandana said derisively as he tossed some blankets and stale bread out from the back of the wagon.

"Please, sir, that really is all we have. You're going to deprive us of our blankets?" Ringo pleaded. "We are not wealthy merchants."

"Yeah, I can see that," the young man replied spitefully. "But there's no way you were planning on going to Vodavi with nothing but stale bread, blankets, and a small bag of copper coins. You're hiding something from us."

One of the larger goons began snooping around the front seat of the wagon. Ringo sighed as the man pulled up the seat and found the hidden compartment. "Quinn!" he said excitedly to announce his find.

"Well, stars be damned, so you were hiding the good stuff from us," the young man, Quinn, remarked tersely as he headed toward the front of the wagon. He pulled out the coins Ringo had hidden, along with some other items, among them the star pendant, the rest of Franko's berry candy, and the toy wooden sword. When he spotted the broken sword, he looked it over briefly. "A broken blade? Why are you keeping this trash?" he asked with a scoff as he tossed it to the ground.

Quinn studied the star pendant with an almost lecherous look in his eyes. "Now this here—this is paydirt!"

"No, please!" hollered Ringo as he approached Quinn. He was quickly knocked to the ground by the large goon who stepped in to stop him.

"Father!" shouted Franko as he ran towards Ringo.

"Back off!" shouted the large man as he backhanded Franko across the face, sending the boy to the ground with a thud.

"You bastard!" Ringo hollered as he rose to his feet and punched the brute in his mouth.

The massive oaf stepped back, holding his hand to his lip, and looked at Ringo with a murderous glare.

"You're dead!" he snapped as he headed toward Ringo. Evidently, there were two among the group of Forest Folk who spoke the common tongue well.

"That's enough!" shouted Quinn. "We got what we need and then some. We're not gonna rough up some man and his kid for no reason. Got it, Bric?" he said firmly to the large man.

Bric reluctantly stopped in his tracks, then turned his attention to Franko's wooden sword, set on the ground nearby. "Fine," he said grudgingly, "but the brat loses his toy," he added as he grabbed the toy sword and broke it over his knee.

Ringo was about to charge the man when Quinn pointed his knife at him. "Don't move, merchant," he said in a low tone. Quinn then directed his gaze to Franko, the boy's face contorted as he started to sob, tears streaming down his face.

Quinn shook his head and sighed. "Dammit, Bric. Look what you did. He's just a kid," Quinn huffed as he dug through the stolen sack of copper and tossed a few coins at Franko's feet. "Here, kid. Maybe that'll be enough to buy another one. Sorry about that, Bric takes things too far sometimes."

"Please, Quinn. The pendant is very special to me," Ringo pleaded.

"Don't push it, merchant," Quinn barked back. "You lied to me and then attacked one of my men; you're getting off easy," he said, holding up the pendant in front of him.

It was then that a dagger zipped through the air, narrowly missing Quinn's head. A cloaked figure swooped in like a gray blur, striking Bric with a vicious knee to his jaw, planting him on his back. Quinn tried to collect himself, but was taken down by a swift kick to the gut, followed by a spinning elbow to his face. The cloaked figure quickly jumped up into a tree, climbing up with the grace and skill of a wildcat. The figure stood atop a high branch, overlooking the group. It extended its hand out, displaying the star pendant, which it tossed on the ground toward Ringo and Franko.

The group of Forest Folk all collectively gasped at the sight. "The demon! The Forest Demon!" one of them said in a heavy, broken accent, horrified.

Bric slowly came to and helped a startled Quinn to his feet, who was breathing heavily after the brief confrontation.

"De... Demon," he heaved, voice trembling. "This... this has nothing to do with you!"

"Quuuinn..." the female voice said in an ominous, booming tone. "This has everything to do with me if I decide it does," the voice rang out from the cloaked figure.

"L-look," Quinn stuttered. "We've seen you around before, lurking in the shadows. We've never bothered you, whatever you are. We're just... we're just trying to survive. We aren't out to hurt anybody," he pleaded.

"Is that so, Quinn?" the female figure asked. "That's not what I just saw. Hitting a child isn't hurting anybody, Quinn?"

"That, uhh..." Quinn sighed in resignation. "I take full responsibility for that, for not keeping my men under control. I'm sorry," he said, his voice sounding soft and sincere.

"Yes, Quinn. I know," the demon replied. "That's why your life has been spared today. If you had tried to hurt that child further, the dagger I threw would have landed in your skull. Now get out of my sight."

"Y-yes, we will," Quinn said as he nervously swallowed a lump in his throat. "Let's get out of here!" he hollered. He and his crew of Forest

Folk quickly scampered away, still managing to carry an armful of stolen goods with them.

Ringo and Franko watched the group leave, then turned their gaze back to the mysterious figure in the trees, only to find she was no longer there.

"Father, who was that? Was that really the Forest Demon?" Franko asked in amazement.

"I already told you, son. There's no such thing as demons," his father replied, still scanning the tree tops. "Do you think that's who you encountered earlier? The one who gave you those squirrels?" he asked as he looked back at his son.

"I'm not sure, but I think so," the boy replied, rubbing the side of his face where the big brute had struck him.

"Well, whoever that was, thank the stars they were around," Ringo remarked as he placed his arm around Franko's shoulder and began heading back toward the wagon.

The two got back on their wagon and cautiously moved ahead, the Forest Demon watching them in the distance from the treetops overhead.

Chapter 9

An Introduction

As the sun began to set, the two pulled aside to set up camp for the evening, their nerves still wracked by the events of the day.

Franko had started writing a letter for Gwendolyn, in part to help ease his mind. He found putting words on paper seemed to help calm him. He read over the letter once more before folding it up and putting it in his satchel, with hopes of having the letter delivered once they reached the next town.

Dear Gwendolyn,

Father and I have had quite the adventure since we left. You wouldn't believe who I saw. We got jumped by some Forest Folk, but The Forest Demon chased them away. I met her the other day as well. I didn't get a good look at her, but she tossed me some squirrels for Father and I. I can't wait to tell you and Bruno all about it. I will add more to this letter later, when we reach town to let you know we're okay.

Franko

"Franko, it's getting late. Why don't we gather some firewood together? After that, we might still have time to catch some fish for dinner," his father said as he straightened his son's shirt for him.

"It'll be dark soon, Father," the boy replied. "I don't think we'll have time for both. I can get some firewood while you try to catch some fish."

Ringo paused for a moment. "Franko, are you sure? I don't want to ask you to do anything you're not comfortable with. Especially after what happened earlier."

"I don't think those Forest Folk will be bothering us again anytime soon, Father," he replied. "But if you would rather I go with you, I can."

Ringo mulled it over for a moment, thoughtfully scratching his beard. "Okay, son. But I want you to take my blade with you. Don't hesitate to use it, do you understand?"

He placed his hands on his son's shoulders and bent to look him in the eye. "You holler if you so much as even think you see something, got it?"

"I will, Father," the boy answered.

***

While his father was fishing in the stream, Franko ventured out a bit from camp and began gathering some decent-sized dry sticks for a fire. He didn't notice at the time that he was being watched by a cloaked figure perched on top of a tree branch.

As Franko was putting sticks into a pile to be carried, he heard branches creaking and turned around. He flinched and looked around the tree tops.

Oh no, is it her again? Is it the Forest Demon? He asked himself, his heart thumping in terror.

"Frankooooo," the raspy voice of the Forest Demon again echoed through the trees. "Frankooooo."

It is, it's her again! What does she want with me?

"Oh, it's you," he replied, trying his best to sound calm. "Um... Thank you for your help with the Forest Folk earlier. And for the squirrels."

"Frankooooo," the voice repeated. "You've been a bad boy, Franko."

He felt himself begin to panic. "What? I—I haven't done anything. I swear!" he pleaded.

"But you did, Franko," the voice of the Forest Demon replied. "Do not lie to me. These are my woods. You *know* what you did."

What is she talking about? Is it the letter? He asked himself.

"I don't know what you mean. I promise, I didn't mean to do anything wrong," he replied desperately.

"But you did. You mentioned me in that letter you wrote, didn't you?" she asked, accusingly.

"I don't understand," he said, his eyes darting around in confusion. "How did you know about that?"

"Ah, so you *did* write about me. You just admitted it."

"But I don't—"

"I don't want people talking about me, Franko," she interrupted. "Place the letter on the ground and stay where you are. Do not mention me again, understood?"

"Oh...okay," he replied nervously. "I'm sorry, I didn't know—"

"Just put the letter down and do not leave, Franko. I want to speak to you for a moment," she interrupted again. "I am aware that you did not know. This is your first and last warning. Do not do it again. Do you understand?"

"I'm sorry. I didn't know—"

"Do you understand!" the demon barked.

"Yes, I understand," Franko answered, his voice trembling.

"Good," she replied calmly.

Franko reached into his satchel and set the letter on the ground before him. “Okay, there it is. Can I go now?” he asked as he again scanned the tree tops and saw no sign of her.

He heard a rustling of leaves behind him and nearly leapt out of his skin when he turned and saw her standing just inches in front of him.

The boy was about to scream, but she reached out and clasped her hand over his mouth, her vice-like grip grabbing him by the face so tightly it muffled his screams, and he couldn't escape. He felt the sides of his teeth cutting the inside of his cheeks.

As he looked at her, up close for the first time, he saw that her hood covered most of her face. He could barely make out the lower half of her profile, and couldn't see her eyes. He saw that it appeared she wore paint on her face, white paint with black around her mouth, nose, and what he could see of her eyes, resembling a skeleton's skull. It was impossible to make out her age; she seemed short for an adult and barely a head taller than he was. He went to reach for his father's broken blade tucked in his belt. She effortlessly swatted it out of his grasp with her free hand. He frantically tried to break free of her grip, but to no avail. He tried to scream, but little more than a muted whimper escaped through her hand.

She held her finger to her mouth, "shh," she whispered. "Don't make a sound. I’m not here to hurt you. I just want to talk. Do you understand?"

Franko nodded, his mouth still covered by her hand and his eyes wide in terror. He could smell an odor coming from her hand; it smelled of the same earthy mixture of herbs he recalled from his dream. The intoxicating aroma made him light-headed, almost calming.

“Good,” the Forest Demon replied as she released her grip, and Franko backed away, rubbing his reddened cheeks where she had grabbed him so tightly.

"I'm sorry if that hurt you. I couldn't risk you screaming and drawing any attention," she told him, her voice still soft, yet raspy and barely audible. "Now that the matter of the letter is taken care of, we can talk. The trees say that you're a friend, but I'm not so sure. I want to see for myself. Tell me, what are you doing in my forest?"

Franko eyed her cautiously. He spotted his father's broken blade lying on the ground nearby and reached down to grab it.

"Don't even think about it!" she snapped as she stepped on his arm, causing him to drop to his knees. "That blade is useless against me."

"I—I won't try anything," he said quickly, his chest shaking. "It's my father's. I can't lose it," he added as he felt a warm tear running down his cheek and wiped it away. "Please... don't hurt me," he quietly pleaded, his lip quivering, unable to bring himself to look up at her directly.

"Pathetic," she scoffed as she took her foot off his arm. "I asked you a question, Franko. What are you doing in my forest?"

The boy grabbed his father's sword and tucked it back in his belt, his hands shaking. He didn't acknowledge her question, hesitated to answer, and offered her no information. She made him uneasy, and he was unsure of her intentions. He recalled how easily she had dispatched Quinn and Bric; it made him even more worried. He slowly stood back up as she paced around him in a circle, like a predator toying with its prey.

“My father and I, we’re just passing through. How do you know my name?” he asked, his voice shaking.

“I know much about you, Franko of Greencourt,” she replied with a sinister smile.

Terror struck him as he noticed her teeth; her canines were sharpened like fangs. It reminded him of a monster from the scary campfire stories his father would tell him.

“Your father is Ringo, the merchant, isn't that right?" she asked. "Just two destitute vagrants trying to make their way in the world," she remarked with mock pity in her voice.

Franko's eyes went wide, and his heart began to pound with fear at this strange and intimidating figure circling him. *How does she know all of this? And what does destitute vagrants mean?* He had never heard that term before, but the sound of it didn't sit well in his gut.

"I..." his words failed him as his nerves were set on edge. “I had a dream about you the other day. Do you—.”

“*Though real this may seem, it is just a bad dream*,” she interrupted. “Or was it?”

His eyes shot wide at her response. “So it was real?”

She stopped circling him and started to walk straight toward him, a mischievous grin on her face. He stepped back, tripped over a tree root, and fell to the ground. As the demon kept advancing on him, he scooted back as quickly as he could and found himself seated with his back against a tree trunk.

The Forest Demon kept slowly approaching Franko until she loomed over top of him as he sat, pinned against the tree. She crouched down, her face inches from his. He closed his eyes tightly and turned his head, his face grimacing and his breathing erratic.

"Do I frighten you?" she asked, her raspy voice now sounding almost playful.

Franko could feel her breath against the side of his face; it smelled of wild berries and pecans. *She's enjoying this, but why?* he wondered.

He swallowed and finally managed to steady his breathing. "Uhh... no," he responded, his voice still slightly shaky and his head still turned to the side.

"Liar," she said with a scoff. "*Please don't hurt me*," she said mockingly. "I can smell the fear on you. You *should* be frightened. You saw what I did to those big, bad Forest Folk back there. I could do much worse to you if I wanted," she added as she brushed the side of his face with the back of her fingers. "You pulled a weapon on me, Franko. Why? *I* didn't pull a weapon on *you*."

"I—I'm sorry," the boy stammered, a shiver going up his spine when she touched him. "Wha—what do you want with us? And how do you know who I am?" he asked, doing his best not to sound scared, but his voice was quivering.

"You heard Quinn, I'm the Forest Demon, the trees tell me what's said in these woods. As I already have stated, I know much about you, Franko," she responded. "And to answer your first question, I wanted nothing more than to introduce myself. That is all... And," she added as she grabbed his chin and forced him to face her, "look at me!" she snapped. He cautiously opened his eyes to meet her gaze, fear welling up inside of him as he caught the close-up sight of her skull-painted face and yellow eyes with two small horns protruding from her forehead, just below her hairline. "And—to let you know that these are *my* woods. The trees have put you under their protection, but you will still respect my forest while you are a guest here, understood?"

"Y—yes," he whispered in response.

She leaned her face toward the side of his. His body tensed, and he closed his eyes tight again, *oh no!* he thought, terrified.

"Oh stars. Please don't bite me!" he pleaded.

The mysterious figure was so close he could smell her clothing. She had the scent of wildflowers and pine. She leaned her face toward his ear and whispered, "I... will be watching you, Franko of Greencourt. Be mindful of that. And don't tell your father about our little chat, understood? Oh, and one last thing. Go ahead and write your letter again tonight, just leave me out of it this time."

"Okay," he answered with a quick nod as she stood up. By the time he opened his eyes again, she was gone.

He quickly scanned his surroundings, trying to see where she had gone. "Who is she?" he quietly asked. "What is she?"

He heard a voice echoing from the tree tops. "I am the guardian of these forests. Some call me a demon, some call me a spirit, others call me a ghost," she replied. "I think that's the one I prefer. You can simply call me, *Ghost*."

"Ghost?" Franko asked nervously. But there was no response. He looked around but saw no signs of her.

The boy did his best to steady his nerves and collected up the firewood before heading back to meet his father, running as fast as his wobbly legs could take him. The bizarre meeting with the Forest Demon playing over and over in his mind. He noticed that he started to feel relaxed, almost unnaturally so, given the recent encounter he just had. *That odor on her hand,* he thought, *it was the same from that time she jumped me before.*

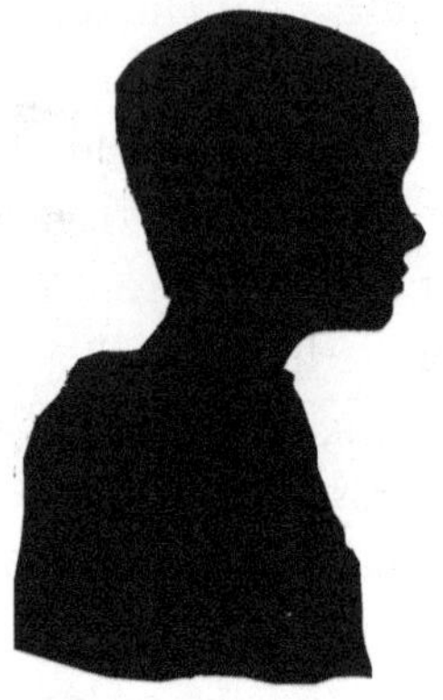

Chapter 10

Destitute Vagrants

When Franko got back to their campsite, he saw his father was already there cooking up some fish he'd caught. Franko's mind was still startled from the encounter with the mysterious Forest Demon, but his body was getting so sleepy that he could barely keep his eyes open. He forced himself to stay awake because he knew he needed to eat, and because he wanted to write another letter to Gwendolyn.

"Everything okay, Franko?" Ringo asked, a concerned look on his face. "You took quite a while out there, so I decided to grab some wood for the fire myself and get to it. I was just about to start looking for you."

Franko swallowed nervously, the words of Ghost echoing in the back of his mind, *don't tell your father about our little chat.* "I'm sorry, Father. I just got a little turned around out there, I guess," he lied.

"You should have called out for me, son," his father chided him as he handed the boy a piece of fish. "You don't have to do everything by yourself, you know."

"I'm sorry, I will," Franko said as he nodded uncomfortably and sat down to eat. He sat silently for a moment, reflecting on what Ghost had called them-"destitute vagrants." He didn't know what that meant.

"Father," the boy asked, "what does *destitute vagrant* mean?"

Ringo stopped chewing and looked intently at Franko. "Where did you hear that from?"

Franko froze for a moment; he couldn't mention his confrontation with the Forest Demon. "It was... from someone from back at the capital last time we visited."

"The capital? Figures," Ringo scoffed as he started chewing again. "It means someone who's poor and doesn't have a real home. That's what we are to the world, Franko. I've tried my best to protect you, but the fact is, the world looks down on people like us—*Destitute vagrants*," he added derisively. "Anyone who calls you that thinks that you're beneath them."

His gut tightened upon hearing his father's words. "Are we, Father?"

Ringo's jaw tightened. "No," he said flatly. "We can't control how others perceive us, Franko. But we can control how we perceive ourselves. Next time someone calls you that, let me know. Nobody talks to my son that way."

Franko's heart sank. *This is how the world sees us?* he asked himself. *Are we nothing but poor trash?*

Ringo studied his son's expression. "Did something happen to you out there, Franko?" he asked inquisitively. "And why are your cheeks red?"

"No, nothing happened," the boy quickly replied. "I told you, I just got lost. I must have just been still on edge over those bandits."

His thoughts started racing, *Should I tell him about Ghost?* he thought. His father had always told him never to keep secrets with an adult. That the only grown-ups who would do such a thing are the ones who hurt children. But he also remembered how adamant she was not to tell anyone about her. *And besides*, he thought, *she didn't hurt me. Not really. She just wanted privacy, I guess.*

"What about your cheeks?" Ringo asked again.

Franko's head jerked up. "What?"

"Your cheeks, Franko," Ringo said, leaning toward his son, his face stern. "What happened?"

"Oh, that," Franko replied as he touched the side of his face, still tender from where she had grabbed him so tightly. "It must be from when that big guy hit me earlier."

"That bastard!" Ringo grunted as he picked a fishbone out of his mouth and threw it on the ground in anger. "Stars be damned, Franko, I'm sorry that happened to you."

"It's okay, Father," the boy responded. "I'm just glad we're all okay. Thanks to that demon lady," he said. His heart jumped when he realized that he thoughtlessly brought her up. *Oh, stars!* he panicked. *She told me not to mention her. But that was about my meeting with her, not the earlier confrontation. Hopefully, she'll understand*, he thought as he realized the panic had quickly settled and his eyes felt heavy.

"*Forest Demon*," Ringo scoffed as he licked his fingers. "You know I don't believe in that garbage, Franko. That was just some poor, lost soul, probably a runaway. More than likely, a bandit just like those others. Or even worse, a witch."

Ringo sat silently for a moment, thinking over his words. "Having said that, sometimes I can't help but wonder if the old tales have some truth in them. Those stories from The *Tales of the Star Sage*, about Garel and demons and whatnot," he paused and shook his head. "Either way, Franko. Whoever, or whatever, that woman was—I'd advise you to stay away from her. I don't care if she gave you those squirrels or chased those bandits away. I still say they're all trouble."

Franko didn't respond; his nerves surged again despite his fatigue. "Father," the boy asked, desperate to change the topic.

Ringo looked at him, his eyebrows perched. "Yes."

"Could you tell me more about Mother?"

His father sagged his shoulders and drooped his head. "I've already told you, Franko. I don't want to talk about it anymore."

"Well, could you at least tell me her name?" Franko pleaded. "You've never even told me that before."

Ringo lifted his head and sighed. "Riva... her name was Riva, okay? I don't want to talk about your mother anymore, understood?"

Riva? he thought. *That's a pretty name.*

"Yes, Father," the boy replied, so fatigued that he was having to fight to keep his eyelids from drooping. "I can barely stay awake any longer. If it's okay with you, I might write a quick letter for Gwendolyn and then lie down for the night."

Ringo stared straight ahead and responded with a slight nod and a slow wave of the hand as Franko rewrote the same letter he had before—this time, with no mention of Ghost.

After he finished the letter, Franko lay down, falling asleep as soon as his head hit the rolled-up blanket he was using as a pillow—the name of his mother on his lips. "Riva..." he whispered.

Chapter 11

A Farewell

When Franko awoke the next morning, he found his father gone. He stood up frantically, scanning his surroundings. As the boy rose, he heard something fall and hit the ground. When he looked, he noticed a small cloth sack lying on the dirt at his feet. It had been tucked into his cloak and fell out when he stood. He opened the sack to see the berry candy inside, the candy that Quinn and the Forest Folk had taken from him during their encounter the previous day.

Did the Forest Folk come back and leave this with me? He asked himself, puzzled.

As he gave the matter more thought, he noticed that the letter he had written for Gwendolyn was missing as well. *The Forest Demon, Ghost,* he concluded.

He looked around to see if he could spot her watching him and was about to call out for his father when he saw Ringo walking toward him, his hair soaked.

"Father, where have you been?" Franko asked anxiously.

"Well, you were sleeping like a baby, and I didn't want to wake you, so I went to the stream and took a bath," Ringo said as he handed his son a bar of soap and walked to the back of the wagon. "Your turn, son. Don't take too long, we've got to get moving," he hollered as he finished getting dressed.

Franko popped a candy in his mouth, then put the sack of sweets in the front seat of the wagon before heading toward the stream, grabbing a handful of what he believed were goldberries, edible yellow-colored berries from a bush along the way. He put them in his satchel, planning to eat them when he finished washing up.

As he continued to make his way down, he couldn't help but wonder why he had slept so soundly after the events of the previous day. Then, the thought occurred to him. *Her hand, it smelled like herbs or something, just like it did before. Did she... drug me with some sort of sedative? Why?*

He approached the stream, and then he remembered what the Forest Demon had said the day before, her eerie and raspy voice playing in his head, *I will be watching you*. The thought unsettled him, and he decided to keep his breeches on as he jumped in the stream to wash off.

When Franko had finished with his bath, he stepped out of the stream, only to be startled by the sight of Ghost perched on a low-hanging branch, facing him.

"Did you enjoy the candy?" she asked, her voice playful yet still unnerving to Franko. She had a smirk crossing her painted face and had her hood pulled back slightly so he could now see most of her features.

"So it *was* you," he responded as he quickly got dressed and put on his cloak.

"Of course it was me. Who else?" she asked as she tilted her head almost like an owl—a motion that made the boy's skin crawl.

"How did you get it back from them?" he asked pensively.

"It took a little... persuasion," she replied. "I saw that big oaf, Bric, about to reach into the bag with his grubby hands, and suddenly the back of his head ran into the bottom of my boot. Then I showed him my knife and told him I'd cut out his tongue if he didn't give it to me. He found my argument compelling and handed over the bag of candy. I went ahead and rearranged his face anyway for the trouble."

Franko looked at her, appalled.

"Oh, don't look at me like that," she said. "Have you seen that ugly pig? I did him a favor. It's an improvement if you ask me."

"Why did you do all that over candy?" Franko asked

"Let's just say, sometimes forest guardians get bored too."

The boy drew a deep breath, strengthening his resolve. "Did you do something to me to get me to sleep like that? I smelled some sort of herb on your hand yesterday."

"Very astute, Franko," she said with a hint of admiration. "Yes, I figured you could use some help getting settled for the evening. Plus, I didn't want to take a chance of you stirring awake while I returned your candy, so I rubbed some slumber root on my hand before our little chat."

"I don't understand," Franko said. "Why did you do all that to me? The slumber root? The candy? And my letter? What do you want from me?" he asked, his voice shaky yet determined.

"I already told you, Franko of Greencourt," she responded. "There's nothing I want from you. Yesterday was an introduction, today is a farewell."

"But why? I don't understand... And where's my letter?" he asked. "I promise I didn't mention you."

She maintained the same sly grin on her face and kept her eyes fixed on his as she reached into her satchel and held up a folded piece of parchment between her index and middle fingers. "Here you go," she said as she flicked the paper toward his feet.

He took his eyes off of her for a brief second to reach for the paper, and she lunged at him, wrapping her arm around his neck from behind and bringing him to his knees. She wasn't choking him, but her hold was firm, and he couldn't break loose. She was far stronger than her petite frame would suggest.

"Not the best survival instincts, I see," she whispered in his ear. He could again smell her sweet, earthy scent as she held him in place, his back pinned against her.

His breath quivered nervously. "What are you—"

"These are pyrberries," Ghost interrupted as she reached into his satchel and pulled out the golden-colored berries he had picked earlier. "They look like goldberries, but see the red flecks? They are *not* goldberries; they will make you sick," she remarked as she tossed them aside.

She then pulled out a handful of yellow berries from her pouch and held them in front of his face. "*These* are goldberries. No red spots. They are safe to eat," she told him as she placed them in his satchel.

Franko gulped, his breathing frantic. "Okay, pl... please. Let me go," he pleaded.

She scoffed and slowly let go of the boy. "Don't you know it's unbecoming for a man to beg like that, Franko of Greencourt?" she rasped.

After she let him go, Franko turned around, a look of frustration and bewilderment on his face as he saw Ghost back up and sit perched on a low-hanging branch just behind him. A mocking smile upon her face.

"I heard you were talking about me to your father last night, Franko," she said accusingly.

Franko held his hands out in front of him. "Oh, no, I didn't say anything about our meeting. I promise," he said pleadingly, a panicked expression on his face. "We only talked about the first time we both saw you. That's all, I promise."

"I know that, Franko," she chided. "I told you—*I heard*."

"Look, whatever I did, I'm sorry. I won't tell anyone about you. You won't have to worry about seeing me ever again. I promise," he assured her.

Ghost's expression changed suddenly. Her head jerked back, and her eyes opened wide, as if she was offended. "You didn't enjoy my company? Was I not hospitable to you?" she asked defensively.

Franko's eyes darted around anxiously. "Oh, no. I didn't mean to sound like that!" he replied. "I just thought you didn't like me being here. I thought—"

He cut himself off when she hopped off the branch she was perched on and started walking toward him intently.

"No, please," he pleaded as he started to back away. "I'm sorry I said that. I didn't mean—"

She grabbed him by the lapel of his cloak and pulled him close to her, leaning again toward his ear.

"I told you before, the trees say that you're a friend. They'd be happy to host you again," she whispered. "You may come back anytime you wish... You *will* come back and be our guest again. Understood?" she said adamantly.

"O—Okay," he replied, his voice trembling. "I'm sorry if I—"

She jerked his cloak toward her again so that they were now face to face. "Stop apologizing to me!" she demanded.

Franko swallowed a nervous lump in his throat. "Okay, I will," he replied, making sure not to add another apology.

She let go of his cloak and took a few steps back.

"Why are you so interested in me?" he asked with a hint of frustration in his voice.

She stood silently for a moment before answering. "Normally, when I come across a child separated from their family, I devour them," she replied. "But the trees forbade me from doing the same to you. This caught my interest."

She studied him with her eyes from head to toe. "But," she added. "They never said I couldn't have a little fun with you, Franko, son of Ringo," she said mockingly. "Or should I say, Franko... son of *Riva*," she added as her lips curled into a sadistic smile.

He snapped his head toward her and glared at the demon-like figure.

"Oh," she said as she raised her eyebrows. "Does that name make you feel unsettled?" she asked. "You were mumbling it in your sleep last night."

Franko tensed up as he stared her down. "Don't you say her name again," he demanded, his teeth clenched.

"Is the little trout finally growing a backbone?" she asked in a playful tone as she approached him again, but this time he didn't back down. Ghost leaned her face toward his, so close that they were almost touching. "Riiiiiivaaaaa," she rasped.

"You shut up!" he shouted as he lunged, taking a wild swing at her and striking the demon right across her face.

Franko gasped in disbelief. *I can't believe I just did that! Father would be furious with me if he saw me raising my hand at someone like that,* he thought in shame. *He told me never to let someone's words drive me to violence. He would be so disappointed in me right now.*

She smirked at his reaction, the hit having evidently no effect on her. “Yes, that’s it!” She grunted in approval. “That’s the kind of spirit that I like. That's the kind of fire the forest needs, Franko.”

“I’m sorry I struck you like that,” he said in resignation as his nerves began to steady. “I know you just said that to tease me. I shouldn’t have gotten so upset.”

She turned her back toward him. “I thought I told you to stop apologizing to me, Franko,” she responded flatly. “Besides, you have nothing to apologize for. You stood up for one you loved. That is a noble thing.”

There was an awkward silence between the two of them for a moment before Ghost spoke back up. "I am sorry if I hurt you yesterday, Franko," she remarked, her tone now serious.

Franko went to rub his cheeks, still slightly reddened from when she grabbed him the day before. "Oh, that. It's okay, they're a little tender, but it doesn't really hurt."

"I'm not talking about that," she replied. "I'm talking about what I said. When I called you *destitute vagrants*. I'm not used to talking to children." She paused for a moment. "That hurt you, didn't it?"

Franko stood silently. *Yes*, he thought, but didn't respond aloud.

"You are not beneath anyone, Franko," she said firmly. "The trees are fond of you, and if the trees regard you, so do I. Understood?'

"Yes," he replied as he exhaled, his mind easing slightly.

"The trees say that they enjoyed your company, Franko of Greencourt," she said over her shoulder. "It was a pleasure meeting you. I look forward to your next visit."

He nodded uncomfortably. "Okay... thank you," he said as he stood upright and slightly bowed his head, remembering his manners. "It was nice meeting you, too, Ghost. And... uhh... the trees."

She smiled and nodded her head. Then, the enigmatic Forest Demon dashed back into the woods, effortlessly leaping from branch to branch like it was second nature before eventually disappearing out of sight in the dense canopy of the forest.

Franko ran his hand through his hair and sighed in relief before making his way back to his father. *One thing is for certain,* he thought, *I'll be glad when we get out of this forest.*

***

As Franko dreamt that night, he found himself in an unfamiliar place. It was nighttime and he was somewhere deep within the forest. But the darkness of night was lit up by flames. He heard the screams, shouts, and cries of people in the distance.

The boy checked his surroundings and saw what appeared to be a town in the forest not far from him. He spotted tents, wooden shacks, and small cabins scattered about, all engulfed in flames. Mysterious figures wearing crimson cloaks were setting the village ablaze and attacking its inhabitants. Among them was one holding a large battle axe, with blue-tinted blades.

There were some attempting to flee, while others were doing their best to fight back. Amid the mayhem were several bodies scattered about.

"What is happening?" Franko asked as he watched on in horror. "Who are these people?"

As he approached, he saw what he believed to be a young girl, not much older than himself, escaping the carnage with several of the cloaked attackers on her trail.

"No!" Franko shouted. "Stop this! Leave her alone!" But they didn't appear to see or acknowledge the boy's plea.

"Please be safe, little girl," he whispered to himself as he tried to catch up. *Maybe I can help her*, he thought desperately.

He chased after her, shouting with all his might to get someone's attention, but to no avail. The girl swiftly dove into some brush, in the hopes of throwing her attackers off. She crawled out the other side and sat leaning with her back against a tree trunk. As Franko finally caught up to her, he noticed that he couldn't make out her face. It was as if a shadow was covering her. But he did see tears falling to the ground as she sat sobbing.

"Are you going to be okay?" he asked her gently.

No response. She just sat there, weeping.

"Can you hear me?" he asked. "My name's Franko. What's your name, girl?"

Again. No response.

From behind him, he heard a voice, the voice of a woman, wicked and shrill.

"So, you thought you could make it out of this alive, did you?" the voice asked, her tone full of mockery and disdain.

As Franko turned around to see who it was, he awoke from his dream.

Chapter 12

A Different Path Back

The two finally exited the northern forests of Wyverly the following day. They crossed the border into Vodavi and entered a small village called Findale. The visit to town was largely uneventful, aside from several villagers and some soldiers they came across, who gave the two Wyverly visitors suspicious glances. A guard interrogated Ringo and inspected his wagon. When it became apparent that the two were little more than poor merchants, they were free to move about as needed.

Findale was a lumber town, and with an abundant supply of the Vodavi red cedar, Ringo knew he could get it at a low price and sell it for a nice profit, perhaps at the Wyverly capital. The two stayed there for a few days, trading fish to the lumberjacks in exchange for some valuable Vodavi quality timber and working odd jobs for a few coppers here and there. It wasn't much, but there was enough coin for food, and it had the potential for a decent payday once they sold the lumber they had acquired.

Franko finished his letter to Gwendolyn, adding that they arrived safely in Findale and might be in the area for a while. He wanted to find a courier to mail the letter while he was in town, but his father told him he doubted anyone in Vodavi would be willing to risk crossing the border into Wyverly to deliver it. The boy's heart sank, but he kept the letter in his satchel, thinking again of how Ghost took his last letter. *I'll make sure she won't get her hands on this one.*

The two entered a general store in town after putting in their last day of work in town before they left for Wyverly the next morning. They had a decent haul and made some coin. Ringo was picking up some supplies while Franko looked at some books on a shelf. There were some history books and some fairy tales, but the one that caught his interest was about sword fighting. He picked it up and was about to thumb through it when his father interrupted him.

"Books, son?" he inquired, perplexed.

"I wouldn't mind learning how to fight with a blade, Father," the boy replied. "I feel I'm old enough to start."

"Eh," Ringo grunted with a dismissive wave. "You want to learn sword fighting? I'll teach you, son," he added as he playfully patted Franko on the back.

"You know sword fighting?" Franko asked, surprised. "You never mentioned that before."

"You never asked," his father responded with a shrug. "Your old man knows more than you think."

"Well, I still think I might buy the book," the boy replied. "Seems like a good way to learn."

"Son, if you want to learn about something—read about it. If you want to learn about something quickly—listen to someone who's already read about it," Ringo stated as he playfully wagged his finger like a professor. "You don't need to waste good money on that book. Not when you've got me."

"You've read books on sword fighting?" Franko asked skeptically as he put the book back.

His father held his head high, a haughty expression on his face. "I have both read and practiced."

"Well then, maybe you could teach me since you suddenly know so much, Father," Franko responded playfully.

"Maybe I will," Ringo replied. "Once we get back to Wyverly, I will show you everything I know."

Franko smiled at the thought of his father being some sort of master with the sword. But his smile quickly faded as he thought of their trip back. *Would we be taking that same route?* He thought. *Would we run into Quinn and the Forest Folk again... or even Ghost?*

"Something wrong, son?" Ringo asked when he noticed Franko's worried expression.

"Can I talk to you about something... outside?" he whispered as he nervously glanced around.

His father's eyes darted around as he straightened up. "Okay..." he said pensively.

Ringo went to the counter, paid for all their supplies, and then took Franko out to the wagon.

"Tell me what's bugging you, son," Ringo said in a low tone as he leaned toward Franko.

"I'm nervous about taking that same route back," he whispered. "Remember when I told you about that demon attacking me in the woods and we thought it was just a dream?"

Ringo hesitated for a moment. "Yes, what about it?"

"It wasn't a dream. It was real," Franko replied, his voice uneasy.

Ringo eyed his son skeptically. "And how do you know this was real, Franko? I thought we talked this over already."

"She told me," Franko answered. "I didn't tell you this before because she made me promise, but after that happened, that demon lady confronted me twice while I was alone back there."

Ringo's eyes went wide in a mixture of shock and rage. "Franko," he scolded, "you should have told me about this."

"I know, Father. I'm sorry, but she frightened me," the boy said, his voice shaky. "She knew things, Father. She knew who I was, who you were, she knew about Greencourt, about my letter to Gwendolyn. She told me the trees could hear everything we said. I was scared, Father."

Ringo's face went red with rage, his teeth gritting. "Did that witch do anything to you, Franko?" he interrogated. "Did she hurt you in any way?"

Franko shook his head quickly. "No... not like that. I mean, she was a little rough with me, but I don't think she meant to hurt me at all. She told me I was under the tree's protection."

Ringo stood silent for a minute, studying his son's face. "Maybe that little witch is some sort of demon after all," he grunted. "I wonder if she has some sort of connection to the Garelians. They study dark magic."

Franko had never seen his father so visibly upset before. He noticed he hadn't been the same ever since that day in Greencourt when he got that broken sword back. Something about that blade changed something in Ringo.

"We are going to take a different way back, Franko," Ringo said through his clenched teeth. "And you are not to leave my side, no matter what. And if I run into that little forest witch, I'll make sure she knows to never lay a hand on you again."

"Father," Franko pleaded. "She said we were welcome to come back. I really don't think she's a threat—"

"This isn't up for debate, Franko!" his father snapped. "We're taking a different way back, and that's final."

Ringo grabbed his son's arm firmly, and they walked back into the general store together. He took a sack of coins and slammed it on the table in front of the clerk.

"I want the sharpest dagger this money can buy," he barked to the man behind the counter.

The clerk looked through the sack of coins before handing Ringo a dagger from a display case nearby.

"The next person who thinks they can put their hands on my son is gonna catch the wrong end of this blade," Ringo told the boy flatly as he slid the dagger into his belt and left the store.

The two headed toward the inn to buy a room for the evening. Ringo stayed up all night, watching over Franko like a sentinel. He woke him at daybreak, and they hopped into their wagon and headed farther east, on a different path back to Wyverly.

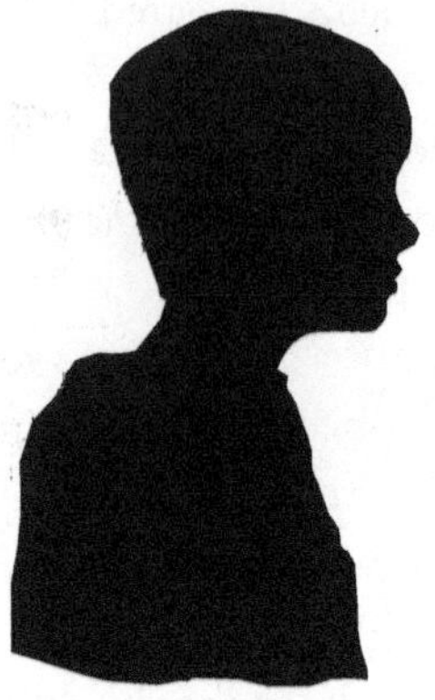

Chapter 13

An Unfamiliar Route

It was a couple of days into their travels when they approached a mountain pass near the Vodavi-Wyverly border. The quiet of the pass was unsettling, and the wind blowing through the narrow path made a howling that put young Franko on edge. *Maybe this was a mistake,* he thought.

Ringo had hardly spoken a word since Franko told him about his encounters with Ghost. He had kept a rigid expression on his face ever since, barely even looking his son in the eye. He could tell that his father was disappointed in him—the worst feeling in the world for a young boy.

"Is everything okay, Father?" Franko asked as they were navigating the mountain path.

Ringo inhaled sharply through his nose. "You should have told me about that witch before, Franko."

"I already told you I'm sorry, Father," the boy replied defensively. "I promise I won't do it—"

"We aren't a family that keeps secrets, Franko!" his father snapped.

Franko's eyes began to well up, a mixture of fear and anger. "Really, Father?" he shot back. "What about Mother? You won't tell me hardly anything about her! I had to beg you just to tell me her name. And you shout at *me* for keeping secrets?"

Ringo turned toward the boy and grabbed him by his cloak, pulling him close. "You do not speak to your father that way! And do not speak of things you know nothing about. Everything I have done for you, your whole life, has been to protect you. Your mother is gone, that's all you need to know. I will not speak of her with you again. Understood?"

Franko quickly nodded without a word. Ringo let him go, and the two went back to riding along the path, looking straight ahead, without speaking a word to each other.

A short time later, Ringo slowed the wagon down, seeing that their path was blocked by a fallen tree up ahead. "Stars be damned," he sighed as he got off to inspect the large tree. "It would take forever to cut through this with nothing but a small dagger and this blade," he remarked as he looked at the broken sword in his hand. "We'll have to turn around and look for another path."

As he turned back around to face the wagon, Ringo froze in place. There was a figure in a crimson colored cloak atop the wagon, with a blade to his terrified young son's throat.

"The Garelians!" Ringo gasped in horror at the sight. "No!" he hollered. "Please, that's my son. We're just poor merchants, we—"

"Silence, you worthless rat!" barked another crimson-hooded figure who stepped out from behind a large boulder. "You are nearing Garel's holy temple. This is an act punishable by death," he snarled. The man pulled his hood down. He looked to be middle-aged, tall, and muscular with a clean-shaven head and claw marks tattooed across his face. He was holding a double-sided axe with blue-tinted blades at his side.

"Lace!" Ringo screamed as he saw the man. He stood, his chest heaving, fear and anger both raging inside of him. "Damn you, leave my son alone!"

Lace looked at Ringo, his expression perplexed. "And who are you? How do you know my name? Nobody who knows my name lives." As the words left his mouth, his countenance changed to that of amusement. "Ahh, I remember you now. You're the man who was with Riva. The coward who ran all those years ago. The one who was too afraid to fight."

Franko watched on helplessly, terrified by the cold steel blade Lace's henchman had pressed against his neck.

"Just leave my son alone, please. We want no trouble with you. We promise we won't tell anyone we saw you here," Ringo pleaded.

"A coward as always," Lace scoffed. "I see nothing has changed." He looked over to Franko, then back at Ringo. "You are on holy ground, fool. The Star Temple lies just ahead. The throne of Garel. You would dishonor the mighty King Garel, son of the fallen star?"

"I promise you," Ringo said, his voice quivering. "We want nothing to do with any religious conflict. Like I said, we are just poor merchants."

"I don't care who you are!" snapped Lace as he lifted his axe in front of him. "Normally, I would give poor souls such as yourself an opportunity to join us or die. But since it's you, I'm going to finish the job this time."

Franko watched as Lace raised his axe to come down on his father's skull when he saw him narrowly dodge the blow. He tried to stand up, but the man holding him hostage drove his knee into the boy's gut. He keeled over and gasped for air, unable to stand and fight off the man and aid his father.

Ringo used the edge of his broken sword and sliced across the left side of Lace's face, causing the Garelian to howl in pain. He then pulled the small dagger out of his belt and threw it with precision at the man who had been holding his son hostage. The knife landed square in the man's temple, killing him instantly.

Franko sat paralyzed and tried to inch himself away from his fallen attacker, and looked over at his father, who had directed his attention back to Lace. He struggled to steady himself, the wind still knocked from his lungs.

"Run, Franko!" he hollered. "Run for your life!" Ringo swung his blade again at Lace, aiming for his head, but the Garelian leader lifted his arm just in time to divert the lethal strike. The attack put a gash in Lace's arm, causing him again to groan in pain.

Ringo was about to strike again when a voice called out from a nearby cave. "Yellow Fang!" boomed the female voice, and a wave of yellow energy struck Ringo, causing him to drop his weapon and hold his hands over his eyes, screaming in agony.

"My eyes!" Ringo shrieked.

Lace had a look of intense rage on his face as he lifted his axe and brought it down across Ringo's back, sending him to the ground in a heap.

"Father!" screamed Franko, and he ran toward him.

Ringo slowly lifted his head toward his son but gurgled out his last words, "Run, Franko. Dammit, run for your life," he rasped as he collapsed and fell limply to the ground.

As Franko kept running to his father, Lace lifted his axe again. "And now it's your turn, little rat!"

Lace took a swing with his axe at Franko, but the injuries from Ringo's attacks prevented him from landing his blade on the boy's head. Franko lifted his arm up, and the handle of Lace's axe came down on his forearm. The boy felt a jolt of intense pain shoot through his forearm and fell to the ground screaming.

Franko immediately stood up and ran toward the forest beyond the pass.

"Stop him!" shouted Lace.

The woman who had cast the spell on Ringo came out of the cave. She was a thin, middle-aged woman with bright blonde hair tied in a tight bun. She clasped her hands together in front of her chest and heaved, "Yellow Fang!" A yellow wave of energy again shot out from her, narrowly missing young Franko as he fled.

"After him!" the woman shouted.

Two cloaked figures emerged from the cave behind her, pursuing Franko, daggers in hand.

The boy ran as fast as he possibly could, favoring his right forearm and gasping desperately for more air. All he could hear was the heavy breathing of his pursuers and the sounds of twigs and branches snapping as they ran.

Franko kept speeding through the forest, looking for a way to escape the Garelian killers. He slid down a steep hill, dirt and pebbles pelting his face, getting in his eyes and mouth as he slid.

He got up and ran across a stream and up another hill, now screaming desperately, "Somebody help me, please!"

He saw a dagger whizz by his head, missing him by a hair and sticking in a tree. He could hear his pursuers gaining on him now; his legs were aching, and his lungs were burning. He kept running as fast as the rough terrain would allow him.

Franko felt something hard smack against the back of his skull. One of the Garelian assassins had thrown a fist-sized rock that struck the boy on the head. His vision blurred, and he collapsed to the ground. He felt his stomach rise to his throat, feeling as if he were about to vomit as he gasped for more air on the leaf-covered forest floor.

"Looks like your time is up, boy," one of the attackers said, taunting him.

"Please," Franko whimpered. "Please don't kill me."

"Beg all you want. It won't help you. You're a coward, just like your father was," mocked the other attacker.

As the attackers brandished their blades, a sickening squelch sound could be heard, followed by one of the Garelian killers falling to the ground dead, a dagger in the side of their neck.

The remaining attacker looked around frantically to find his partner's killer, only to meet the same fate seconds later. Another dagger was sent through his throat, and he fell down dead.

Franko tried desperately to lift himself, but collapsed again from pain and exhaustion. He tried to scan his surroundings, but his vision remained distorted, and it felt as if his head were swimming.

As he slipped out of consciousness, he spotted her, the Forest Demon, looming over him.

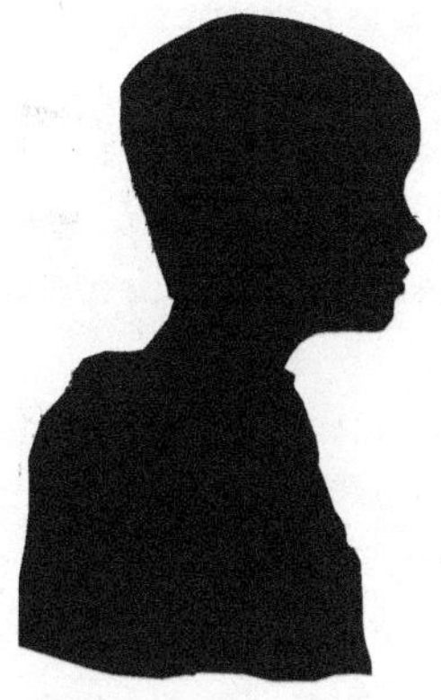

Chapter 14

Surprisingly Human

It was night by the time Franko came to. He opened his eyes in a stupor, hoping his last memories were nothing but a bad dream. He was trying to focus his vision when he noticed he was lying by a campfire, and someone was crouching across from him on the other side.

"Father?" he groaned as he went to touch the back of his aching head, only to wince as his fingers touched the spot where a rock had struck him.

"Franko," a voice replied, low and soft. "I see you've awoken. How are you feeling?"

"Uhh," the boy moaned as he tried to collect himself. "Father, where is he? I saw him getting attacked. Is he—"

"Don't try to move too much, Franko. You were badly hurt, but you're safe now," Ghost replied.

"Ghost? Is that you? What... what happened? Who were those people who attacked us?" Franko asked as he went to rub the sleep from his eyes, but noticed he couldn't move his right arm. It was bound to his body with a rope, and a makeshift wooden splint was tied to his forearm.

"You broke your arm. Don't try to move it," she said.

"What happened to Father?" he asked desperately as the fog in his mind slowly started to clear.

The Forest Demon sat silent for a moment before speaking up. "He... he was killed. I'm sorry, Franko. You're lucky to be alive yourself. If it hadn't been for me intervening, you would have joined him."

He felt as if he was going to vomit; he grimaced at the news of his father and started to sob. "Father," he cried, "I'm so sorry... this is all my fault. I shouldn't have said anything!"

Franko wiped the tears from his eyes and noticed that Ghost had her hood pulled down. He saw her full face for the first time. However, it was still difficult to make out her features, as it was still painted to resemble a skull. The expression on her face seemed genuine sorrow. It was the first time he had ever seen a sincere emotion like that in her. He couldn't help but notice, upon seeing her face, that, in spite of the small horns on her head, she looked surprisingly human. She had yellow eyes and her hair was a deeper shade of red than he'd ever seen in a person's hair before—as red as blood.

Ghost remained crouched in front of the fire, staring blankly at the flames. "He was a good man. He did not deserve this fate," she said thoughtfully. "And it's not your fault, Franko. It was the Garelians who did this. They are to blame—no one else."

The Garelians, he thought. *And that man, with the axe, were they the people from my dream the other night? The ones who attacked that forest village?*

"Do you know them, the Garelians?" he asked.

"They are a dangerous cult and should be avoided at all costs," she replied bitterly. "They terrorize the forest and all who they come into contact with."

Franko couldn't bring himself to respond. He lay on his side, his heart heavy with grief for his father, the only person who truly loved and cared for him. "I don't know what I'm gonna do," he said, his voice strained.

"Father was all I had. I don't know if I can go on living like this. I hate that the last time we spoke, we were angry at each other."

"You are grieving, Franko," Ghost told him. "This is to be expected. Do not make any rash decisions. Right now, you just need to sit and feel it. Feel the pain, but don't let it take over."

Franko could do nothing but sit and weep uncontrollably. His heart broken and his mind weary.

"Take all the time you need, Franko," she said as she stood up and turned her back to him. "I am going to get some more medicinal herbs for your wounds and something to relax you so you can rest. There are some nuts and berries in a sack beside you; help yourself to as many as you like. I will be back shortly, just yell out if you need anything."

Franko offered no response as she walked away into the darkness, leaving him alone with his thoughts and his grief. He looked hopelessly out into the night sky, shooting stars periodically illuminating the darkness. *If only a wish on a star truly worked like they said,* he thought. *Why is the world such a cruel place?* He asked himself, hopelessly. Then the cryptic words his father had said to him back in Greencourt the evening before they left crossed his mind. *The world is cruel to a broken blade.* Tears ran down Franko's cheeks as he tightly closed his eyes and clenched his jaw. *You were right when you first said it, Father. We... are broken.*

***

The following hours passed like a blur to Franko. Time was meaningless, sometimes dragging along and other times, racing like a chariot. He noticed his right arm began throbbing intensely, the pain returning as whatever medicine she had given him was beginning to wear off.

He wasn't sure how long he had been waiting by the time Ghost returned. She had several herbs held in a basket made of willow shoots, no doubt something she had made herself. She also held Ringo's broken sword, placing it on the ground next to him.

"I thought you might want this," she remarked, motioning toward the sword.

"You... went there? To where they attacked us?" he asked as his heart sank. "Was Father there? Did you—"

"Yes, I came across your Father's body. It was earlier, while you were still unconscious," she answered. "I made sure to give him a proper burial. I do hope that's okay with you. I didn't feel it was wise or beneficial to have you see him in that condition."

Franko's eyes welled up again. He was somehow hoping she would say that she found him alive, that he somehow survived, and everything would be okay. But he knew better; his father had died right in front of him as he fled from the battle.

The boy's chest began heaving as he sobbed once again. *If only I had been stronger. If I could have stood up and fought with him.*

"If you're beating yourself up right now for not rescuing your father, you need to stop," she told him. "You're no older than ten; there's nothing you could have done other than get yourself killed. Your father died fighting for you. Do not disgrace his sacrifice," she said sternly.

He would have liked to have said her words brought him some sort of relief, but they didn't. He couldn't stop thinking about how he lay there helpless as his father was slaughtered in front of his eyes. One thing that did strike him as he reflected was how his father was able to fight like that. The way he evaded Lace's attack and injured the Garelian priest, as well as killing Franko's captor with the dagger. He had no idea that his father really knew how to fight. Franko thought he was surely joking back at Findale when he told him he knew sword fighting. It had never been mentioned before. *Where did he learn to fight that way?*

While he was thinking back on the events that took his father's life, Ghost had been mixing some herbs and flowers, concocting some sort of medicine for him. She stirred them in a bowl with water and handed it to him.

"Drink," she said flatly as she handed him the bowl. "It's bitter, but it will help with the pain and also help you to sleep."

He choked down the unpleasant-tasting mixture she had made for him as best he could; the medicine numbing his tongue after a short while. It didn't take long for him to feel the effects in his body, as the pain in his arm slowly dissipated and sleep started to weigh on his eyes.

"Good," said Ghost as she stood. "Now, you rest."

She laid the boy on his side and pulled his cloak over him. Before he fell asleep, he asked her something. "I want to learn to fight like you," he said faintly, trying to keep from drifting off to sleep for a moment. "Will you train me?"

She looked down at him, not answering at first. He couldn't make out her expression, whether she was flattered or frustrated. "Just get some rest," she replied. "Once your arm starts to heal, we can talk."

Chapter 15

Time to Heal

The next few days were lonely and miserable for Franko. Ghost would come and go throughout the day to check on him, administer medicine, and bring him food as needed, never saying what she was doing or where she was going when she was gone for extended periods of time. Few words were spoken between the two of them.

He spent most of his time in deep thought. Coming to grips with the reality that his father was never coming back, and wondering what Gwendolyn was up to. *Had she missed me? Is she upset that I never sent her a letter? Will I ever get to see her again?* he would ask himself. Then he realized something: *the letter! Do I still have it?*

He slowly sat himself up and went through his satchel and cloak as best he could, using only his left arm. He checked every square inch to see if it was still there. Nothing. *It must have fallen out when I was running from the Garelians,* he reasoned. *Either that or Ghost took it again*. Franko heaved a sigh in frustration. *Where can I get my hands on another piece of paper and a pencil out here?* He thought, hopelessly. He feared his chances of ever seeing or even writing Gwendolyn any time soon were slim at best. He often found himself lost in anxiety and fear as to what he was to do next, after his arm healed. Possibly, he could go to Greencourt and see Gwendolyn and ask if anyone there would offer him a home, but he felt that was somehow beneath him. *It feels too much like begging*, he told himself. He did his best to push such thoughts away, as it caused him to sink into a state of hopelessness and despair. Nevertheless, it weighed on him heavily, even if it was from the back of his mind.

Ghost returned as the sun was setting, bringing with her some more flowers and herbs, along with some nuts and berries, as well as a couple of dead rabbits she had hunted down. *Must be dinner,* he thought. *It's been a while since I've had meat.*

"I feel guilty just sitting here while you wait on me," he told her as she began sorting out her finds from the day. "Is there anything I can do to help?"

"No," she answered flatly, not even turning her head in his direction as she spoke. "You need more time to heal; any movement can aggravate your injury."

Franko groaned in frustration. "This is driving me crazy, being out here in the middle of nowhere all by myself most of the time. What are you doing when you're out there? Where do you go, and why can't I go with you?"

"Do not be ungrateful, Franko," she responded curtly. "Where I go and what I do is none of your concern."

The boy sat silently for a moment. "Have you thought about what I asked the other night, about training me?" he asked.

"No."

Franko groaned again. "Well, I have a friend in Greencourt. I would like to see them again. Maybe I'll just head there in the morning. Would you help lead me out of this forest?"

"No."

"Why not?" he snapped.

"You are sounding ungrateful, child," she chided him. "I saved your life, I took care of you, and this is how you treat me? You can't travel with your injuries. You need to heal."

Franko closed his eyes and nodded in embarrassment. "You're right," he said humbly. "You have taken good care of me. I'm sorry if I don't sound appreciative. I'm just worried about a lot of things right now."

"You need to give yourself more time to heal, then you can plan what to do next," she responded, not acknowledging his apology or gratitude.

"Well, how long do these things take to heal?" he asked impatiently.

Ghost sagged her shoulders and gazed up in frustration. "It will take at least a few weeks for you to be able to use your arm again," she replied shortly.

"A few weeks!?"

"Yes, Franko. A few weeks. There's nothing I can do about that. I'm not the one who broke your arm. If you aren't happy with the current arrangement, take it up with Lace and the Garelians," she said obnoxiously.

Franko stood himself up and propped up against a tree, pressing the back of his head against it in frustration. "I just don't know what to do. I'm sorry if I don't sound grateful, I'm just going to lose my mind out here."

Ghost didn't respond at first. She started working on getting a fire going. "I sent your letter off to be delivered," she told him over her shoulder.

The boy jerked his head and looked at her with his eyes wide. "You did what?" he asked in astonishment.

"I told you. I had your letter delivered. I saw some merchants on the main route. They said Greencourt was one of their stops. So I gave them the letter along with some coins and asked them to deliver it," she said as a matter-of-factly. "They seemed like decent merchants. I think they'll honor their word and deliver the letter."

For the first time in ages, Franko's heart raced in excitement. "I can't believe it! This is great. Thank you so much!"

Ghost let a slight smirk cross her painted face, "You're welcome."

As Franko gave the matter some thought, something didn't sit right about what she said. *She met some merchants? What, did they just stop and have afternoon tea and a chat with some spirit demon witch with horns who paints her face to look like a skeleton?* "Can I ask you something, Ghost?"

She exhaled out of her nose in frustration at the question. "What is it?"

"It's just... about the merchants you met. You said you spoke with them and delivered the letter," he paused for a moment to think through what to say without sounding rude. "I just remember when we first met. I thought you were kinda—"

"You were scared of me," she interrupted. "And part of you still thinks I'm scary, right?"

He shifted around uneasily. "Well..."

"A spirit can take many forms," she remarked. "We can seamlessly move between different societies and groups as we see fit, dependent upon our wants and needs at a particular moment," she went on. "To you, I'm some sort of demon, here to protect the forest and scare off those who would harm. To them, I was a mere traveler who was in need of delivering a letter for a friend. That is all you need to know."

Franko looked at her in bewilderment. "How did you—"

"I will take no more questions about myself, my activities, or the means by which I choose to pursue them. This is my forest, and I determine the rules. Understood?" she stated adamantly.

The boy nodded nervously. The more he spoke with Ghost, this spirit, demon, witch, guardian, whatever she was, the more uneasy he felt. She set a plate of food down for him and abruptly left, not returning until the following morning.

The days slowly turned into weeks, and Franko's arm began to heal. It was time for him to choose what he would do next.

Chapter 16

When Do We Start?

Tired of having his arm bound up, Franko decided to undo his restraints and remove the splint. It was an eerie feeling to be able to move his right arm freely once again after so many weeks. He hadn't seen Ghost since he went to lie down for the evening the night before, so he took it upon himself to grab his father's broken blade and find an open area to start practicing his swordplay.

As much as he longed to see Gwendolyn, what he desired most was revenge. *Besides,* he thought, *it sounds like my letter got delivered. If Ghost decides to train me, I can find my way to the nearest town and send another letter when I'm not practicing.*

Getting used to moving his right arm again was an adjustment. Gripping the sword felt awkward at first, and swinging it even more so. He figured if he kept using it, his strength and dexterity would return in no time.

For hours, he would swing the blade in different positions and different angles, imagining he was fighting off the Garelians. He found himself drenched in sweat and heaving for breath, but he kept pushing. *I have to get stronger. I have to learn how to use a blade,* he told himself.

As he continued practicing his strikes, he heard Ghost from the treetops. "What in stars' light do you think you're doing?" she asked, her tone almost bored and lackadaisical.

Franko turned to look up, his breathing heavy. "I'm just practicing," he said between breaths.

"Why did you take your splint off? I told you I would tell you when you were ready," she said as she quickly scaled down the tree to meet him.

"My arm felt fine. It's been feeling fine for days now," he retorted.

"I don't care. I told you I would let you know when it was ready," she responded flatly as she approached him. Her yellow eyes were glaring at him in disapproval.

"I don't see what the problem is," he responded defensively.

"Hold up your arm like you're blocking an attack," she said.

"What do you mean?"

"Don't you understand the common tongue?" she asked derisively. "Hold. Up. Your. Arm. To block."

He tightened his jaw and held up his right arm, as if to block an attack. Ghost raised her hand in front of her and swatted his forearm with the back of her hand, doing little more than a flick of her wrist. Franko felt a vibrating pain shoot through his arm and fell to his knees as he hollered in agony.

Ghost stood over him, a look of disdain upon her face. "You should not have removed the splint. I'm not putting a new one on you," she remarked stoically. "You'll just have to deal with the pain now. Do not disrespect me like that again." She turned and started to walk away. "And your swordplay was pathetic. Your footwork was off, and you left yourself wide open. I could have dispatched you with my eyes closed."

"So will you train me or not?" he shouted as she scaled back up a tree to leave.

"I feel like I have to," she hollered back. "You're bent on revenge regardless, and the way you fight now, you won't last five seconds in a battle."

A smile crossed Franko's face as he rubbed his hurting arm. "So, when do we start?"

"Just stay where you are. I'll be back in an hour," she replied. "We'll start our training then."

Chapter 17

Breaking and Putting Back Together

True to her word, Ghost showed up about an hour later, with a couple of wooden staffs in hand. She took her cloak off, which is something Franko had never seen her do before. It appeared that all the skin on her visible body was painted black and white to look like a skeleton. This was a strange spirit, to say the least.

"Are you ready, Franko of the broken blade?" she asked in what sounded like a taunt.

He blinked and furrowed his brows at her question. *Franko of the broken blade, that's a new one,* he thought. "Yes, I'm ready,' he answered.

"We're going to start with footwork; this is the most important part. It's all about maintaining your balance and control. An errant swing need not throw off your balance and expose an opening to your opponent."

For the rest of the day, the two practiced footwork, how to maintain balance, and how to do so while holding a weapon in various positions. Franko had noticed how similar the footwork used for battle was to that of a dance; one looking on without a frame of reference might not even notice the difference.

As the days and weeks progressed, the boy had finally gotten to the point of making the footwork feel like second nature. It was then that attacks and blocks were incorporated. Then, the hand-to-hand element of combat. Everything from punches and kicks to grappling and throws. Whether it was standing or fighting on the ground, they covered combat in virtually any scenario.

Another exercise was as much about combat as it was about survival—persistence hunting. As a means of building his endurance, she would make him stalk and chase prey until it tired, and then catch it with his bare hands. Be it a rabbit, a squirrel, or a deer. He learned how to stalk quietly and run endlessly.

The worst parts of training were what Ghost called the sensory exercises. Sometimes she would blindfold him, other times, she would plug his ears with cloth or wool so he couldn't hear. Then she would attack from different angles, forcing him to rely on his other senses to defend himself. Her strikes were brutally efficient and unrelenting. If he ever showed signs of giving up, she would strike even harder. It took some time and a great deal of patience, but he eventually reached a point where he could fight efficiently with the senses he had.

All this left little time for him to write to Gwendolyn. He was so worn in the evenings that the thought of going to a town to get paper made him groan. But he awoke one morning to find a stack of parchment and a lead pencil by his side. No doubt a gift from Ghost. He thanked her, but she ignored him.

Franko couldn't think of what he should write. He knew Ghost wouldn't allow anything about her to be mentioned, and he was unsure if he wanted to bring up his father's death. He thought this would do nothing but worry Gwendolyn. He decided that less was more and wrote her simple messages, neither lying to her nor telling her everything. He would say that he missed her, that he looked forward to seeing her again soon, and that their travels were taking them longer than expected.

He didn't dare ask Ghost to deliver the letters for him, and she wouldn't allow him to stray from camp. So he would place his written letters folded up on a tree stump near where he would lie for the evening, and they would be gone by the time he awoke. Again, he would thank the strange forest guardian, and again, she would ignore his gratitude.

Ghost's training was brutal and unforgiving. She would push Franko to his limit and beyond. Every day, she would break him, and every evening, she would put him back together with various ointments, medicines, and muscle massage. Few words were spoken between the two; she forbade casual discussion and despised small talk. He was chastised whenever he tried to speak without permission. Though he noticed that she would break such rules as she saw fit herself.

"So, whatever happened to your mother, Franko?" she asked one evening after training, staring blankly at the campfire.

"Like my father, she was killed by Lace. It happened right after I was born," he replied. "Father said she left to visit family and was killed by the Garelians. I never knew her. He wouldn't even tell me what she looked like. I had to beg him even to tell me her name—Riva."

Ghost's face was without any expression; she just continued to gaze at the flames.

Franko decided to risk being chided and spoke up. "I didn't keep my word with you back then," he told her.

She gave him a sideways glance. "What are you talking about?"

"Back when we first met, you told me not to mention our meeting to Father," he said cautiously, worried that she would get upset. "Before we left Vodavi, I told him. I'm sorry."

He looked at her, expecting her to lash out at him or berate him. But she sat there just as before, staring at the fire with an unreadable expression.

"What did he say?" she asked him.

"He was mad," Franko replied, shaking his head in regret. "He was mad that I didn't tell him before. That's what we were upset with each other about before everything happened. And that's why we took a different way back. Why we crossed Lace's path, it's my fault."

Ghost raised her head, looking thoughtfully out into the distance. "It wasn't your fault. I don't want to hear any more of that talk," she said intently.

"I was hesitant to tell you that," he said with relief. "I'm glad you aren't upset with me."

Ghost offered no response; she shifted her focus back on the flames. Staring blankly, the reflection of the flickering light danced on her golden-colored eyes.

Chapter 18

A Dry Blanket

One day, while they were training, they heard crying in the distance. It had been raining steadily throughout the day and just begun to let up.

"It sounds like a child crying," Franko remarked.

"I'm sure her family is close by," Ghost replied. "Let's leave it be for now. But I do think we should hide so they don't see us."

As they sought cover, the crying continued.

"I think we should at least check it out, Ghost," Franko said as he peered around the tree trunk he was hiding behind.

"Very well," Ghost groaned. "But I think we're wasting our time; surely her family is with her."

"It won't hurt to check, will it?" he asked.

"I will go first, I can spot them without being seen. You make too much noise," she remarked as she scaled a nearby tree and began to make her way toward the sound of the crying child.

Franko followed her on foot as quickly and quietly as he could. He heard Ghost whistle, indicating that she had found something. As he approached, he saw her. A young girl, no older than five. She was whimpering and shivering alone in the woods.

"Hey there," Franko said gently to the frightened little girl, who was visibly startled by his approach.

"It's okay," he assured her. "My name is Franko. What's your name?"

The child was hesitant to answer at first, but finally spoke up. "Bella," she said faintly, her lip quivering and eyes watering as she looked at Franko pensively.

"Bella? That's a pretty name," he said softly. "Where is your family? Are you lost?"

"Yes," she said with a sob. "I saw a pretty squirrel, so I followed it. Now I can't find my parents."

"I'm sorry," Franko replied. "I bet that must be scary, and you look cold and wet too," he said as he stooped down to be eye level with the child. "All I have on me now is my cloak, and it's soaked from the rain. Otherwise, I would give it to you."

Just then, Ghost came down from the trees, much to Bella's horror. She eyed the forest guardian with terror as she ran and hugged Franko around the chest.

"It's okay, Bella," Franko said as he patted the little girl on the head. "She might look a little scary, but she's a friend. She protects the forest."

Bella looked hesitantly in Ghost's direction, who responded with a slight nod.

She reached into her pack and pulled out a dry blanket. "Take this, it is dry," she said flatly as she handed the blanket over to Franko to give to the girl.

"A dry blanket!" Franko said, in childlike surprise, to amuse the girl. "What I wouldn't give for one of these!"

He wrapped Bella in the blanket and lifted her up. "I tell you what, Bella," he said as he wiped her tears with a corner of the blanket. "Why don't the three of us go for a walk and see if we can find your family. Is that okay?"

Bella nodded in return, her expression softening as the fear visibly started to leave her. Ghost climbed back up a tree and began to search for her family.

As they were walking, Franko asked the girl a question. "Bella, have you ever put your wings on?"

She looked back at him with a confused expression and shook her head.

"No?" he responded in mock disbelief. "Well, we have to fix that."

He lifted her horizontally over his head and began to run. Bella's breathing was quivering.

"Spread your arms out, Bella," Franko hollered as he ran. "We call that *putting your wings on*. It makes it feel like you're flying. My father used to do this with me when I was younger."

As he kept running, the girl finally began to feel more comfortable and spread her arms. "Like this?" she asked, her face beaming.

"Yes, that's it. That's perfect!" he exclaimed.

"It feels like I'm flying, Franko!" Bella shouted in excitement. "I have my wings!"

It was a short while later when they heard the desperate shouts of Bella's parents looking for her. Once Ghost spotted them in the distance, she whistled again for Franko. He began to follow the sound of their voices and saw them a ways out, hollering Bella's name.

"That must be them," he told Bella as he cradled her in his arms. She could barely contain her excitement when she saw her mother and father in the distance.

"I think it's best if I let you go to them yourself, Bella," Franko told her as he set her down. "It was nice meeting you. Please stay safe, and don't go chasing after any squirrels in the woods, got it?" he said as he got down on one knee in front of her.

"I won't, Franko," she said sheepishly. "Thank you for helping me, and for showing me how to put my wings on," she added as she hugged him and kissed him on the cheek.

"You're welcome, Bella," he replied, patting her head as she turned and ran toward her parents.

Franko hid behind a tree and waited until he saw her parents grab and hold her tight, crying with joy that their little girl was okay.

He looked on, smiling from ear-to-ear at the sight of the reunited family. As he turned around, he was startled to see Ghost standing right behind him, looking on at the happy family as he had been.

"What are you looking at?" she asked sternly, turning her attention to him.

"Nothing," he said with a coy smile. "I just wasn't expecting you to care so much."

She narrowed her yellow eyes. "I don't know what you're talking about," she replied tersely. "This was your idea anyway."

As they began to make their way back, Franko couldn't help but feel some sort of envy over what he had just witnessed. Bella, a sweet little girl, being reunited with two loving parents. With two *living* parents. He found himself thinking about how Ghost had so willingly offered her dry blanket to the girl, without hesitation. *I wonder if she would have done something like that for me?* He asked himself.

"Ghost?" Franko asked, his curiosity getting the better of him.

"What!" she replied from the treetops, in a sharp tone that sounded more like a command than a question.

He swallowed nervously. "Would you have given *me* a dry blanket if I were cold and wet like that?"

There was a moment of silence between the two before she responded. "What a *stupid* question to ask," she chided.

Franko sighed and shook his head without a reply as they made their way back to camp. Not another word was spoken between the two of them for the rest of the day.

Chapter 19

A Shallow Grave

Two winters had passed while Franko lived in the wilderness of the northern forests of Wyverly. His only companion was a mysterious guardian of the forest, Ghost, who didn't have a real name, or at least not one that she ever gave to him.

He had just entered his twelfth year, and his mind and body were both strong, stronger than most grown men. His time training hard in the woods with this elusive figure had made it so, pushing him to the brink over and over. The boy had developed a cast-iron physique, along with unwavering bravery and resolve. He felt he was ready to hunt Lace and the Garelians. *But when should I make my move?* he would ask himself, endlessly wrestling with the thought of what could be his final battle and his only chance at revenge.

***

Then, one night, Franko found himself in a dream. He was near the same forest village as he was in that dream he had a couple of years earlier. He saw and heard the same sights and sounds as before, flames engulfing the homes and shacks of some remote forest village, the shouts and screams of the townspeople as they were mercilessly slaughtered by their crimson-cloaked attackers. He again saw the one holding an axe with blue-tinted blades.

"Lace and the Garelians," he barked bitterly as he watched the carnage unfold once more.

He saw her again, a young girl fleeing for her life with some of the cloaked invaders pursuing her.

"I'm not letting this happen again," he said adamantly as he ran toward the girl as fast as he could.

Franko was stronger and faster than he was last time. He caught up to the girl and followed her through the bushes as she sought refuge behind a tree, if only for a moment.

"Please, listen to me!" he pleaded. "My name is Franko. I'm not here to hurt you. I want to help."

She sat sobbing, offering no response to his pleas. Again, her face was obscured by a shadow, making it impossible for him to make out her features.

"You have to leave!" he shouted. "They'll find you!"

He heard the same shrill, contemptuous voice of a woman behind him as he heard last time. "So, you thought you could make it out of this alive, did you?"

Franko didn't bother to turn around this time. He recognized the voice now. "It's her, the woman who cast that spell on Father," he said between his clenched teeth.

He knelt down and reached for the young girl's face. "Who are you?" he asked. "Why am I here? Why am I seeing this when there's nothing I can do to help you?"

As his fingers touched the shadow obscuring her face, it vanished. He stumbled back and gasped at the sight.

As he suspected, it was a young girl, about the same age as him. But her features were unique: she had hair as red as blood, yellow eyes, swollen with tears and panic, and sharpened canines. Her face slowly started to warp into something else. Horns grew out of her forehead and what was once the face of an innocent looking young girl turned into a black-and-white skull-painted face that he recognized.

“Ghost?” he asked softly. “What is this? What are you doing here?”

There was no response. Franko sat back in disbelief as the dream faded and he awoke.

***

When he got up that morning, instead of heading to his usual training spot, he put on his cloak, placed his broken sword in a scabbard on his belt, and grabbed a wooden staff he had been using to train. He had gone through many staves over the past two years, but this one proved to be the strongest. Never breaking after countless strikes. He had just sharpened one end of it with his sword, to use as a more fatal weapon moving forward. He set his sights toward the Northeast, where he had last seen them. From there, he hoped to find the path that led to an old star temple they claimed was actually the throne of their demon king, Garel.

He had tried asking Ghost for help over the last few weeks, but she flatly refused and forbade him from going alone. "They practice powerful dark magic," she told him. "They cannot be easily defeated. The most we can do is what I've been doing the whole time. Keep them at bay, attack the ones who are not magic users if you must." But the problem was, Franko had never seen the Garelians again after that fateful encounter two years ago that claimed his father. They knew something ominous lurked in the forest and rarely ventured out, which explains why none were sent to recover their comrades who were slain by her back then.

Franko had had enough just waiting around for them to stumble upon him—he was ready for revenge and could wait no longer. So he wrapped his cloak tightly around himself, pulled up his hood, and marched.

That dream, he thought. *Why was Ghost there? Why was she a little girl?*

It was a couple of hours before he got there, the place he hadn't seen since that day two years earlier. The day that changed his life forever. The mountain pass where he first encountered Lace and the Garelians. There was nothing there from back then; the wagon was gone, no doubt either scrapped by the Garelians or claimed by some looters. There were no blood stains, washed away by the countless rains that had fallen since then. Even the fallen tree was gone, along with any trace of the Garelians. *But,* he thought, *this was their territory; surely they would come back to check on it at some point.*

He walked around the site, pain tearing his gut as he relived the last moment he was there. Then, he saw it, where the pass turned, and the forest began, behind some boulders—a shallow grave.

There were sticks tied together in the shape of a star sticking out of the dirt. "Father," he whispered with a pang of longing, his face wincing as tears streamed down his cheeks. Ghost had given Franko's father a proper burial, just as she had told him long ago. He leaned against the boulder and sobbed openly for the first time in ages. But his grieving didn't last long. He heard footsteps approaching.

Franko quickly hid himself behind the boulder, listening in as the footsteps and whispers of whoever was coming his way got louder. They were close enough so that he could now hear them.

"Madame Rayla insists that this pass be monitored, but we haven't seen a soul here in ages. This is a waste of time," rasped one of them.

"Master Lace has the utmost faith in Madame Rayla's judgement. If she tells us to patrol, we do it. No questions asked," said the other.

Garelians, Franko said to himself. *Two of them, but by the sound of it, they're just underlings. This may bode well. I can dispatch one of them and then get more information about these freaks. Where this star temple is and where this monster, Lace, came from. The more I know about him, the more I can use to take him down and the rest with him.*

The boy wasted no time; he leapt out from behind the rock and swung his staff with brutal efficiency, disarming both of them of the staffs in their hands in a matter of seconds. As one reached for a knife in his belt, Franko impaled him through the neck with his staff, causing the Garelian guard to fall dead to the ground. The other went to flee, but the boy dropped his staff, jumped on the boulder, and leapt onto the man's back. Franko pulled out his blade and held it to the man's throat.

"Tell me where this temple, this *throne of Garel* is, and I'll spare your life," he whispered in the man's ear as he pinned him to the ground.

The man's breath was quivering, but his jaw was clenched. "I will tell you nothing, boy. And you just threw your life away."

"That's fine," Franko growled. "I'm already broken," he said as he grabbed one of the man's arms, lifted it, and struck his right forearm against the Garelian's forearm, causing the man to scream in anguish as Franko broke his arm.

"Now do you feel like talking? Or should I break the other one?" he asked as he lifted himself off the guard, who was writhing in pain.

"Damn you!" the man shouted. "You're dead, you know that?!"

"Tell me where the temple is and everything you know about this Lace, or else I'm breaking your other arm," Franko told him slowly. The man didn't respond, only looking back at him in contempt.

"Fine," Franko said casually as he went to grab the guard's other arm.

"Stop!" the man shouted. "I'll tell you what I know," he growled between his clenched teeth. "What difference does it make? You'll just die in that temple anyway."

"Where... is it?" Franko said adamantly.

"It's about a half-day's journey east of here, you can see it from the cliff, a couple of miles from where we are now," the man groaned.

"And what about Lace? What can you tell me about him?"

"He's of the Sedowin people—a warrior tribe. I don't know much beyond that," the man said, wincing in pain. "Except," he added, "they were all wiped out several years ago. When they wouldn't bow their knee to Master Lace." The man was breathing heavily and looked up at Franko, raw hatred in his eyes. "And you will meet the same fate, you fool."

He glared at the Garelian guard, then began to turn to walk away. Just then, the man reached for the knife in his boot to lunge at the boy. But this proved a fatal mistake. Franko quickly dodged the attack and cut the man across his throat with the blade. The guard fell down dead, just like his partner.

"Who's the fool now?" Franko asked dryly as he turned to head east.

Chapter 20

Shattered

Franko made his way to the cliff that the Garelian guard had told him about. It was perilous terrain, but nothing he couldn't handle given his training and living circumstances over the last two years. He was more concerned about Ghost finding him and what she might do to him if she did. She wasn't one who tolerated disrespect, as he learned the hard way on the handful of occasions when he talked back to her during their training. Franko never knew his mother, and as much as he dreaded her discipline, part of him appreciated it. Almost as if it proved that someone out there still cared about him. He caught himself almost chuckling as a thought occurred to him, *Ghost is the closest thing to a mother I've ever known.*

It wasn't long before he arrived at the cliff. Sure enough, off in the distance, there stood what appeared to be old temple ruins. It had spires like claws reaching to the sky. A massive stone structure covered in ivy and moss. It looked as if several bricks were missing. *How old is that place?* He thought.

As he stood, studying the structure and trying to plan his best path to reach it, his thoughts were interrupted.

"Enjoying the view," said a sinister-sounding voice from behind.

He turned to see a man in a garnet cloak—an older man, tall and thin with salt and pepper hair and a matching well-trimmed beard. Two guards in similar garnet cloaks flanked him.

"Just passing through," Franko said as he tightened the grip on his staff.

"Oh, I'm sure," the man replied with an arrogant smirk. "My name is Ponzer, servant of Master Lace of the Garelians," he added with an insincere bow. "You know, we had two guards on patrol who are yet to report back. You wouldn't happen to know anything about that, would you?"

"Can't say as I do," replied Franko.

"Of course," the man said. "I'm sure you and your blood-stained staff had nothing to do with it," he remarked facetiously.

The two guards advanced on Franko, their staves held, ready to attack.

He immediately struck the first guard's arm, then did a spinning strike, connecting directly into the other man's gut with the dull end of his staff. He spun his staff around and was about to stab the first guard when the two stumbled out of the way, and Ponzer clasped his palms together in front of his chest, took a breath, and heaved, "Red Fang!"

Before Franko could even react, he was hit with a wave of red energy. A deafening squeal rang in his ears. He dropped his staff and placed his hands over them, but it offered no relief. He fell to his knees, howling in pain as the two guards grabbed each of his arms. Then he remembered the training that Ghost had put him through, how she would place that cloth in his ears and have to simulate deafness while he'd spar with her.

He fought through the immense pain and loss of hearing and rose up to knee one guard in the groin and deliver a vicious elbow to the other guard's nose. But before he could turn to attack Ponzer, the man struck Franko in the back of his knee with one of the guard's staffs. He fell to his knees again and then felt one of the guards kick him off the ledge of the cliff.

Franko fell hard on the cliff's face and had his body badly scraped as he slid down. He landed on another small cliff edge about fifty feet below. The fall had delivered some serious damage, but he was still conscious. The two guards were frantically looking around for the quickest path to the lower cliff edge when Ghost had arrived at Franko's side, shielding him from their view.

The three Garelians looked in bewilderment at the Forest Demon. "You," Ponzer said scornfully as he eyed the mysterious figure.

"Who is that? Should we go down and kill them?" asked one of the guards.

"No," Ponzer said, his voice grinding in frustration. "No one who has ever chased after her has returned. She's more trouble than she's worth. But I do have something for her," he said as he again clasped his hands together and heaved, "Red Fang!"

Another wave of red energy shot out from him, but Ghost knew it was coming, so she quickly grabbed Franko and leapt off the lower cliff into the forest below.

Ponzer looked on and inhaled sharply. "Damn that witch," he said bitterly. "Let's go. We'll report what happened to Lord Lace."

Ghost carried Franko over her shoulder until they got a safe distance away from the Garelians. She set him down and examined his wounds. He was covered with cuts and scrapes from head to toe.

"Dammit, Franko!" she hissed as she looked him over.

"I'll be fine," he groaned as he slowly stood up. "I've been through worse."

"Are you sure you're okay?" she asked.

"Yes, I'm good. It's just a few cuts and bruises," he replied.

"Good!" she snapped as she punched Franko in the gut, knocking the wind out of him and causing him to fall to his hands and knees, gasping for air.

"You fool!" she said sharply. "You would have been dead if it wasn't for me... again!"

Franko slowly stood back up, holding his stomach. "I'm sorry," he gasped. "I just couldn't wait around anymore. I thought I was ready. I wanted to–"

"Shut up!" she yelled as she slapped him across his face. "I told you not to confront them! Their magic is too powerful for you!"

"I see that now," he replied as he tried to catch his breath. "I'm sorry. It won't happen again."

She grabbed him by his shirt and leaned toward his ear. "You will not disrespect me like that anymore. Do you understand?"

He nodded as she let him go. "Thank you for helping me out there–"

"I don't want to hear it," she interrupted him as she made her way back, disappearing into the forest.

Franko slowly made his way back to the area of the forest that had become his home of sorts. He figured that Ghost wouldn't bother helping him bandage his wounds this time, as had become her unspoken policy for when he got himself hurt. So he rinsed his cuts off in the stream and placed crushed marigolds on them to help them heal faster. He had made a point to find out what some of the plants and herbs were that she used for these sorts of things.

When Franko got back to where he usually set up his campfire, he looked through his meager belongings and pulled out his father's star pendant–something he hadn't worn since the day he was killed. As he held it, he felt the same shame and helpless frustration he had that day. How he was unable to help his father back then, and how he failed in his attempt to avenge him today.

Tears of rage began to roll down his cheeks as he began to sob for the second time that day. "All this training and I still can't avenge you, Father," he said through his tears. "You were right the first time you said it. You told me later that we weren't broken, but you were wrong. I... am broken!" he shouted as he threw the star pendant against a tree, shattering it into pieces.

Upon seeing the shattered pendant, Franko immediately started crying in remorse for his outburst. Never noticing that Ghost had been perched up in a tree, watching him the entire time. He went to gather the broken pendant, regret twisting his gut. Then, he noticed something.

There was a folded-up piece of paper that had fallen from it. It wasn't just a simple pendant—it was a locket.

"What?" Ghost whispered in disbelief.

Franko looked in bewilderment at the folded paper on the ground, covered with shattered fragments of the pendant. As he reached for it, Ghost had swooped in to grab it before him.

"What are you doing?" he hollered. "Give that to me!"

"That does not belong to you," she said sharply.

"It was my father's! It's rightfully mine. Give it back, now!"

"It's mine now, child," she responded, her voice firm as she placed the paper in a satchel on her belt.

He went to grab her, but she quickly struck him with an open palm strike to his collar bone, followed by a knee to his gut and a hammer-fisted strike to the back of his head, sending him to the ground with a thud.

He stretched his arm out, and she stepped on his hand with her heel, twisting her foot to grind his hand into the ground. Franko groaned in pain. "Why are you doing this?" he grunted through his clenched teeth. "You... have no right."

"I make the rules in this forest," she growled. "And you... are done here," she added as she drew her leg back and kicked him across his head, knocking him out cold.

Chapter 21

I'll Find a Way

When Franko came to, the sun had just begun to peak. He scanned his surroundings to see Ghost looming over him. He also noticed that he was seated on the ground, his arms were tied around a tree trunk behind him, and there was a rag tied around his mouth to gag him.

Ghost crouched down, almost on top of him, her face almost pressing against his. "You... will never challenge me like that again," she said in a low growl. "Do you understand?"

Franko couldn't speak but just glared at her in anger instead.

"I see," she replied, "Then we'll just have to do things the hard way from now on."

She walked over and picked up a birch switch that she had prepared. "I know some like to teach their children respect this way," she said in a menacing tone as she waved the switch in front of her. "From now on, you will get reprimanded with this when you disobey."

Franko looked at her defiantly and began to lift himself up in spite of his arms being bound. She responded by whipping him on the side of his leg, beside his knee, causing him to groan in pain and fall back down into a seated position.

"I see it's working already," she rasped as he tried desperately to work himself free of the gag on his mouth.

"Is there something you feel the need to say?" she asked him, her voice taunting.

Franko nodded, not shifting his intense gaze from her yellow eyes. She reached down and pulled the gag out of his mouth. "Go ahead, speak," she said firmly.

"I'm done with you. With your training. With these woods. All of it," he snapped, his voice quivering in anger.

She leaned in close to him. "Your training is not complete."

"I don't care. I'm done," he said adamantly. "You can't keep me here. I'll find a way to escape you. I don't care if you're some sort of demon or spirit or whatever in stars' light you are. I will get out of here."

She stared at him silently for a moment. "Very well," she replied. "I will not keep you from leaving. Consider our arrangement over," she said as she tossed the switch aside and turned to leave.

"You could at least untie me," he hollered scornfully.

"Boy, if you can't get out of that, then my training has failed," she replied with a dismissive wave of her hand. "You have done well, Franko of the broken blade. The trees will miss you. They'd be happy to host you again sometime," she added with a mischievous smirk as she climbed a tree and dashed off into the woods.

Over the next few hours, Franko grimaced and groaned to break himself free. Rage and hatred were burning inside of him, toward the Garelians, toward Ghost, and toward himself.

"Ghost," he hissed. "Damn her. The last piece of my father was in that locket, and she took it from me. Just to show me that she could."

Then, he thought back on that dream again. The forest village getting slaughtered, the young girl who resembled Ghost.

She knows something, he thought, his mind boiling with bitterness and resentment. *About Lace and the Garelians. Damn her, she knows something!*

"Ghost!" he shouted up toward the forest canopy. "I know you can hear me."

He continued to struggle against the restraints. He felt the back of his leg burning from when she had lashed him with that switch. He felt the side of his head throbbing from where she had kicked him. "Damn you!" he cursed.

"I understand now!" he hollered. "I understand how demons operate now. You knew this was gonna happen to me, didn't you? You knew because it happened to you. They killed you and all of your people, didn't they? That's why you took me in. You wanted someone else to join you in your suffering and despair, and you want to drag me down with you. Well, I'm free from you now, from your tricks. I'm gonna come back someday and I'll be stronger. When I do, I'm gonna kill every last one of them—none of them get to live. I'll burn down the whole forest if I have to! And if you get in my way, you'll burn with it!"

Franko was finally able to work his way out of the binds that she had tied him up with, but not without adding more scrapes to his arms. Once he was free, he grabbed his cloak and his broken sword along with a small sack that was sitting next to it. When he opened it, he saw the shattered pendant inside. Ghost had gathered all the pieces and put them in there for him.

Looking upon the remains of the pendant she had collected for him, he was now even more confused about what to think of the Forest Demon than ever. He shook his head in disbelief and remorse over some of the things he had just said. *What sort of creature is she?* he asked himself as he gathered his belongings and made his way out of the forest for the first time in two years. He knew exactly where he was heading first.

Greencourt.

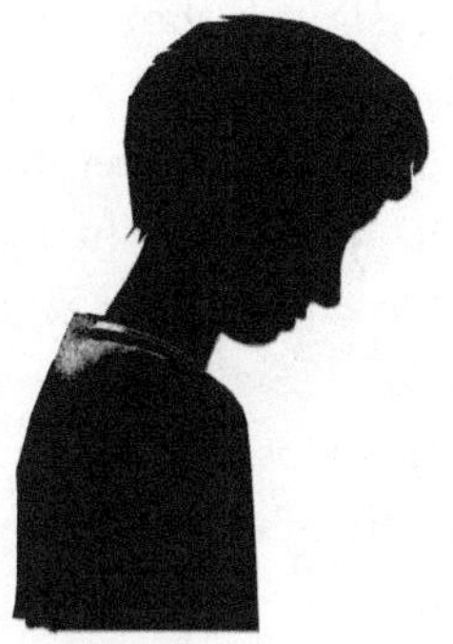

Chapter 22

If Only for a Moment

It took Franko a couple of weeks to make it back to Greencourt from the eastern side of the northern forest. As he approached the town, his knees began to shake, and his heart raced in anticipation. *Did she get the letters?* He wondered. *Does she still want to see me again? It's been two years, maybe she doesn't care anymore.*

Walking through the town entrance was almost like walking back in time to Franko. Nothing had changed in Greencourt since he was last there. Meanwhile, everything had changed for him. He was a completely different person than he was when he and his father left that town with a bag full of coins and a plan for the future.

He walked through the quaint little town, nodding to Mr. Chambers and his wife, who were standing out in front of their bed and breakfast, helping some guests unload. They waved back at him, though Franko was unsure if they recognized him. He had gotten much taller and leaner since they last saw him, and the trials of the last two years were visible on his face.

He passed by the blacksmith's shop, the shop run by Gwendolyn's adoptive family. He saw Bruno working, but Bruno didn't see him. Franko's priority was her; he would greet Bruno and the others later.

He walked toward the field where he had first met her, the events replaying in his mind. How her bright blue eyes mesmerized him the first time he met her gaze. How he made a fool of himself trying to play rushball with the other kids, and how embarrassed he was. A smirk crossed his lips when he thought about how he punched Bruno in the face for mocking his father.

His father... Franko had to fight back tears as he thought about him. He was so caught up in training for revenge with Ghost in the woods that he had almost forgotten what he had lost. *Father was the finest man I'd ever known.* He thought to himself. *We were poor, but he always made sure I had food and kept me safe. Father could have killed Lace at the mountain pass, but instead he threw a dagger to kill my captor, and that act cost him his life... Father... you were everything to me—the only thing. And now you're gone. Forgotten by the cruel world that you were so kind to. Do you remember that time in Velldale, Father? We were struggling—more than usual. We didn't know where our next meal would come from. Our wagon needed repair, and we had no coin to pay for it. I remember what you told me back then, when I saw a cart of apples, briefly left unattended by the man who owned it, and asked if I could steal one, hunger gripping my insides. You told me you'd rather die in a ditch than steal from a working man. You were so noble, Father. The most noble man I've ever known.*

"Franko?" a young female voice asked, interrupting his reverie.

He turned around to see her—Gwendolyn. She was somehow more beautiful than he remembered. She was taller and more slender, and her eyes glowed when he met them.

"Gwendolyn!" Franko said excitedly as he turned toward her. "I've thought about you every day. I'm so glad to see you." He ran up to her, and they embraced, a feeling he had been longing for ever since he left.

"I got your letters," she said, her eyes welling. "Thank you for writing them. I wish there were some way I could have written back. Where exactly have you been? Where is your father?"

He stiffened up at her questions—the excitement on his face at first seeing her changing to a sullen expression.

"Franko?" Gwendolyn asked, concerned. "Did something happen to you out there? I can see on your face that you've changed. More than just the kind of change from two years of growth."

Franko looked down, fighting back tears. He never mentioned in his letters what happened to his father. Gwendolyn walked up to him and grabbed him gently by the chin to lift his face. "Franko," she said softly, "What happened?"

Franko told her about how they had gotten ambushed by the Gare-lians, and his father died in the attack. How he had been stuck in that region for two years training, but he didn't mention Ghost. He was worried about what she would think of him living two years with a forest spirit in the wilderness. He kept the details of his time and training vague, but she didn't press him for specifics.

"Oh, Franko," she said, eyes welling with sympathy. "I'm so sorry to hear that. I know how much your father loved you. I wish there were something more I could do," she told him as she pulled him into another embrace.

The two stood hugging each other silently for a moment as Franko felt so much of the pain from the last two years melt away, if only for a moment. "Gwendolyn," he said as he let go of her and grabbed her hand. "Do you mind if we go for another walk in the woods, like we did before?"

She smiled and nodded as she interlaced her fingers with his. "I'd like that."

As the two made their way through the woods, back toward the lake, they skipped rocks two years earlier. Gwendolyn looked at him and smiled.

"What is it?" Franko asked, chuckling when he noticed her smiling at him.

"I'm just glad you wrote, even through all that."

Franko smiled back at her and nodded. “I wish I had written more. That I had told you what really happened. I just didn’t want to make you sad or worried,” he replied.

This made him think of Ghost, the strange spirit who kept her word and had the letters sent out. Just as she had followed through with giving his father a proper burial, he felt bad that things had ended the way they did with her, but he couldn’t help but have a deep sense of admiration toward the mysterious figure. She had crossed his mind often since he left. He had felt a strange connection with her that he wouldn’t dare tell anyone about, especially Gwendolyn.

“Are you okay, Franko?” Gwendolyn asked, noticing he appeared distracted.

“Oh, yes. I’m fine, sorry,” he said as he set his focus back on her. “I’ve just had a lot of things going through my mind lately.

“We’re here,” she told him as they approached the lake and sat down on the same boulder that they stood on the last time they came out.

Franko looked deep into her eyes again, getting lost in them just as he had before. He leaned in and kissed her on her cheek.

"Franko!" she said in shock as she placed her hand on her cheek. "What in stars' name was that?"

"I like taking risks," he said with a confident smirk on his face.

Gwendolyn blushed and then leaned in and gave him a peck on the lips. "I like taking risks too!"

They enjoyed each other’s embrace before cuddling together to watch the sun set. Franko found himself cradled in her arms. He lay his head on her lap and stared off into the distance, his heart overflowing.

She ran her fingers through his hair and began to sing him a song.

They say that stars will answer your call
They say that a wish is welcomed by all
They cry at the sound of a broken boy’s heart
They shine at the sight of one true as you are
They know of the love we’re too shy to speak
They give of their glow the answers we seek
They hear of your wish be it large or so small
They shoot through the sky for one and for all
They allure us all with their bright dance in the air

They'll grant us our wish if ask them we dare

Franko fought back a tear as he grabbed her hand and pressed the palm to the side of his face, a type of warmth that he hadn't felt since the last time he was here, when he held her hand. For a brief moment, it was as if the pain of the last two years had never happened.

"Thank you for that, Gwendolyn. That was beautiful."

She looked down at him, his head still resting on her lap. "You're welcome. I'm glad you liked it."

He exhaled in relief, as if a burden was lifted off of him. "I guess we should head back to town. It's going to be dark soon."

They got up and made their way back toward her home. "So, Franko. What are you planning on doing with yourself now? You're going to stay here a while, right?"

Franko sighed as some of the weight had returned at the thought. "I will stay for a little while. But I have to bring those bastards to justice. They killed my father. I can't let them get away with this, Gwendolyn."

"Franko," she pleaded. "You don't need to live your life this way. Is this what your father would have wanted?"

He shook his head in frustration. "Probably not, Gwendolyn. But I know if it were me who got killed out there, he would seek revenge, too."

"Franko, please," she begged. "You have your whole life ahead of you. Don't spend it chasing these peop—"

"I'm not arguing about this, Gwendolyn," he told her firmly. "This has been my plan all along. I just wanted to come here and see you first. I will stay for a few more days, then I'll have to move on. I need to get stronger. I promise I will come back for you... if you promise you'll wait for me."

She sagged her shoulders, cast her eyes to the ground, and raised her hand with her pinky extended in front of him. He wrapped her pinky with his own, and they pressed their foreheads together.

"I promise," she said softly.

Gwendolyn offered to have her family clear out some space for him to stay the night, but he opted to take a sleep sack out into the woods and sleep under the stars.

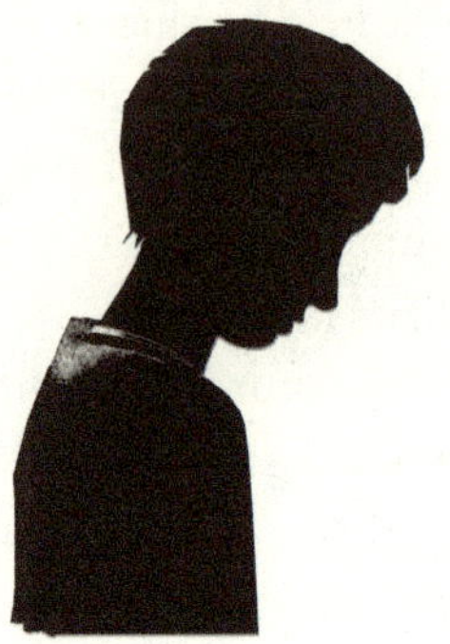

Chapter 23

I've Killed Two Men

The next few days were a pleasant change of pace for Franko, compared to what he'd been through. He met briefly with Bruno to make sure there were no hard feelings and spent the rest of his time there with Gwendolyn, as she was free to do so. She had promised not to bring up his leaving, so they talked instead about what she had been up to over the last two years, about her starting an apprenticeship with the local seamstress, and about how she planned to eventually live in the Capital when she was done with her schooling.

Franko never mentioned it further to her, but he wanted to get stronger, to find some way to take out the Garelians, but he had no clue where to start. He had considered seeking out a group of mercenaries or bounty hunters, but neither of those was especially appealing to him. His father always looked down on mercenaries, and he didn't see a group of bounty hunters finding any value in hunting deadly enemies with powerful magic who didn't even have a bounty on their heads.

Then, one morning, it happened. A recruiter from the Capital came to sign up some new soldiers. At that time, it was required that all men join the Wyverly Guard upon turning eighteen and serve for a minimum of two years. Women could volunteer, as could boys from the age of sixteen.

Franko approached the officer, a soldier by the name of Captain Aldo, but was told he was too young.

"Please, sir. I promise I can fight as good as any of your recruits, better even," Franko pleaded. He knew this might be his only chance to get stronger.

"I'm sorry, kid. But these are the rules, and they always have been. I respect the fact that you want to sign up, but you're just too young," Aldo replied as he took down the names of the handful of young men who came to register.

"Isn't there a youth brigade? Why can't I join them?"

"Youth brigade is for sixteen-year-olds, kid. You're still too young."

"There's got to be something," Franko begged. "Don't you have some sort of program for young prodigies?"

The Captain rolled his eyes and finally looked at the boy. "Are you saying you're a prodigy? From Greencourt?"

Franko put his hands in a placating gesture. "I don't mean to sound arrogant, sir. But I have been doing hard military-grade training for the last two years. I've gone to battle against grown men and defeated them. Dangerous ones."

"I'm sure, kid," Aldo scoffed. "But being in the guard isn't some friendly competition. People die out there. You may have to kill or be killed."

Franko straightened up and drew a deep breath. "I've killed two men." The words almost made him dizzy when they came out of his mouth, his heart racing. He had never really reflected on that before, but he did. He killed those two Garelian Guards before facing Ponzer.

Captain Aldo immediately shot his gaze over at Franko and straightened up, glaring at the boy directly in his eyes as if he was studying his expression. "You're serious, aren't you?"

"I am," he replied flatly.

Aldo slowly lifted his finger and pointed directly at Franko's chest. "Son, you're gonna tell me exactly what happened out there. Don't lie to me."

"My father was killed by a group of outlaws at a mountain pass by the northeast forest of Wyverly. I killed two of their members," he told him, leaving out the specifics.

Aldo studied him for a moment and then spoke up. "And how do you feel about that, son?"

Franko's eyes darted around nervously; he hadn't really thought about that at all until just now. "I'm not sure, sir. I don't know if I would say I'm glad, but they were with the group that killed my father. If I hadn't killed them there, they would have killed another person. I did what I had to."

Captain Aldo nodded slowly and stood silently for a minute. "I can't make any promises, kid. But if you come to the Capital, you may be able to get a sponsor. That's the only way for someone your age to get admitted."

"A sponsor?" Franko asked. "How do I find one? Can you sponsor me?"

The Captain shook his head. "I can't. Only members of the Shattered Star Brigade can do that."

"Shattered Star Brigade?"

"They're a group of highly-skilled soldiers, nobody knows their identity outside of that brigade and a small handful of other people. Not even I know who they are," Aldo said. "But, I can write a letter for you to take to the recruiting office in the Capital. They can have it sent to the Shattered Star; they may or may not choose to speak to you. So your trip to the Capital may be wasted if that's the case. You'll have to assume that risk."

"I'll do it," Franko replied adamantly. "I see no other choice."

The Captain nodded slowly again, then wrote a note on a piece of paper, placed it in an envelope, and affixed his seal on it. "This can only be opened by someone at the recruiting office. If they see it's been opened by you or anyone else, they'll discard it. Understood?"

Franko nodded and took the letter. He and the Captain parted ways with a nod, and he headed off to ask a favor of Bruno and say farewell to Gwendolyn.

Aldo watched the boy walk away, respect and pity filling his eyes. “Dammit, boy. Be careful.”

Franko stopped by Bruno’s shop first to ask for a favor. He wanted his broken blade polished and sharpened, but not fully restored. Bruno graciously agreed to take care of it for him while he went to say goodbye to Gwendolyn.

He looked through the town for Gwendolyn, but saw no signs of her. He figured she might be by the lake, so he made his way out there, grabbing a wild rose with pink petals he spotted on the way.

As Franko got closer, he heard singing. The beautiful, melodic voice was soothing to his soul; he could tell it was Gwendolyn. He saw her from behind, her hands crossed over her chest as she sang.

"Gwendolyn," Franko hollered out.

She was startled and turned around. "Franko," she said as she brushed her hair behind her ears. "Here to say goodbye, I take it."

"I am. How did you know?"

"I saw you earlier talking to that recruiter. I knew what you were up to. You're going to join the Wyverly Guard, aren't you?"

"Yes, that's my plan. He said I'm too young, but I may be able to find someone to sponsor me in the Capital."

"I see," she said solemnly as she looked down.

His heart sank as he saw how sad the news had made her. "I got you a flower. It's a wild rose. I thought you might like it." He dropped down to one knee with a playful smile on his face. "For you, my dear. A sweet-smelling flower, just like you."

Gwendolyn smiled and shook her head at the display. "Thank you, Franko," she said as she took the flower. "Please get up, you look ridiculous on one knee like that. You look like you're proposing marriage."

He stood up and brushed the dirt off his pants. "I think we *should* get married, Gwendolyn."

Gwendolyn couldn't stop herself from laughing. "Franko, don't joke about stuff like that, please."

He gently grabbed her by the chin and looked her in the eyes. "I'm not joking, Gwendolyn. When I come back, I think we should get married. I'll never meet someone like you again. You're the only one for me."

Gwendolyn gently took his hand off her chin. "We're far too young for this talk, Franko." She turned to look out over the lake, smelling the rose he had just given her. "I tell you what. When you return from this... quest for vengeance, or whatever it is you want to call it. Come find me. If I see you're still the same Franko you are now, we'll talk. But we're still a few years too young to be doing anything like that."

Franko nodded with a smile. "I like the sound of that," he told her as he pulled her in for one last kiss. "I love you, Gwendolyn. I want to spend the rest of my life with you when this is over."

Gwendolyn's eyes went wide and watered at the sound of those words coming out of his mouth. "I love you too, Franko. Please, whatever you do. Don't let the world corrupt you. Do you hear me?"

"I won't," Franko said softly as he brushed her cheek and turned to head back to town.

Gwendolyn sat on the boulder they had always shared, wiping the tears from her eyes as she looked upon the pink rose.

Franko stopped by to pick up his sword, which Bruno had polished and sharpened. As he admired it, he saw how the blade reflected like a mirror, its edges sharp enough to slice through a hair. He thanked Bruno and then joined a caravan heading to the Capital.

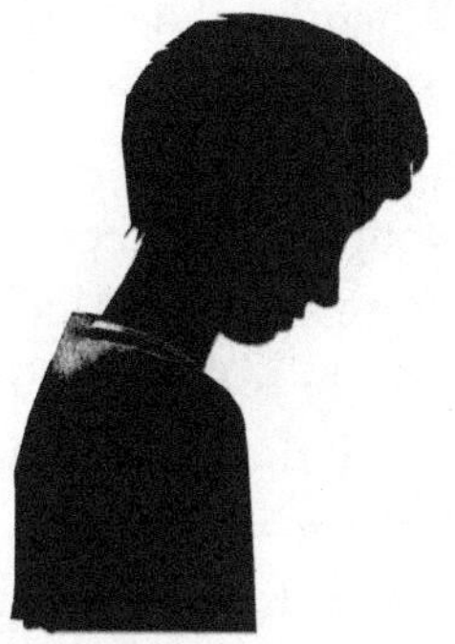

Chapter 24

Of Pencil Pushers and Priests

A few weeks later, Franko arrived in the Capital. The city was named Wyverly after the Kingdom itself, which was named after the Star Sage, who is believed to have sealed away Garel. Most citizens simply called it the Capital to avoid confusion. The massive city, full of cobblestone streets and large, multi-story buildings, was by far the largest the boy had ever been to. He and his father had been there numerous times when he was younger, but they were always in and out after a day or two, and Franko never left Ringo's side.

The boy was on his own now, but all he needed was to find the recruiting office and hand in the letter that Captain Aldo had given him. As he made his way through the crowded streets, he spotted some soldiers and followed them around for a while. They gave the twelve-year-old a sideways glance when he asked for directions to the recruiting office, but still told him where he needed to go.

Once he arrived, he saw a middle-aged man with reading glasses rifling through some papers. When Franko cleared his throat to let the man know he was there, the clerk looked at the boy with a perplexed expression on his face.

"Are you looking for your older brother, young man?" the clerk asked.

"No, I have a letter from Captain Aldo. I was told to hand it in," Franko replied as he passed the sealed envelope to the confused clerk.

The clerk cautiously took the letter from the boy and opened it in front of him. He blinked a few times and shook his head as he read through it. "Are you Franko?" he asked in astonishment.

"I am, sir," the boy replied.

The clerk cleared his throat. "Uh, well... yes," he mumbled as he appeared to read Aldo's note over again to himself. "Well, this is certainly unusual." The man appeared to be muttering to himself quietly as if to make sure he was reading it correctly. He folded it back up and placed it on the side of his desk. "I'll make sure to pass this along. In the meantime, I suggest you find your own sponsor. Their time is very valuable, and there's no guarantee they'll bother to read this letter or seek you out on their own."

Franko stood there, confused. "Where do I find a sponsor? Is there somebody I'm supposed to talk to or meet?" he asked.

"I can't tell you that," the clerk replied flatly. "All I know is that a boy your age needs a sponsor to get admitted. I don't know who's in the Shattered Star Brigade, but that's who would need to sponsor you."

"If you don't know, then how am I supposed to know?" Franko asked with an edge to his voice.

The man leaned forward. "I don't know who's in the Shattered Star Brigade, young Franko," he said in a low and serious tone. "I guess you'll just have to figure that part out yourself. This sounds like a job for an ambitious young man who wants to demonstrate that he belongs here. Asking around seems like it might be a good start," he said as he motioned toward the door.

Franko took that as his invitation to leave, so he turned and walked out, even more confused than he was when he walked in. As he stepped out onto the cobblestone streets, he started to think about how in the world he was supposed to know what questions he had to ask people he didn't know, not knowing where to look or where to even start.

He spent the next several hours wandering aimlessly through the streets of the Capital. He had asked a few soldiers he spotted, but they either weren't interested or weren't able to give him any guidance—several scoffing at him for even asking about the Shattered Star Brigade.

"A kid like you? This has got to be a joke," a gruff-looking young soldier with a scar on his chin remarked with a cynical laugh as he shoved past Franko.

The boy's frustration was starting to build, as was the hunger in his stomach. He still had a few coins left that were in his belongings from when he left Ghost and the forest. Money left over from when he and his father were together. He wanted to save it for an emergency, which he didn't realize he would be facing on the first day in the city. Franko knew there was no guarantee that he'd get in, but he didn't consider that he'd be literally dumped in the streets to fend for himself as soon as he arrived.

More hours passed, and the evening was fast approaching. He walked past a Star Cathedral, a relic of Wyverly's past worship of the stars. It was a belief that most held onto out of sentiment and nostalgia, but there were still several devoted practitioners. It was the only faith allowed to be practiced in Wyverly. Outside, there were a couple of men wearing white clerical robes; one was a pleasant-looking, tall man with salt and pepper hair and a matching beard that went down halfway to his chest. The other appeared to be a younger man, not quite thirty if Franko had to guess. In all likelihood, a protégé of the older man.

"Greetings, young master," the older priest said to Franko as he spotted the boy.

Franko stopped as the man greeted him. He had never met a priest before and wasn't sure how to conduct himself. "Uh… hello. I'm Franko from Greencourt," he said nervously, doing his best to mind his manners. "I'm looking for someone and not sure where to start exactly."

"Ah," the older gentleman said as he tilted his head and arched his eyebrows. "You're looking for a sponsor, are you not?"

Franko's head shot back in astonishment. "How did you know?"

"The stars know everything, young master," the man replied. "Plus, you've been asking around all day. Word travels fast, even in the city."

"Well, can you help? Do you know someone who could sponsor me?" Franko asked desperately.

The older man clasped his hands together in front of his chest and gazed up thoughtfully. "Hmm... perhaps," he said as he slowly swayed back and forth.

Franko looked at him, puzzled. "Well, who do I need to talk to? Where should I start looking?"

"You know someone, Lord Jaron?" the younger man asked the older one.

"I may," Jaron replied as he tilted his head towards the young protégé. "He's not a member of the Shattered Star Brigade any longer. But he might be willing to at least speak with you, young master."

"Please, sir," Franko pleaded. "I've been walking around this damned city all day. Do you have his name? Can you tell me where I can find him?"

Jaron let out a brief chuckle. "Oh my, young master. Giving you his name will do you no good. He remains well hidden. His name won't help you find him."

"I'll take anything I can get at this point. I'm about to give up," Franko replied, shaking his head.

"His name is Sassporo, young master. But again, that name will do you no good," the old priest replied.

"Sassporo?" the young protégé gasped. "You know him? He's still around Wyverly?"

"I know of him," Jaron replied. "But as I said to the young master, his name will do you no good."

"Sassporo..." Franko muttered. "Who is this man?" he asked.

"He was an elite soldier back during the first war with Vodavi," the younger priest said excitedly. "He was a member of the Shattered Star Brigade, one of the most decorated soldiers Wyverly has ever seen. There have been rumors he's still around, but nobody has seen him in ages."

"Sassporo," Franko repeated, a slight smile crossing his face. "Well, that's more information than anybody else has given me today. Thank you, both of you," he said with a slight bow. He'd just assumed that's the kind of thing people did when talking to star priests.

Jaron bowed back with an amused expression on his face as Franko took off down the street. "May I ask where you are headed to now, young master?" he hollered.

"The library. My father used to tell me, *If you want to learn about something—read about it. If you want to learn about something quickly—listen to someone who's already read about it.* Maybe there's an old man like you hanging out at the library that can tell me where I might find Sassporo." Franko shouted back as he headed down the street.

"Wise words, young master," Jaron hollered back. "I do hope this Sassporo can help you out," he said with a laugh as he and his young protégé headed back into the cathedral.

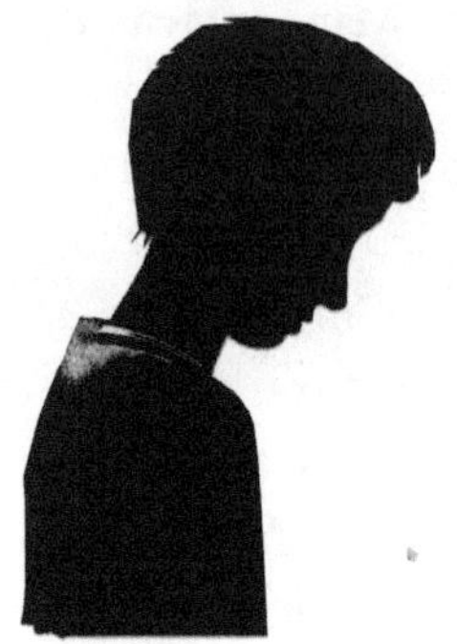

Chapter 25

Seeking Sassporo

Franko finally made his way to the library, but it was too late. It was closed for the day. He sighed and sat on the front steps, anger and hunger building up inside of him. *What a waste of a day*, he thought as he hung his head in frustration. *All this time, wasted. What good did Aldo's letter do me? It'll sit on that clerk's desk for a week before anyone sees it. Then, who knows if they'll actually want to sponsor me or even talk to me.*

As he leaned his head against the handrail of the library steps, drained and defeated, he heard sluggish footsteps approaching. When he looked to see who it was, he noticed a familiar looking young man with a scar on his chin. It was that same soldier with the bad attitude who shoved him aside earlier, along with two others, all reeking of cheap mead.

"Stars be damned, look who it is?" the soldier slurred as he approached Franko. "It's the newest recruit to the Shattered Star Brigade," he said mockingly. He studied Franko and noticed the broken sword at his hip. "More like the Broken Blade Brigade," he said as he and his buddies laughed at the boy. "You can't even own a decent blade, and you expect to be a soldier like us?"

"I do expect to be a soldier, but definitely not one like you," Franko sneered.

"I think the mouse just made a joke, Rondo," one of his buddies chimed in facetiously.

"Oh, is that it?" Rondo replied. "The broken blade thinks I'm the joke? Let's see if he's still laughing when I knock his teeth out and leave him in a heap on the library steps."

"It's not worth you getting in trouble," Franko replied. "Just go home, you're drunk."

"Oh, I won't get in trouble," Rondo responded. "I'm a member of the Wyverly Guard, and I've got two witnesses. They won't touch me."

Franko stood up on the steps and glared at Rondo. "Boys, it's time for you to leave," he said firmly.

"Boys?!" Rondo replied as his eyes widened. "It's time we put this little wannabe down. Let's make it so he doesn't get back up," he said as he lunged toward Franko.

Franko quickly parried Rondo's attack and headbutted him right in the nose, causing the soldier to stumble back and fall. The other two went to reach for their friend's attacker, but the boy kicked the first one in the side of the knee, causing him to collapse immediately. The third thug went to take a swing, but Franko crouched down and punched him firmly in his liver, causing him to fall with the other two.

"It's over. Go home," Franko said with authority.

"Not til you're in a puddle of your own blood!" shouted Rondo as he went to charge Franko again, but was met with a hammer fist to the side of his neck that put him back on the ground.

While one soldier remained on the ground, clutching his knee, the other slowly got back up and pulled out a long knife.

"Don't do this," Franko warned. "This isn't worth losing your life."

Franko pulled out his broken blade and took a defensive stance. The man advanced on him, knife in hand. Franko steadied his blade and was about to cut a brutal gash in the man's arm when two hands came out of nowhere—one grabbing the arm of the attacker, and the other grabbing Franko's.

The man twisted both fighters' arms, causing them both to holler in pain and drop to one knee. "Enough!" said a booming voice as both Franko and the attacker struggled.

Franko looked up to see Jaron, the priest, holding both him and the other man. He was so deeply focused on battle that he tried to stand up and pull out of Jaron's grip when the priest twisted harder and sent him back down to one knee, moaning in pain.

"I said, *enough*!" Jaron commanded. He did a quick flick of his wrist on the attacker's arm, causing him to drop his blade and scream in agony.

Jaron let the man go while Rondo and his other friend got up and stumbled away in fear. He maintained his hold on Franko and looked at the boy.

"My, such impressive technique, young master," he said with admiration as he kept his grip on the boy's arm. "You are like your blade, young master. Broken, yet still very dangerous."

"What are you doing here, Jaron?" Franko asked through his clenched teeth. "Were you following me? Why are you seeking me out?"

Jaron let the boy go and clasped his hands together. Franko rubbed his hurting wrist. "You have it wrong, young master. It is *you* who have been seeking *me* out."

"What are you talking about?" Franko snapped as he sat, favoring his hurting arm. "I'm not *seeking* you out, I'm looking for—" he stopped himself for a second as a realization hit him. "Sassporo?" he gasped as he looked in astonishment at Jaron.

Jaron smiled warmly at the boy and bowed his head slightly. "At your service, young master."

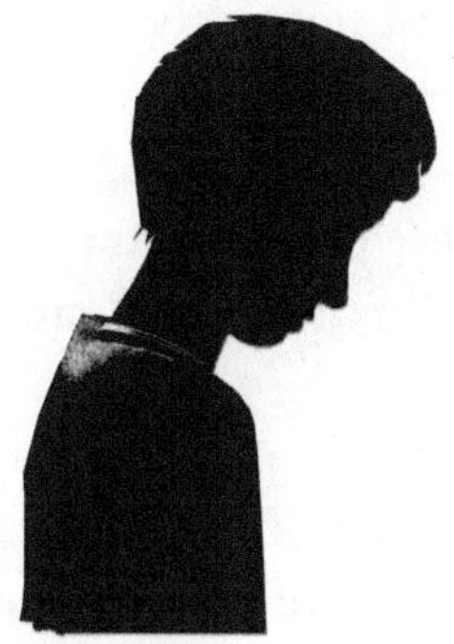

Chapter 26

Restrained Strength

Franko sat dumbfounded in the streets of the Wyverly Capital, staring up at the priest who turned out to be none other than the famed warrior himself, Sassporo.

"Sassporo!" he said in disbelief. "I don't believe it. Why didn't you tell me earlier?"

"There are many reasons I have for concealing my true identity. I cannot simply have this information known by all who would seek to find me," Jaron, or rather, Sassporo, informed him.

"I don't understand. You're a hero," Franko replied, perplexed.

"To many, yes," Sassporo responded. "There are also many who might consider me an enemy. Or worse, there are those who would seek to prove themselves by challenging me. There are those who may seek me for their own personal gain and glory. Quite simply, young master, I have found that it is best to only reveal myself to those whom I feel need to know."

"Okay," Franko replied cautiously. "You've hidden your identity, even from your own protégé? I noticed he seemed surprised that you even knew Sassporo."

Sassporo nodded slowly. "Yes, young Baxton does not know who I truly am, nor does he need to. I feel the fewer people who know this about me, the better it is for them and for me. Young Baxton simply does not need to know."

Franko nodded and stood up. "I see," he replied. "So why did you decide on now to reveal yourself to me?"

"I would love to answer all of your questions, young master. Perhaps we should head back to the cathedral and discuss this further over some hot tea," he said as he motioned for Franko to walk toward the direction of the Star Cathedral.

As they entered the cathedral's sanctuary, Franko looked around in awe at what he was seeing. The immaculate architecture, the vaulted ceiling seemed immeasurably high, with stained-glass windows featuring images of warriors of old, the star sage Wyverly, who defeated the Demon King Garel, and countless icons of stars, both depicted shooting across the sky and standing freely.

"This is amazing," Franko gasped, having never seen such a building from the inside.

"Yes, the ancients who oversaw this construction felt the stars deserved only our best efforts," he said with the humility of a man who had seen this thousands of times but still appreciated its splendor. "Come along with me, young master," he said as he walked down an adjacent hallway.

Franko followed the man into his office. It was almost as impressive as the sanctuary. Hand-carved oak furniture with intricate designs, again with stars being prominent among them. The walls were lined with bookshelves. If he had to guess, there would be a thousand books or more lining the walls on every side.

"Wow," Franko gasped as he took it all in. "These... These are a lot of books. Have you read most of them?"

Sassporo sat down at his desk, his fingers steepled in front of him as he wore a thoughtful expression, as if giving the boy's offhand question serious consideration. "I have read many in their entirety; I would not say *all*. Though I tend to use most for reference, just reading bits and pieces here and there regarding specific topics." He drew a deep breath, "I suppose if I had heard the words of a wise man who once said, *If you want to learn about something—read about it. If you want to learn about something quickly—listen to someone who's already read about it.* That certainly could have saved me a great deal of time and coin over the years," he added with a wink as he motioned for Franko to take a seat.

As the boy sat down, he couldn't help but notice how Sassporo's wit, humility, and quiet strength reminded him of his father in many ways.

"So, as I was asking before, Sassporo. Why was it you chose to reveal yourself to me out there?" Franko asked eagerly.

"Well, young master," he began as he took a sip of hot tea that Baxton had left for the two of them. "I had heard a young boy was asking about a sponsor from the Shattered Star Brigade. I couldn't help but be curious—a boy your age seeking to join the guard," he said as he tilted his head toward Franko.

"I see. But what was it about me that made you feel that I was someone who should know who you really are?"

Sassporo tapped his fingers together, looking not at Franko, but through him. As if gazing out into the distance. "It was the way you handled those thugs in front of the library. I could already tell by the way you carried yourself that you knew how to fight. You could have easily destroyed those young men had you wished to, but instead, you showed incredible restraint. Doing everything in your power not to cause unnecessary harm. That, young master, is the way of a Wyverly soldier—*Restrained strength*. It is the principle behind the Soldier's Creed, and it appears to be already instilled in you."

"The Soldier's Creed?" Franko questioned, with his brow furrowed in confusion.

"Yes, young master," Sassporo replied as he began writing something down on a sheet of paper. "*Assess, but don't hesitate. Act, but not rashly. Attack if you must, defend at all costs. The people of Wyverly, they are the lifeblood of the nation. Without them, we have nothing to fight for*," he recited from memory as if he had done so a thousand times before.

Franko nodded as he listened to Sassporo state the creed. "I like it."

"Good, young master. Because you're going to be hearing it a lot," Sassporo said as he stood up and handed Franko a sealed envelope. "Here is your letter of sponsorship, young master. Welcome to the Wyverly Guard."

Chapter 27

Above the Rest

Much to the clerk's astonishment, Franko handed in his sponsorship letter from Sassporo the next morning. The man scampered down the hallway, hollering for some of his fellow clerks and, it would appear, his superior to look over the letter. He could hear bits and pieces of the conversation.

"How is this possible?" whispered one.

"How did he find Sassporo?" said another.

"There's no doubt about it, this insignia is real," said the clerk's elderly superior. "This letter is from Sassporo."

The clerk headed back to the front desk, where Franko was still waiting, accompanied by his superior—a man well into his seventies, with wispy white hair and spectacles on his face.

"Young man, I suppose you aren't going to tell me how you found Sassporo, are you?" he asked with a hint of amusement.

"I'm afraid I can't do that. Sassporo prefers to remain private," Franko responded, just as Sassporo had requested.

The elderly gentleman smiled and nodded. "I figured that was the case. Couldn't hurt to ask."

The clerk spoke from behind his desk, avoiding making eye contact with Franko. Possibly embarrassed, or maybe jealous, that the precocious young lad had actually met the legendary Sassporo. "There will be a wagon arriving in another hour, making its rounds. You are free to wait outside until then," he said as he motioned to the door just as he had done the previous day.

Franko disregarded the clerk's invitation to leave this time and instead grabbed a piece of paper and wrote a quick letter to Gwendolyn. Just letting her know that he made it to the Capital safely, was sponsored to enter the guard, and was about to be on his way to orientation.

He placed the paper in an envelope and handed it to the clerk. "Can you place this in your outgoing mail for me?" he asked, noticing the clerk looking back at him pensively, obviously uncomfortable that Franko had decided to wait inside. "And *then* I'll go out and wait for the wagon," he added with a knowing nod. The clerk breathed an obvious sigh of relief and took the envelope from him, placing it with the outgoing mail.

The wagon came on time, as promised, and Franko hopped on with some other recruits, all of them several years older than him, casting a sideways glance at the boy but not saying anything out loud. This didn't concern him too much; he knew he would soon prove himself to the rest once the training started—and that he did.

It was obvious to officers in charge that Franko, despite being by far the youngest recruit, was well above the rest. His stamina and skill with a weapon were beyond compare. Though it did bother him that he was not allowed to use his broken blade as his primary weapon, he did choose a staff instead and proved himself more than capable with it. When asked how he had acquired this level of skill, he lied and said his father, a former mercenary, taught him.

He ignored the hostile glares and backhanded remarks of the other recruits, chalking it up to little more than jealousy. He knew if he wanted to take down Lace and the Garelians, he would need to get as strong as he could and make connections with soldiers who were as powerful as those in the Shattered Star Brigade.

There were a couple of recruits who took kindly to Franko. Deni and Jac were both just sixteen and were admitted with their families' permission. They weren't near Fanko's skill level, but they were eager to get better. Deni was a big, clumsy oaf with dark hair and an infectious smile. Jac was the complete opposite; he had blond hair and was as skinny as a rail. Franko would often spend free time in the evening helping them hone their skills and giving them tips.

They went around tying red handkerchiefs around every recruit's arm, signifying that they were new soldiers. "Red, for the blood that's been shed under the stars that guide us," they said after doing each and every recruit. Franko used this moment to ask some of the officers in charge what it would take to get a chance to join the Shattered Stars. He was verbally reprimanded and told that the topic wasn't to be discussed openly. "If you're a Shattered Star, they'll see you first. You don't see them," he was told with a stern warning not to bring it up again. Franko discarded the handkerchief after they left, as did several of his comrades.

The training lasted several weeks. Halfway through, the recruits were allowed to send one letter, yet were not allowed to receive any themselves, except in emergencies. Franko didn't feel he had a great deal to say, but he didn't want to miss his chance.

Dearest Gwendolyn,

Things are going about as expected. I'm doing well in my training, and I think the officers have taken notice. I hope this will lead me to my next step. I don't want to say too much, as they prefer the specifics of what goes on here to not leave the camp. I did make a couple of friends here, though. I don't think I've really had friends before with the way I'm used to living, so that's been a nice change of pace.

Sadly, they told me that I can't receive letters unless it's an emergency. Maybe Bruno will drop an anvil on his big fat foot, and that will give you cause to send me one.

I don't know what they'll have me do at this time, but I promise that I will visit again as soon as I have an opportunity.

Love,

Franko

Once training was over, the recruits were sent back to the Capital and put into a dormitory. They were allowed to choose their own dorm mates, so Franko was able to room with Deni and Jac. When they arrived at their modest accommodations, the two older boys groaned at the sight of their tiny shared room, with a couple of bunk beds and a footlocker for each of them.

Franko couldn't help but laugh at their disappointment. This is the closest thing to a house he'd ever known. Save for a handful of nights where he and his father were able to sleep at an inn or a bed and breakfast, he'd always slept either in their wagon or out in the open air.

"This is great!" Franko said as he plopped down on one of the beds.

"This place is a dump, Franko," Jac retorted as he hopped up on a top bunk and sighed in frustration.

"It's better than the barracks, but I was hoping for something a little roomier," groaned Deni. "This is where we'll be staying for stars know how long."

"Well, you won't hear me complaining," Franko said as he lay with his arms crossed behind his head and let out a satisfying sigh.

"How could you say that, Franko?" Jac asked in disbelief. "What kind of place did you live in growing up anyway?"

It was too late, Franko was sound asleep.

"That kid is something else, Jac," Deni said as he kicked off his boots and lay down.

***

Little changed over the next several years. Franko, just past his eighteenth birthday, would be assigned random duties, often with Deni and Jac: serving as a bodyguards for important guests, breaking up bar fights, chasing petty criminals, and being sent on patrol to various regions of Wyverly. Always making sure to visit Greencourt anytime he was stationed remotely close. Whenever a position opened up for a placement nearby, Franko would always volunteer and was often chosen. He would receive a letter slid under his door every year that stated that the Shattered Star Brigade was watching him and impressed with his performance, but did not have any missions suited for him as of yet. Though he was frustrated with the lack of progress in pursuing a position with the Shattered Star, he was excited that he got to visit Gwendolyn more in those few years than he ever had before.

He had hopes of taking leave soon to go visit her again, but before he could, there was an important event for the kingdom coming up.

The annual Festival of Celestial Lights.

Chapter 28

The Festival of Celestial Lights

The kingdom's most celebrated annual holiday was upon them—The Festival of Celestial Lights. Homes all across Wyverly were decorated with star-themed decor. Songs were sung throughout the streets, communities would gather together, and hearts were merry. It was the most joyous time of year for all. All that is, except for the Wyverly guard. For them, it was the time of year that had to be most alert, especially for this year's festivities.

As various parades and celebrations were held, the people would tend to let their guard down, making them easy targets for some. Though most of the criminal element to be dealt with was from thieves and scammers, this year, the recently crowned King Roland of Wyverly had invited a special guest, an ambassador from their rival northern kingdom of Vodavi.

The two kingdoms had been enemies for decades, but King Roland had promised to pursue peace with their long-time adversary. This came as a delight to many, but there were others who didn't wish for peace.

The king and the ambassador were to be part of the parade as it went through the streets of the capital. Franko, along with Deni and Jac, were assigned to go undercover amongst the crowd, maintaining a safe distance from the ambassador in order to keep an eye out for any suspicious activity.

As the chariot carrying the ambassador and the king was being ridden through town, the crowd was all looking at the special guest, while Franko and the others were looking at the crowd. Most people were cheering with excitement, some were looking on with expressions of mixed emotions, while others weren't looking at all—almost as if they were *trying* not to look.

This, of course, wasn't enough justification to confront these individuals, but it did call for special attention. Franko signaled to Jac and Deni, who were scattered in the crowd, but always within sight, to keep an eye on the possible suspects. He held up three fingers for his comrades and motioned with his head toward the direction of three hooded figures who were themselves spread out in the crowd, but always managing to stay within line of sight of each other, as well as the ambassador and the king.

The suspects must have realized they were being watched. Franko noticed one of them motioning to the others. He held up three fingers himself for his own comrades to see, followed by a tap on his bicep. Franko saw this and felt that this was an indication that they knew that he, Deni, and Jac were watching. *A tap on the bicep*, he thought, *the same arm where guard members would often wear their red handkerchief. He must be signaling to his friends that three guard members were watching them. This must mean they plan on either making their move or losing us.*

Franko thought back on the creed that they were all taught upon entering The Guard. The same one he had first heard from Sassporo.

Assess, but don't hesitate
Act, but not rashly
Attack if you must
Defend at all costs...

There was no question in his mind—it was time to act. Franko held up three fingers for Jac and Deni to see. He pointed in the direction of the suspects and then bumped his fists together. *We confront them now!*

The suspects read his signs and took their chance to attack. All three lunged with alarming speed at the caravan holding the ambassador and the king.

"Assassins!" hollered Franko to get the attention of the king's personal guard.

The crowd scattered as the royal guard members drew their weapons and covered King Roland and the Vodavi ambassador. When the three suspects noticed, they shot Franko a vicious glare and cursed before fleeing.

Franko, Deni, and Jac all pursued the would-be assassins, who had all gone in different directions. Several guard members wearing blue vests with decorative golden embroidery immediately pursued the suspects along with Franko and the others. He had heard about what those vests meant—these were elite guard members, the best of the best, some of whom were no doubt members of the Shattered Star. When they showed up, the rest of the guard was to stand down and let them take care of business. But now was not the time; there was imminent danger, and he had to act.

He kept up his pursuit of one of the assassins. The man was fast, but not as fast as a young man who practiced persistence hunting for two years in the forests of Wyverly. Franko quickly caught up with the man, tripping him up and subduing him in a matter of seconds.

As Franko bound the man's hands and feet, he was met with a swift kick to the face, seemingly out of nowhere. He fell off the assassin and stood up to see that he was facing a dozen cloaked figures, all armed with short swords. *Those are weapons issued by the guard?* he said to himself. *What are they doing with them?*

"You fool," one of them said as he stepped forward. "You're nothing but a low-ranking lapdog of the crown. That imbecile, King Roland wants peace. But there is no peace to be had with the likes of Vodavi," he spat.

"I don't care who you are or what you think," Franko retorted as he pulled out his broken blade and stood ready. "Nobody is gonna get assassinated under my watch."

The man snickered in response. "I am Gundo Ray, a former elite guardsman. We left the guard after King Roland accepted the crown. We want nothing to do with him or Vodavi," he stated. "You seem quite skilled, young one. I will give you one chance. Join us or die," he said as he drew his blade.

Franko had heard this kind of talk before. Lace and the Garelians were known to make the same kind of ultimatum. He had no use for Gundo, Lace, or anyone else who would threaten people this way.

"Get lost," Franko replied as he held his blade steady.

"I should have figured," Gundo scoffed.

He charged at Franko, and their blades met. Gundo's technique was fast and flawless, leaving no openings for a counter from the young soldier. He grazed Franko's shoulder with his blade, but Franko quickly recovered and performed a spinning strike that cut Gundo's forearm. Both men were bleeding, but neither was relenting.

He swung his blade toward Gundo's head, but was blocked by the former guardsman's sword, who countered with an elbow to Franko's jaw. He took a half step back and kicked Gundo in his knee, but Gundo kept his frame and did a backhanded slice toward Franko's face that narrowly missed. There was no doubt about it, Gundo was an elite.

The two backed away from each other, both gasping for breath.

"We don't have time for this!" Gundo grunted. "Take him out!"

As his comrades drew their weapons and began to advance on Franko, they were interrupted by three soldiers wearing elite vests. They swooped in and quickly dispatched half of Gundo's goons. Leaving only about half a dozen of them in a standoff. As Franko looked up, he saw that Aldo was among them.

"Stand down, soldier," Aldo said firmly as he held his palm out toward Franko without looking at him. "We've got it from here."

"Gundo Ray," the elite soldier said knowingly as he glared at Gundo and the others. "I should have known. You're under arrest."

"Aldo," Gundo spat. "You've got to be joking."

He and his comrades charged the elite guard members all at once. Their weapons clashed, and the elite guard proved their skill by overcoming Gundo's thugs in a matter of seconds. Gundo was holding his own but soon realized he was badly outnumbered.

"No sense in dying at the hands of you!" he shouted as he pulled out a vial of purple liquid and threw it on the ground.

"Back up!" shouted one of the elite guards as a cloud of purple smoke arose from the broken vial.

Franko noticed they all covered their faces and backed away, so he did the same. He noticed Gundo had lunged toward him to run his blade through his gut and flee. He could barely make out Gundo's movement and couldn't react in time to stop the attack.

"Star Shield!" the voice bellowed out as a wall of translucent white energy appeared in front of Franko. Gundo crashed into the mysterious force field and fell to the ground, groaning as if he had just hit a brick wall.

Franko turned around to see Sassporo standing there with his arms extended out in front of him.

"Sass—I mean, Jaron!" Franko gasped in shock. "Where did you come from?"

Sassporo quickly nodded at the boy but kept his eyes set on Gundo. "Gundo Ray, you are under arrest!" he shouted with authority.

Gundo moaned and got up to one knee as his eyes met Sassporo's. "Jaron?" he said faintly as he recognized the priest. He looked around and saw the elite guardsmen closing in on him. "How did you—" he stopped himself as he realized there was no getting away this time. Gundo placed his hands behind his head, and the guardsmen tied him up.

"Thank you, preacher," Aldo said as he looked cautiously at Sassporo while all but one of the elite guard members left with Gundo and his gang. "I can't help but wonder how a priest knows this kind of star magic."

"The stars hold many mysteries," Sassporo replied with a coy smile.

"I know," Aldo replied. "And there's only one person who truly understands their power," he turned to the rest of the elite guard who were standing there. "Tremlee," he said to the guardsman who had stayed back, "We're in the presence of greatness. Priest Jaron must be none other than the legendary Sassporo."

Tremlee looked wide-eyed at Aldo, then at Sassporo. "Lieutenant Magnus Tremlee," he gasped as he introduced himself, fumbling to shake Sassporo's hand. The star priest bowed his head slightly, the expression on his face showing that of resignation rather than delight.

"At your service," Sassporo replied flatly.

Franko couldn't help but chuckle at the priest's discomfort. He knew Sassporo preferred to keep his true identity hidden, a fact he reminded the two of as before they left.

Once they were gone, Sassporo turned toward Franko. "You were enjoying that entirely too much, young master," he remarked.

"I don't think I've ever seen you that uncomfortable before, Sassporo," Franko replied with a smirk.

"Of course," Sassporo sighed. "Come now, young master. I'll get a bandage for that wound on your shoulder."

Chapter 29

It's Best This Way

Sassporo brought Franko to his office and put a bandage on the cut Gundo had given him on his shoulder.

"You did quite well, young master," Sassporo noted as he examined the bandage. "You held your own against an elite guard member. Quite impressive. And quite dangerous to attempt that on your own."

"I like to take risks, Sassporo," Franko replied wryly. "Who was that guy anyway?" he asked as he favored his shoulder.

"Gundo Ray," Sassporo sighed. "A zealot who wishes to remain at war. He used to be an elite guard member, but he left when King Roland assumed the throne. I had no idea his intentions were so murderous," he said with a tinge of bitterness.

"Did you know him?"

"I knew *of* him," Sassporo shrugged. "He was a fine soldier. Brave, noble. But it would appear he lost his way and chose the wrong path," he said as he shook his head in despair. "This is why we need to weigh heavily the choices we make on a daily basis, young master. We need to examine our own motives and hearts. The broken path is one often chosen by the brightest stars."

"I see," Franko said as he sat and nodded as he took in Sassporo's words.

"What was that you did back there?" he asked. "Was Aldo right? Was that star magic?"

Sassporo nodded slowly as he sat in his chair, facing a nearby window.

"So that's real?" Franko asked in astonishment. "I thought that was all just part of the old fairy tales."

"*Old fairy tales*," Sassporo said with a quick laugh. "Yes, that's what everyone says these days. It's probably for the best."

"What do you mean?" Franko pressed.

"There are important stories and lessons to be learned by the Star Sage's words, fairy tales or not," Sassporo replied. "But the power of the stars can be dangerous if not used properly. It's too much power to be trusted to a human."

"What about you? Is it not too much for you?"

"It dies with me, young master," Sassporo said as he shook his head and thoughtfully stroked his beard.

"So I take it you won't teach me?" Franko asked with an edge in his voice.

"As I said," Sassporo replied, "It dies with me."

Franko sank back in his chair in frustration. "That doesn't sound fair," he retorted. "Someone taught you, obviously. You won't pass it on?"

"It's best this way, young master."

Franko sat in silent frustration for a moment while Sassporo continued to stare out over the streets of the capital, lost in thought. "Who taught you anyway?" he asked.

Sassporo turned back toward Franko with his eyebrows arched, as if startled by the question. "Sometimes we call upon the stars. Other times, the stars call upon us," he replied, his voice low and heavy.

"What does that even mean?" Franko asked, frustrated.

Sassporo sighed wearily. “It means, young master. That all may prostrate themselves to the stars in their time of need, though few do with a sincere heart, while others are called upon. Destined, if you will. I’m afraid I can’t elaborate on the mystery of it all.”

Franko shook his head hopelessly. “Thanks for explaining that to me, Sassporo,” he said sarcastically. “I do appreciate all of your help today for saving me from that lunatic. But I think I’m gonna call it a night,” he added as he got up to leave.

Sassporo gave a slow nod and waved his hand before returning to whatever reverie he was in before.

“I would like it if you were to come and listen to my sermon tomorrow, Franko,” Sassporo said with his back turned to the young soldier as he was leaving.

Franko turned around, stunned. That was the only time Sassporo ever called him by his name. “Uhh... sure... I’ll make a point to be here tomorrow.”

Chapter 30

It's Yours Now

"We all have made a wish upon a shooting star in our lives at some point. Some of us have made many," Sassporo, or rather, Father Jaron had declared in the morning sermon after the Festival of Celestial Lights. "We all laugh at it now, seeing it as some sort of children's tale. Or perhaps we hold on to these beliefs out of pure nostalgia. Oh, what a waste of such a beautiful gift we have access to," he went on. "How the stars long for us to prostrate ourselves before them and humbly ask for that which we need and desire," he said as he made an expansive gesture with his arms.

Franko sat in a pew a few rows back, perplexed at the message he was hearing. This was his first time ever in a Star Cathedral. He had heard much of this before, how everyone could make one wish on a shooting star. He had never made a wish and never thought he would bother ever making one. His father told him about Wyverly lore before. Everyone knew the gist of it. Wyverly had been called the Kingdom of the Shooting Star. The mythology ran deep in the kingdom, but few took it seriously anymore. Though Ringo, Franko's cynical father, believed there was still *something* to it, even if much of it was romanticized over the years to make it more palatable to children.

Jaron went on to conclude his hour-long sermon on the glory of the stars to an inattentive audience of nobles who were most likely there just to be seen.

"Sometimes, we call upon the stars," he said, "And other times, the stars call upon us," he added, looking directly at Franko.

Jaron finished with a chant to the stars and sent the crowd home. Franko sat in bewilderment, confused as to why Sassporo had looked directly at him in his closing message. *Sometimes the stars call upon us*, the words echoed in his mind.

After the service was over, Franko visited Sassporo in his office.

"That was the same thing you told me last night," Franko said as he paced around Sassporo's office. "You mind telling me what that was all about?"

"You don't need to read into my message too much, young master. Nobody believes in the old fairytales anymore," Sassporo replied as he thoughtfully rubbed his hands together at his desk. "As I said before, I think it's best that way."

"You keep saying that. So you're a priest that doesn't believe in his own message?" Franko asked cynically.

"I never said that. I simply said I think it's best that way."

"Because you don't think we can be trusted with the star's power?"

Sassporo inhaled sharply. "It has proven to have been the case too many times."

"Ah, but you said we can prostrate ourselves before the stars and ask, didn't you?"

Sassporo raised his eyebrows and nodded. "Have you ever made a wish upon a shooting star, young master?"

"No, the stars don't want to hear what I have to say," Franko replied with an edge in his voice.

"So be it," Sassporo said with a sigh.

There was silence between them for a moment before Sassporo spoke back up. "We've destroyed them. All but one," he said aloud, as if he were talking to himself.

Franko turned to him. "Destroyed what? Why do I always feel like you're talking to me in mid-conversation?"

"The enchanted weapons," Sassporo replied.

"Enchanted weapons?"

"Yes, there were eight of them. Weapons that corrupted Star Mages had enchanted and sold to the highest bidder," Sassporo answered. "That is why I say it's best for star magic to die with me."

"This is the first I've ever heard of this," Franko said with interest as he took a step toward the star priest.

"Yes, we have worked hard over the generations to help the people forget."

"So how does that work? Enchanted weapons?" Franko asked as he studied Sassporo's expression.

"Star magic is only granted to those worthy, young master," Sassporo replied. "But it certainly does not promise that those who possess it will not be corrupted. Past mages were captivated by the allure of fame and wealth. They couldn't enchant a person with star magic, but they realized they could enchant a weapon. This would give its wielder a certain degree of magic."

"So where's the last enchanted weapon?" Franko asked earnestly.

"We don't know," Sassporo shrugged. "We know nothing about it, only that it has never been accounted for."

Franko shook his head and rubbed his eyes in disbelief. "If you had told me any of this stuff two days ago, I would have thought you were crazy," he said with a cynical chuckle.

"If only that were the case," Sassporo replied with a click of his tongue. "If you'll excuse me, young master. I have some business to attend to," he said as he rose from his chair and removed his vestments.

Franko nodded and began to make his way out. But before he turned, he noticed a blue and gold elite vest in Sassporo's wardrobe when the priest opened it.

“By the stars, is that an elite guard vest?” Franko asked, impressed. “I should have known, I guess. I just can’t picture you wearing one. No offense,” he added.

Sassporo laughed as he grabbed the vest and tossed it on the chair nearest Franko. “Very well, young master. You may have it.”

Franko jerked his head back and waved his hands. “Oh, I didn’t mean it like that!”

“Please take it, young master. You have more than shown yourself worthy,” Sassporo replied as he put his cloak on. “You saved the kingdom from untold tragedy yesterday. Many have no idea it was you who alerted the royal guard, but I know."

“But Sassporo,” Franko pleaded. “These vests, don’t they need to be issued by some sort of official ceremony or something?”

“That, or given by the previous owner,” Sassporo responded. “Please take it, young master. It wasn’t an offer, it was an order. It’s yours now.”

“Sassporo,” Franko stammered. “I’m honored. I’ll wear it with pride.”

“Please do,” Sassporo quickly replied.

Franko immediately took off his old vest and put on Sassporo’s elite guard vest. It fit him well.

"Sassporo, can I ask you for another favor?"

"Of course, young master," Sassporo replied eagerly.

"Will you teach me how to use star magic?"

Sassporo stood in contemplative silence for what seemed like an eternity.

"Come back here at sundown today, young master, and we'll talk about star magic."

Chapter 31

Like Leaky Bucket

The sun had set, and Franko was eager to learn more about star magic from Sassporo. He had to excuse himself from the nightly card game with Deni and Jac, citing an important top-secret shattered star meeting, which was true enough.

When he arrived at Sassporo's office, he was handed a note by Baxter, *meet me in the woods on the eastern outskirts*, was all it said.

"Great, it'll take me an hour to get there from here," Franko muttered.

By the time he arrived at the impromptu meeting location, it was already dark out. *It's gonna be tough training with no light. This is like Ghost's training all over again,* he thought.

Ghost... I wonder what she's up to now, he reflected. *What a strange being she was. I do miss her, though. I feel like I owe her an apology for what I said to her back then. For threatening the forest. For threatening her.*

Franko walked in the woods and saw Sassporo in the distance. They were a good ways away from the capital at that point, well out of earshot of anybody. He noticed Sassporo was kneeling, with his arms spread to his sides, gazing up at the stars, muttering something.

"Mighty stars, if it is in your will, lend me your power," he petitioned. Sassporo took a deep breath and exhaled. "I see you made it, young master," he said with his back still to Franko.

"What was that?" Franko asked.

"Prostrating myself before the stars, asking them to lend me their power," Sassporo answered as he rose to his feet.

"Does it work?"

"It doesn't hurt, young master," Sassporo replied as he brushed some dead leaves off his pants and approached Franko.

"All may wish upon a shooting star one time. After that, we must humbly ask for that which we desire. If they favor us, we may get some of their power in our hour of need," he added.

"Sounds risky," Franko replied with a note of cynicism.

"I thought you liked taking risks, young master," Sassporo quipped with a playful smile.

Franko shrugged indifferently. "When can we get started with this?"

"Ah, yes," Sassporo said as he clapped his hands together, "let's begin." He knelt down once again and motioned for Franko to do the same. Which he hesitantly did.

"You heard my petition just now, I presume. That's all one with a noble and upright heart needs to do," Sassporo instructed.

Franko followed Sassporo's instructions, though he was obviously uncomfortable in doing so. He fumbled through his plea to the stars and felt no different afterward.

"Is this just for show? How exactly am I supposed to know if this worked?" he asked tersely.

"You call it *show*, I call it *reverence*. Semantics can reflect the heart, young master," Sassporo responded. "The stars give their power to whom they see fit. It is ultimately *they* who call upon *us*. Though I like to believe our humble petitioning doesn't hurt," he added, his eyes closed as he faced the sky.

"And how does this work, exactly?" Franko asked irritably.

“Think of star magic as filling a bucket with a small leak full of water. Once it gets filled, you will know. And it will stay full for some time before it needs to be replenished. And you may not realize or care that you have water, that is until you are thirsty."

Franko looked at him, his eyebrows furrowed. "Not a word you just said makes any sense," he said indignantly.

"It will someday, young master," Sassporo replied patiently. "Like a leaky bucket, it will stay full for quite some time. Until either the bucket slowly gets drained by the leak, or until it is forcefully drawn out. Once it's empty, you simply need to fill it again."

"It seems like if this worked, everybody would be doing it," Franko asked skeptically.

"The stars do not deem most worthy of their power. It is a mystery, young master, even to me," Sassporo retorted. "As I've said before, I think it's best this way. Man has shown me time and time again that we cannot be trusted with this power."

"But you're teaching it to me?"

Sassporo sat silent for a moment. "Yes... I can't quite explain it, but I believe you can be trusted."

"So I just need to wait for my hour of need, and hope this worked? How do the stars know when my time of need comes?"

Franko had seen enough magic with his own eyes to know there was something to it, from the dark magic that the Garelians used, to Sassporo's magic that saved him from Gundo.

Sassporo sighed and shook his head. "As I said, it's a mystery. Part of it's also about knowing *how* to call upon it. Sometimes we call upon the stars in our hour of need, and sometimes they call upon us, lending us their power without our asking."

Franko sagged his shoulders and hung his head. "So that's the lesson today? Ask the stars for help and hope someday it works? How do I call upon it?"

Sassporo stroked his beard anxiously. "Let me show you something, young master," he said as he got back up and stood a few paces in front of Franko.

"Now, try to strike me," he ordered Franko.

Franko's eyes darted around. "Are... you sure?" he asked pensively.

Sassporo glared at him intently, without a word. Franko took the hint.

"Okay, here it goes," Franko sighed as he charged Sassporo and threw his fist straight at the star priest's nose.

"Star Shield!" Sassporo hollered as a translucent dome of white energy encapsulated him, similar to the wall of energy that had protected him against Gundo Ray's attack from the other day.

Franko struck the barrier with so much force that it felt like he was hitting a brick wall. He held his fist and growled in pain. "Thanks, Sassporo, but I already knew about that one," he grunted as he rubbed his hurting hand.

"Now, go grab a large stick or stone or something of that nature and try to strike me with it," Sassporo said, not acknowledging Franko's pain from hitting the star shield.

Franko stood hesitantly. "If this is the star shield again—"

"Just do it!" Sassporo barked.

Franko grabbed a fist-sized rock nearby. *I'm not gonna bother getting too close to him,* he thought, *I'll just throw it from here.*

He threw the rock at Sassporo, only to notice that the star shield had already dissipated.

"Oh no! Watch out!" Franko shouted.

"Shattered Star!" Sassporo yelled, a white glow enveloping his hand. He raised his hand toward the rock heading toward him. As soon as the stone touched his hand, a loud crack echoed through the woods, and the rock shattered into a heap of pebbles.

Franko stood in shock, his mouth agape. "What—what was that?!"

"The Shattered Star, young master," Sassporo replied, beads of sweat forming on his forehead. "The *Star Shield* repels any attack that is not a spell or from an enchanted weapon. *Shattered Star* destroys any weapon or object once it touches the part of you that has been enchanted. These spells are temporary if they are cast on a person. Weapon enchantments are permanent. Please understand, Star magic is primarily for defense, young master," he added as he went to his bag of belongings and pulled out a short sword. "Except this next one."

Sassporo held the sword in front of him, his eyes gazing upon it in a focused fury. "Blade of the Shooting Star!" he bellowed out. The sword lit up with a white glow as he lunged at a nearby tree and sliced his blade through it like he was cutting through air. The massive tree trunk was severed and then toppled over.

Franko gasped at the sight; if he didn't know that there was something to star magic before, he knew then without a doubt. "That was... unreal."

"*The Blade of the Shooting Star*, it can turn any blade into a powerful weapon that can cut through anything," Sassporo heaved, as some signs of fatigue were beginning to show. "There are other spells, of course," he added, "but we would need someone with Dark Fang magic in order to demonstrate how they work. They are defensive spells against such magic," he added as he sat down on a large stone nearby.

Franko nodded thoughtfully. "Dark Fang magic? That must be what they used on Father and me."

Sassporo jerked his head and looked at Franko. "You've encountered this?"

"Yes," Franko replied. "That Garelian witch, she cast a spell on my father that blinded him before he got killed. Then that man cast a spell on me that made it so I couldn't hear for a while."

"Yellow Fang and Red Fang," Sassporo said as he arched his eyebrows.

"You know about that?" Franko asked, his voice sounding shocked, though he quickly remembered who he was talking to.

"Yes," Sassporo replied as he thoughtfully stroked his beard. "There are defensive spells for both of those. I would say that I hope to show you someday, but then again, I would hope to never have to face a Dark Fang user either. It's very powerful magic."

Franko rubbed his face and began to pace around. *So Dark Fang magic can be defeated?* He thought. *If Sassporo had been with us back then, we could have killed those damned Garelians, and Father would still be alive.*

"Something on your mind, young master?" Sassporo asked as he noticed Franko seemed distraught.

"Oh, it's nothing," he replied. "Just thinking back on how things could have gone differently if you had been there when Father was attacked."

"Ah, yes," Sassporo said as he nodded thoughtfully. "We all wish to change the past at some point, don't we?" He stood up and put his hand on Franko's shoulder. "I know you still miss him dearly. I'm sure he was a good man to raise a boy like you."

Franko could do little more than nod in agreement. "He was..." he sighed.

"I tell you what, young master," Sassporo said as he turned to grab his belongings. "You have yet to take leave this year. I think if anyone deserves a break, it's you. Why don't you take some time off? I hear there's a young lady in Greencourt who you haven't seen in a little while."

Franko's expression changed to one of joy. "You mean it?" he asked excitedly.

Sassporo smiled broadly and chuckled. "I do. I say your vacation starts tomorrow morning."

Chapter 32

This Can Work

Franko quickly left for Greencourt the next morning, hoping he would be the one to surprise Gwendolyn. But this time, when he visited, it was Gwendolyn who surprised him.

"What!?" Franko asked in shock as they sat on the boulder at the edge of the lake.

"You heard me. I just turned eighteen, so I'm signing up!" Gwendolyn said with excitement.

"Gwendolyn, it's dangerous," he pleaded. "Joining the Wyverly Guard? I can't believe it."

"Well, it's too late now. Guess you'll just have to protect me since you seem so convinced that I can't protect myself," she said as she turned her back to him and crossed her arms, huffing in playful anger.

"Gwendolyn, I'm serious. And I can't be there for you all the time anyway. You're just another soldier to them."

"Then I'll just have to make do, won't I," she replied as she turned back to face him.

"There is a way we can be roomed together and get put on more missions with each other. Well, unless I get a Shattered Star mission..." he said with a mischievous smile.

"Oh, Franko. Don't do this again," she begged him.

It was too late, Franko scooped up a handful of dandelions and daisies, dropped down to one knee, and proposed. "For you, my love, if you agree to marry me," he said, presenting her with the flowers.

"Franko, don't joke about this," she told him sternly.

"It's not a joke anymore, Gwendolyn. Marry me, we'll be together more often. This can work," he replied.

"Franko...," she groaned. "We talked about this already. We agreed this would be after you take down those cultists. I can't marry a man with that kind of vengeance still at the forefront of his mind all the time."

Franko cupped her chin and pulled her close to him. "What are you saying, Gwendolyn? What do I have to do to get you to marry me right now?"

"Franko, you know. But I can't ask you to give that up. You need to make that decision yourself," she told him as her eyes welled up.

He stood silent for a moment. "Fine, Gwendolyn. I'll give it up. For you."

Gwendolyn stepped back in shock, her eyes shot wide. "You really mean that? Starting today, you're giving up on pursuing those men?"

"No, Gwendolyn. Starting right now. It'll be just you and me," he told her firmly. "If you say yes, that is."

"Are you sure, Franko?" she asked hopefully. "Are you sure you're ready for a commitment like this?"

Franko smiled and held his arms off to his sides as he shrugged. "I like taking risks."

Gwendolyn stared at him intently for a moment, then a smile beamed across her face. "Me too! Then the answer is yes! Let's get married!" she shouted as she sped into his arms.

Franko embraced her tightly, tears of joy running down his cheeks. “Perfect. We can get married in the Capital. I know the priest there, I’m sure he’ll be happy to conduct the ceremony.”

Gwendolyn and Franko both put in a request for an extended leave with the Wyverly Guard. They traveled to the Capital and got married by Jaron.

Chapter 33

I Never Said Thank You

Gwendolyn was sent out for orientation and basic training shortly after. While she was out, Franko woke one morning to a letter that was slid under his door.

Mission placement for the Shattered Star Brigade

Danger level: (3) Moderate

Scope: As the mission has been defined as moderate level 3, a guard member is allowed to be accompanied by no more than two soldiers of their choosing to serve as backup.

Shattered Star member is not allowed to discuss their membership in the Brigade with any others, including the soldiers accompanying them on the mission. Failure to follow this order could result in membership in the Shattered Star Brigade being revoked. Depending on the nature and severity of the offense, a member may be removed from a general guard position with the Wyverly military entirely.

General Scope: A military cargo wagon was robbed while traveling across the main trade route near the northern forest. Drivers were held at knifepoint, and supplies were stolen. No fatalities. Subjects were described as a band of forest folk led by a young male in a blue bandana who spoke the common tongue fluently.

Note: The Shattered Star member is to lead the mission with the objective of apprehending the subjects with minimal fatalities. Lethal force is only to be used only if necessary. Subjects are armed. Shattered Star member has four hours to gather a team and leave the Capital. If member has not dispatched within this timeframe, mission will be transferred to another member. If assistance is needed with gathering a team, a Shattered Star member may go to the recruiting station and request backup. The only information they require is your guard number, along with a verbal statement of the danger level and general scope. Once again, do not disclose that this is a mission for the Shattered Star Brigade to any person.

The ink on this letter will fade one hour after seal is broken.

Franko read the letter over again. *Subjects were described as a band of forest folk led by a young male in a blue bandana who spoke the common tongue fluently.*

"Quinn..." he whispered as the ink on the letter began to fade. He hadn't thought about Quinn and Bric in years. It was their confrontation that marked the beginning of that fateful trip. It's how he was introduced to Ghost and was part of what ultimately led to his confrontation with the Garelians.

Franko knocked on Jac and Deni's dorm room door. Thankfully, they were still there and hadn't been assigned any guard duty as of yet.

"Franko," Jac remarked, pleasantly surprised. "To what do we owe the honor?"

Franko's demeanor was stern and serious; they could tell it wasn't a casual visit. "I need two soldiers to accompany me on a mission. We leave now."

"What kind of mission, Franko?" Deni asked as he slowly arose from his bed.

"It's a danger level 3 apprehension mission by the northern forest. Bring your weapons of choice and let's go," Franko replied flatly.

"A level 3?" Jac asked cautiously. "Franko, Deni and I have never done anything beyond level 2. Are you sure we're the right ones?"

"We'll be fine. I'll take over if things get out of hand," he assured them. "Just follow my lead."

The three left the Capital within the hour and headed off toward the northern pass, wearing civilian clothes and bringing a wagon full of sour wine and moldy bread to serve as a decoy.

***

A few days later, they arrived at the spot. It was an old, overgrown path that hadn't been commonly traveled in decades or longer. Back when Franko was ten, his father had chosen that route to get into Vodavi, because the official trade route leading there was well guarded and only those with forms from the crown were allowed passage. This route proved to be a back door. So he turned onto the path, retracing his steps from so many years ago.

"How did you know to turn here?" Deni whispered. "It's completely overgrown, you can't even see it's here from the main route."

"Call it a hunch," Franko remarked dryly as he kept his eyes forward. His heart was thumping, and something told him that Quinn and Bric would be making an appearance shortly.

The three struggled to maneuver their way through the overgrown path, intentionally being loud and breaking branches as they went so as to draw attention. *Come on, Quinn. I know you're around here somewhere.* Before he knew it, Franko felt cold steel at his throat.

"Not the most cautious of travelers, I see," Quinn whispered into Franko's ear as Bric and forest folk emerged, stolen swords and spears in hand.

"You two, step back," he said, motioning for Deni and Jac to back away. "That's right. Now we're just gonna see what goodies you brought for us, and you'll leave here looking back at this as nothing more than a bad dream."

"Quuuinn," Franko whispered back fiendishly, unconcerned with the blade at his throat. He knew a killer when he saw one, and Quinn was no killer.

Quinn bristled at the sound of his name being spoken that way. It was the same way the Forest Demon said it when she had taunted him all those years ago.

"What!?" he barked. "How do you know my name?"

"Your misdeeds have caught up with you, Quinn. It's time to pay," Franko said in a low and raspy tone.

"You shut up!" he shouted. "Or I'll cut you. I swear—"

Before Quinn could finish his sentence, Franko grabbed the arm holding the knife, pulled it across his chest, braced the bandit on his hips, and tossed him over like a sack of dirt. He then wrenched Quinn's wrist, causing him to groan in pain and drop his knife. Bric charged the young soldier, who spun out of the way and kicked him in the side of the knee, followed by a swift strike to the back of the brute's skull.

Jac and Deni pulled out their weapons to battle the rest of the Forest Folk, who immediately abandoned their leaders.

"Forget them. Tie him up!" Franko hollered to Jac and Deni, who stopped their pursuit of the other Forest Folk and jumped on Bric to bind his arms and legs with rope.

With Quinn still on the ground, Franko pressed his knee into the bandit's side and pulled out his broken sword, pointing it at Quinn's face, eyes wide in shock.

Quinn's breathing was ragged as he stared in astonishment at the end of the broken blade. "No way... It's you. That kid."

"You're going down, Quinn," Franko taunted. "But first. You're gonna tell me what you know about the Garelians."

Quinn looked back at him, perplexed. "The Garelians? How do you know—"

The bandit howled in pain as Franko dug his knee further into his side. "I'm asking the questions here. There's no way that you've been out here all this time and never encountered them. What is your relationship with them?"

"I—I can't talk about that!" he groaned through his teeth.

"You can and you will!!" Franko grunted as he pressed the end of his blade against the side of that bandit's neck.

"Franko, take it easy," Deni pleaded. "This was just a level three. That means no lethal force unless absolutely—"

"Back off, Deni!" Franko shouted. "This is my business. This is why I joined. He's gonna talk, or he's gonna die."

Quinn's chest was quivering as he struggled to breathe. "Look... I know who they are. I don't mess with them, though. They leave us alone, and we do the same."

"There's no way, Quinn," Franko rasped. "They kill on sight anyone who knows about them. You're involved with them in some way. Tell me, now!"

"I swear," Quinn pleaded. "We're not involved with them. It's a truce, at best. We've seen them before. They threatened us, but said they would spare us as long as we never told anyone about them. I think the only reason they didn't kill us is that we helped keep people away. That's the truth!"

Franko looked deep into Quinn's eyes and could tell he was speaking the truth. He put his blade back in his scabbard and pulled the bandit up. Jac and Deni bound his arms and legs like they did with Bric and loaded him on the wagon. They started to turn around and head back.

"You guys go ahead, I'll meet you back at the Capital," he said as he looked out into the distance.

"What are you doing, Franko?" asked Jac. "You should come back with us."

"I just need to check on something, that's all," he said passively, still peering through the tree tops.

"He's gonna meet with his demon girlfriend, I bet," Quinn sneered from the back of the wagon.

Deni and Jac both looked at each other, puzzled, and then at Franko.

"Don't think we didn't notice, kid," Quinn continued. "We saw you from a distance. You and that demon were pretty close for a long time. Weren't you?" he said with a taunt. "I wonder what the guard would think if they ever found out."

"Shut up, Quinn. You don't know what you're talking about," Franko replied.

"What *is* he talking about, Franko?" Deni asked. "What demon?"

"It's nothing. He's a superstitious fool. Just running his mouth," he replied with a dismissive wave of his hand. "Like I said, you guys go ahead. I'll catch up later. Don't worry about me."

Jac and Deni cautiously made their way back to the main route while Franko walked deeper into the forest, searching for his old mentor.

"Ghost! Are you here, Ghost?" he hollered once he knew he was out of earshot from his comrades. "It's me, Franko."

After a period of silence, he finally got a response. "Franko of the broken blade," the voice said, ominously from the treetops. "My old protégé. My, how you have grown."

"It's good to hear from you," he replied, still not able to spot her among the high branches.

"And you've become quite the warrior; it would seem. I guess our time together has served you well."

"It has," he responded. "I never said thank you for that, either. I just wanted to come out here and let you know what that meant to me. I'm sorry for how things ended between us and for those hateful things I said about you. I didn't really mean any of it. I hope you aren't still upset with me."

"Upset with you?" she replied. "No, I'm not upset with you. The trees are happy that you've come to visit."

"I'm glad to hear that," he said as he continued to scan the tree tops, looking for her. "Can I see you? It's been a very long time."

He didn't hear a response, but he did hear the sound of leaves rustling behind him. He quickly spun around, but saw nothing. As he was about to turn back, he felt a hand clasp over his mouth; it was Ghost.

He didn't react with fear this time, he just playfully raised his hands in the air and wiggled them in surrender.

"My apologies, Franko of Greencourt," she said in her low, raspy voice. "Force of habit," she added as she released him.

"Ghost, it's good to see you again."

"Likewise," she replied with a slight bow of her head.

She pulled her hood down and wore a half smile. Franko noticed that she looked no different, other than he was a head taller than her now. Her blood-red hair and the skull paint covering her face, along with her piercing yellow eyes and small horns protruding from her forehead were all the same. He could see why that would terrify a ten-year-old child.

He continued to study her face, as she did his. It was impossible for him to tell how old she was, or how old she appeared, that is.

"You have grown into a fine young man, I see," she stated as she began to pace in circles around him, as she had when they first met. "I believe *handsome* is the word the people use these days."

Franko chuckled uncomfortably. "Thank you... Uhh... you as well... look..."

"Spare me, Franko," she replied with a rare chuckle of her own.

He rubbed the back of his neck and smiled awkwardly. "I'm really glad to see you again. I wish I could spend more time out here. I just wanted to see you once more and tell you how much I appreciate what you did for me back then. Saving my life twice, teaching how to defend myself. It means a lot to me."

"Of course, Franko of Greencourt. It was my honor to do so," she said with another quick bow of her head.

"I would love to come and visit you again sometime, if that's okay with you," he said politely.

"The trees are always happy to host you, Franko," she replied.

Franko swallowed nervously as Ghost watched him, her eyebrow arched in curiosity.

"Is there anything else, Franko?" she asked expectantly.

"Can I... give you a hug?" he asked pensively. "You're the closest thing to a mother I've ever had, you know."

Ghost's head jerked back, and her eyes went wide for a moment in an expression of genuine shock that he had never seen in her before. Her playful smile was gone, replaced with an almost incredulous expression. She stood still for a moment, then slowly raised her arms in the air, as if in surrender, and wiggled her hands playfully just as he had done earlier.

He walked up to Forest Demon and wrapped his arms around her. To Franko's surprise, she returned the gesture, patting him on the back with one hand and brushing the hair on the back of his head with the other.

They released their embrace at the same time, Ghost's face was expressionless.

"Thank you, Ghost," he said with a slight nod of his own. "I have to get going. Goodbye for now," he added as he turned around to head back.

"I spoke to your father before he died," she blurted out.

Franko quickly spun around, an expression of shock on his face. "You what?"

"While you were unconscious after the Garelians ambushed you and your father, I went to check on him. He was still alive, barely," she said. "He was dying, there was nothing I could do but sit by his side. He told me to tell you that he loved you. He felt bad that you were mad at him. I told him that you weren't upset with him anymore, though."

He stood speechless, his eyes welling up. "Why didn't you tell me this before?" he demanded.

Ghost was silent for a moment. "I'm sorry. I should have told you," she replied. "I don't know why I didn't tell you this before. I'm no good at that sort of thing."

Franko stood silent for a moment and then nodded with understanding. "It's okay, Ghost. Thank you for telling me this now. And again... thank you for everything. Take care of yourself," he said as he turned to leave the forest and meet back up with his comrades.

Ghost watched him walk away—with a tear streaming down her face.

Chapter 34

The Pull to Revenge

Franko caught up with Deni and Jac and hopped on the back of the wagon with Quinn and Bric while the other two sat up front, leading the horses. Quinn sat, still bound, glaring at him.

"So, how was your girlfriend doing?" he asked derisively.

"I'm married to another now, Quinn. She wasn't my girlfriend. Don't talk of things you know nothing about," Franko snapped. "You're going to be hanging from the gallows in a short while, Quinn. You may want to make your peace with the stars while you can."

"I know how things work. More than you think," Quinn replied.

"You're of the Forest Folk, Quinn. You don't know anything about what life is like for the rest of us," Franko said dismissively. "Did you know your friends were all going to abandon you like that as soon as things got violent?"

"You don't know anything about me," Quinn snarled. "They weren't my *friends*; we were just a group of people surviving together. And to answer your question, yes, I did figure they'd abandon me, just like everyone else."

"*Like everyone else*?" Franko asked sarcastically. "Sounds like there's one common denominator there, Quinn."

"Shut up!" Quinn hollered, trying but failing to wrestle free from his bonds. "I grew up traveling across Wyverly with my family," he said bitterly. "My family abandoned me. I was only nine years old, Franko. Nine!" he growled. "I learned quickly that I had to do whatever I needed to in order to survive. And unlike you, Franko, I didn't have some demon taking care of me."

Franko sat in silence for a moment, wondering if he would have gone down a similar path as Quinn had things been slightly different, had it not been for Ghost and Gwendolyn being there for him when he needed them. He pushed away any thought that might suggest his path was no better, a path set on vengeance and blood. Franko had promised his wife that he would walk away from it all, but he couldn't help but feel the pull to revenge.

The group had arrived back at the Capital and dropped Quinn and Bric off at the jailhouse. The three soldiers decided to celebrate their first successful level three mission by visiting a nearby pub. The mead was flowing freely, and their mouths were loosened.

"So, Gwendolyn should be coming back any day now, right?" Jac asked, his words slightly slurred.

"She is," Franko answered, the mead making him more cheerful than usual. "I can't wait. It feels like it's been ages."

Jac looked at Deni and then motioned toward Franko, as if wanting Deni to ask him something.

"So, Franko," Deni said hesitantly. "What's this that Quinn guy was saying about you and a forest demon?"

Franko's demeanor immediately went sullen. "It's nothing like what Quinn made it sound like," he said, with his eyes downcast.

Jac and Deni both jerked their heads back in shock.

"So it's true!?" Jac hollered.

Franko leaned his elbows on the table and sank his head into his hands. “I just told you, it’s not like what he was making it sound.”

“But still, you were keeping company with a demon, Franko,” Deni gasped.

“I was ten, guys. She mended my wounds after I got attacked, and we trained together for a while. That’s it,” he replied, adamantly.

“Does Gwendolyn know about this?” Jac asked, his eyes showing concern.

“No. I never told her. I guess I just don’t think she’d understand,” Franko admitted in resignation.

“Franko,” Deni pleaded. “How long were you with this demon?”

“A couple of winters,” he mumbled. “Guys, I think I’m done here. I just want to go home now,” he said as he stood up and left the pub.

As Franko walked into his room, he noticed that Gwendolyn was waiting for him.

“Gwendolyn!” he cried joyfully as they embraced. “Your training is done? I’m so glad you’re back.”

“I’m glad to be back, too, Franko,” she said as she brushed the hair on the back of his head with her fingers.

He couldn’t help but think of his last encounter with Ghost. How he had given her a hug, and she patted the hair on his head the same way in a rare show of warmth. His conscience began to weigh on him. Jac and Deni were right, he should tell his wife about her.

Gwendolyn noticed by the look in her husband's eyes that something was weighing on him heavily. “Is something wrong, Franko?” she asked, her eyebrows raised in concern.

“There’s something I need to tell you about, Gwendolyn. Something that happened after my father was killed,” he drew a deep breath and sighed. “It’s about what I did for those two years I was away.”

Franko told her everything. How he met the Forest Demon that Bruno had mentioned, who called herself Ghost. How she saved him two different times from the Garelians. How she mended his broken arm and then trained him how to fight. And how he had just seen her again earlier that day for the first time since he left the forest so many years ago.

Gwendolyn backed away from him, her eyes widening in disbelief. "Franko, I can't believe you never told me this before. Why am I just hearing this now?"

"That was a troubling time in my life, Gwendolyn," he said as he reached for her, but she slapped his hand away.

"A demon, Franko? That's inexcusable! And then you hid it from me?" she yelled, her jaw tightening.

"Gwendolyn, please," he pleaded. "It's a time in my life I tried to put behind me. I've hardly even thought of my days in the woods with her until today. You don't understand. After hearing that bandit I brought in today... If it hadn't been for Ghost. I would have turned out like him, or worse, I'd be dead."

Gwendolyn hesitated for a moment, weighing his words. "You really think so, Franko?"

He looked her directly in the eyes. "I know it, Gwendolyn. Ghost saved my life. If it wasn't for her, *we* would have never happened."

Her nerves began to slowly calm. "Okay," she said as her tension eased. "But you should have told me about this a long time ago. No more secrets, Franko. Promise?" she asked as she held her pinky in the air.

Franko wrapped her pinky with his, and they pressed their foreheads together. "I promise," he whispered.

"Good," she said, relieved as she nestled herself into his arms.

He ran his fingers through her hair and smiled at her. "You know what I told her when I saw her today?" he asked, playfully.

Gwendolyn closed her eyes and groaned in dread. "What, Franko?"

"I told her that she's the closest thing to a mother I've ever known."

Gwendolyn tried and failed to stifle a laugh. "Franko, that's somehow disturbing, sad, and funny all at the same time," she said as she sat up and looked deep into his eyes. "That's enough about that. We haven't seen each other in weeks."

She leaned in and kissed him as he held her close. The evening set in on the Capital, with Franko and Gwendolyn lost in the comfort of each other's embrace.

Chapter 35

Consorting With a Demon

A few days had passed, and Franko awoke early that morning to a knock on the door and a note slid underneath. He opened the letter and read it to himself, his heart racing.

Mission placement for the Shattered Star Brigade

Danger level: (5) Severe

Scope: As the mission has been defined as a severe level 5, a Guard member is allowed to be accompanied by no more than two soldiers of their choosing to serve as backup.

This is a scouting mission to be led by a member of the Shattered Star Brigade. Reports have been received of a cult in the north-eastern forests of Wyverly engaging in the murder of numerous merchants and patrols. Suspects are believed to belong to a group of heretics known as the Garelians. Suspects are also believed to be practicing illegal dark magic.

The scouting team's objective is to be limited only to gathering as much intel as possible about the suspects, to include information such as the following: number of cult members, hideout locations, physical descriptions of suspects, and any specifics regarding the dark magic they use, along with any other intel that can be gathered.

Suspects are extremely dangerous, and direct confrontation is only to be used if you are spotted.

Lethal Force is permitted should a confrontation occur.

Due to the nature of this mission. The Shattered Star member has (2) days to find a suitable team. The member may approach the recruiting office for backup if needed.

Franko's heart nearly leapt through his throat. "The Garelians," he gasped. His breathing became ragged as the reality set in. This is what he secretly had been hoping for the whole time. A mission from the Shattered Star to seek out the Garelians. It provided a way for him to keep his promise to Gwendolyn, while also addressing his personal desire for vengeance. *If it was the Shattered Star that requested it, then it was simply a matter of following orders, nothing personal...* he thought.

Gwendolyn slowly rose from her bed as she heard Franko's nervous breathing.

"What's wrong, Franko?" she asked as she studied his face.

"I can't talk about it, Gwendolyn. I'm not allowed to disclose the details," he said in a low voice, not lifting his eyes to hers.

"I see," Gwendolyn said passively. She gazed at his face, then at the paper he was holding, her hands clutching the hem of her gown as she exhaled sharply. "You know, you don't have to do every mission that's requested of you."

Franko jerked his head around to look her in the eyes, glaring at her intently. "It's an important mission for the kingdom, Gwendolyn," he said with an edge of tension in his words. "I'm doing the mission, and I can't talk about the details."

Gwendolyn pursed her lips and straightened up. "Fine," she said coldly. "Just make sure that your mission doesn't cause you to go back on any promises you might have made."

"I'm not talking about this right now, Gwendolyn," he replied through his clenched teeth. "I need to go and prepare." He turned and quickly stormed out of the room. Gwendolyn sat on the edge of the bed, her eyes filling with bitter tears.

Franko didn't feel that Jac or Deni had the experience needed for a level five mission, and besides, he was still a little upset with them over the conversation at the pub the other day. He stopped by the recruiting office and requested two soldiers to be assigned who had experience with missions of this nature. The clerk hesitantly accepted his request and told him they would have some assigned by the following morning.

He anxiously paced the cobblestone streets of the Wyverly capital. Unsure of what he could do to occupy his mind in the meantime. He didn't want to confront Gwendolyn again after their conversation this morning. He stopped by the Star Cathedral to see Sassporo, but he was in the middle of an urgent meeting. Franko then went to the library to see if there was anything about the Garelians. There was little in the way of useful information. All he could find was that they were a heretical sect that worshipped the Demon King Garel, who, according to the famed *Tales of the Star Sage*, had been sealed away forever several millennia ago.

The thought infuriated Franko. *All this trouble, my parents' lives taken from them. All for some crazy cult that believed there was a demon king running around based on tales from a storybook,* he thought to himself, derisively. He read that they were wiped out several centuries ago, but it was believed some pockets of Garelians still existed on the fringes of society.

Tales of the Star Sage was the most famous book in all the kingdom. School children were required to read through it. There were numerous tales, along with songs and nursery rhymes, about the famed Star Sage's exploits in battle and his sayings. Franko didn't read the book much himself, since he didn't go to school like most other children, but he was still familiar with much of it based on stories his father had told him. How the Star Sage was named Wyverly, from which the kingdom got its name. How he somehow defeated this Demon King and sealed him away with a mysterious power known as the Guardian's Glare, of which little was known. Franko never had much use for the stories, but he knew many across the kingdom still looked to it for inspiration, as it was woven deep into the nation's lore.

Once Franko realized that this would all be a dead end, he headed back outside.

To his surprise, he was greeted by a young soldier with a bad attitude and a scar on his chin.

Rondo...

"You're coming with me, Franko," he said aggressively.

"Don't start with me, Rondo. It's not the right time, trust me," Franko said as he pushed Rondo aside and kept walking.

"Stay where you are!" Rondo shouted as he grabbed Franko's arm. "You're under arrest!"

Franko jerked his arm out of Rondo's grip and turned to face him. "Get out of my face, Rondo. I'm warning you," he said, glaring at the soldier.

"Fine, we'll do it the hard way," Rondo said with a smirk as he reached for his baton.

Franko grabbed Rondo's arm with one hand while he used the other to strike him across the jaw as he hooked the back of Rondo's feet and pushed him back, causing the soldier to trip and fall flat on the ground.

Rondo gasped and then blew a whistle that was dangling from his neck. "Help, he's resisting arrest. I need backup!" he screamed.

Before Franko knew it, three more guards showed up. But these weren't just any guards. They were wearing blue vests with decorative golden embroidery like his—elite guard vests. *These soldiers aren't bums like Rondo; they're on a whole 'nother level,* he thought. Franko could recognize the familiar grit in their eyes and their tightened jaws; he had held that same look himself—they were no strangers to violence. They slowly approached with their hands on the hilts of their swords, sizing him up. He knew if he drew on them, they would not hesitate to use lethal force. Franko slowly raised his arms in surrender.

Captain Aldo walked beside them, stepping forward with his arms crossed.

"Franko of Greencourt," he said with an air of gravitas. "It's good to see you again. But you're coming with us. You... are under arrest."

"For what?" Franko asked incredulously.

Aldo inhaled sharply. "For consorting with a demon."

Chapter 36

Who Was It?

Franko was brought to a holding cell until further questioning. His caged neighbors being none other than Quinn and Bric.

"Well, looks like what goes around has finally come around," Quinn taunted, as Bric glared at Franko and growled.

Franko glared back at them. "It was you, wasn't it? You're the ones that told them about all that."

Quinn scoffed. "Nah, I wish I could say that it was, though. They wouldn't have believed me anyway."

"Then who was it?" he asked himself aloud.

"Maybe you have more enemies than you think," Bric said ominously.

Franko ignored him and thought it through as he sat in his cell. *Could it have been Deni and Jac?* he pondered. *But why would they have said anything? Especially since it would have gotten me in trouble. That's just not like them. It had to have been someone who wanted me off these missions. Maybe Rondo, but he didn't know about Ghost. Who else would want me removed from—.* His heart nearly stopped as the realization hit him... *Gwendolyn.*

Quinn could see the rage building up in Franko's eyes. "Don't stress it, kid. Looks like we may all be hanging from the gallows together soon."

"They won't hang their own," Bric sneered.

"You'd be surprised, Bric," Quinn replied. He heaved out a hopeless sigh as he lay in his bed in the cell next to Franko's. "It's too bad. I never got to even meet my baby girl."

Franko jerked his head toward Quinn, startled. "*Baby girl?* You have a daughter?"

"Two, actually," Quinn replied. "I've got a two-year-old and a newborn. Whenever I see the brightest star in the sky, I think of her," he added with a pang of longing in his words.

Franko was astonished at this revelation. "I had no idea. Two girls," he remarked, shaking his head.

"And Bric over there has a son he hardly even knows," Quinn remarked, looking over at his oversized friend. "How old is he now anyway, Bric?" The big man just sneered at his friend and turned over in his bed.

"So, you've got a wife, Quinn?" Franko asked.

"I do," he said as-a-matter-of-factly as he nodded his head. "Though, believe it or not, she can't stand me. Once I make a little coin, I swing by and give it to her. That's about the only time she's willing to put up with me," he added with a cynical chuckle. "The world is cruel to men like me, Franko."

The words of his father echoed in his mind. *A man is a blade, and the world is cruel to a broken blade.*

Just then, they heard footsteps approaching and a lock turning as the iron door to the prison hall opened with a squeal.

"Franko," Gwendolyn called out as she entered, escorted by Jaron, whom she didn't know was also Sassporo. "Franko, are you okay?" she asked softly.

"I don't want to speak to you right now, Gwendolyn," Franko said, his eyes narrowing with rage. "You just didn't want me on that mission, so you did whatever you had to do to get me removed. Didn't you?"

Gwendolyn stood with her jaw tight. "I'm sorry, Franko, but you made a promise," she said firmly, yet caring. "If I had known they were going to arrest you, I would have—"

"Save it, Gwendolyn! I don't want to hear it!"

"Young master," Sassporo chimed in. "I would encourage you to display some self-restraint as you have before."

"Stay out of this, Jaron!" Franko hollered. "Gwendolyn, I don't want to see you right now. Leave me alone."

"Franko," Gwendolyn pleaded.

"Get away from me, Gwendolyn! I don't want to see your face anymore. We're through!" he shouted as he kicked the bars of his cell.

Gwendolyn stepped back, startled. "Fine!" she snapped as she stormed off with tears in her eyes.

Franko sat with his arms crossed, fuming with anger. Sassporo let out a weary sigh.

"Young master," he said slowly and calmly. "I would like to see you in my office."

Chapter 37

The Ghost of the Sedowin

Franko sat across from Sassporo in the priest's office. His thoughts were racing as anxiety was clawing at his gut.

"What did you want to talk to me about, Sassporo?" he asked sharply.

"*Heavy are the words spoken lightly over a bottle of mead*, young master. That's what my father used to say," Sassporo remarked.

"What are you talking about, Sassporo?" Franko snapped.

"Young Gwendolyn told me about your... activities with this demon woman, but the Guard already knew before she even entered my office. Their eyes and ears are ever present in this city, young master. You were overheard by an undercover agent in the pub who handed the information over," Sassporo said as he gazed thoughtfully at his bookshelf.

"You are no longer to be held in custody, young master," Sassporo remarked calmly.

"How's that? Did you pull some strings for me?" he asked cautiously.

"You could say that. But even I couldn't get charges for consorting with a demon dropped if you were guilty of it," he said as he steepled his hands together in front of his chest, as he often did. "I was able to get the charges for assaulting Rondo dropped, however. I simply reminded him that I had witnessed him and his friends assault you a while back. He wisely decided the matter was not worth pursuing."

"But what about the charges about consorting with a demon?" Franko asked, leaning toward Sassporo expectantly.

"Those charges were dropped as well," Sassporo replied flatly.

Franko's eyes darted around in confusion. "But you said you couldn't get those dropped?"

"I said I couldn't get them dropped *if* you were guilty."

"I don't understand," Franko remarked, as he raised his hands to his sides. "I *am* guilty."

"No, you are not, young master," Sassporo remarked as he stood up and stepped over to his window, looking out over the crowded streets of Wyverly. "Your wife informed me in great detail everything you told her of this so-called *demon*. Including how you described her… all the way down to the color of her hair."

"The color of her hair? What does that have to do with anything?" Franko asked anxiously.

"Have you ever heard of the Sedowin people, young master?" Sassporo asked.

The Sedowin, he thought. The name sounded eerily familiar. He had heard that word before. Then, the realization hit him. "The Garelian guard that I fought. He said Lace was a Sedowin," Franko replied.

"Would you mind looking at my bookshelf to your left?" Sassporo said as he motioned to his bookshelf. "The second shelf down. You'll see a book, *The Forest Folk and other Forest Peoples Volume 6*."

Franko grabbed the book and brought it back to Sassporo's desk. Flipping through it to see that it covered the last one hundred years of Wyverly history concerning people of the forest.

"Are you going to tell me what this is about, or am I going to have to read this entire book?" Franko asked obnoxiously.

"A little of both, young master," Sassporo responded. "You remember the old saying, *if you want to learn about something—read, and if you want to learn quickly—listen to someone who reads*, yes?"

Franko sighed in frustration. "What do I need to do?"

"First, go to the section regarding the Sedowin people and their unfortunate fate. It's about halfway through," Sassporo said like a professor delivering a lecture.

Franko opened to that section and read through it:

The Sedowins were a peculiar tribe. Both the men and women of the tribe were known for incredible physical strength beyond their stature. They were able to navigate the forest and the trees as if it were second nature. Unlike the Forest Folk, the Sedowin people spoke the common tongue fluently and were known to go back and forth between the civilized cultures around them as they saw fit, often being called by the slang 'the chameleon people'.

The Sedowin name was derived from the old native tongue. Sedo - meaning 'red,' and Win - meaning 'women'. They were called Sedowins 'Red women' due to the fact that the women of the tribe all had distinct blood-red colored hair.

"Blood-red hair?" Franko gasped. "Ghost had blood-red hair!"

He read on:

The Sedowin people were all killed in brutal fashion by unknown assailants. Initial reports believed that it may have been the Vodavi military, but this claim has been widely disputed. To this day, it is not known for certain who killed off the Sedowin tribe. The massacre was believed to have happened around the winter of 9625 AF.

"So this happened about twenty-five years ago," Franko remarked.

Since the Sedowins were a somewhat secluded people, their bodies weren't discovered until several days after the massacre by scouts who happened upon them. All that is in our records of the people from that time were the names of the royal family, along with their fate.

King Drace. Age at time of attack: approximately 40. Killed in a massacre.

Queen Giva. Age at time of attack: approximately 40. Killed in a massacre.

Prince Lace. Age at time of attack: approximately 20. Body not recovered, assumed to have been captured.

Franko paused for a moment. “Sassporo. The man who leads the Garelians calls himself Lace,” he gasped. "He was their prince!?"

“Yes, we know that now, thanks to you, young master,” Sassporo replied. "Now please... read on..."

Franko looked back at the page. Chills ran through his body, and his eyes welled up as he read the next passage aloud.

"Princess Riva... Age at time of attack: approximately 12. Body not recovered, assumed to have been captured."

Franko’s eyes widened as his mouth dropped. “What... what does this mean?” he gasped.

“It means, young master,” Sassporo said in a low and slow tone as he leaned toward Franko. “That was no demon you were consorting with in the forest... That was Princess Riva of the Sedowin.”

He slowly turned his head toward Sassporo as another realization struck him.

"But Sassporo," Franko said, his voice low and quivering. "Riva was my mother's name."

Chapter 38

I Need to Go

"Does this mean..." Franko's voice trailed off as he held his head with his hands, overwhelmed by what he was hearing. "Does this mean... that Ghost is my mother?"

Sassporo stood silent for a moment. "It certainly sounds like a distinct possibility."

"I..." Franko began gasping for air as he started to heave. "I need to go," he whispered.

"Do what you feel you must do, young master," Sassporo said, his eyes soft with sympathy. "If you will forgive my butting into your personal affairs, I would suggest speaking with your wife before you make any further decisions."

Franko looked over his shoulder at Sassporo as he went to leave and nodded before heading out the door.

He went to the room that he and Gwendolyn had shared, only to see that she left with her belongings. There was a letter lying on the bed.

Franko,

You have made it clear that you no longer wish to be with me. I have honored your request and moved into the ladies' quarters. I have also handed in my resignation from the Wyverly Guard and will be leaving the capital once I can join a caravan to go back home to Greencourt.

I already know that your soul will not find rest until you get your revenge, in spite of the fact that you promised you would not. I will no longer try to stop you. If you change your mind, you know where to find me. If you don't change your mind, don't bother coming to see me again.

Your wife,

Gwendolyn

Franko's teeth clenched with a mixture of rage and regret. "I'm sorry for what I said, Gwendolyn. I know you were just trying to help. But you're right, I will not find rest until I kill Lace and the Garelians. I hope you understand someday, but if you don't... so be it."

Franko paced his now empty room, brewing in anger and grief, plotting out his plot for revenge until the sun set and he could make his move.

***

The night descended on the capital, and Franko was ready. He put on the blue and gold elite guard vest that Sassporo had given him, placed his broken blade in the scabbard on his belt, threw on his cloak, grabbed his staff, and headed toward the jailhouse.

Since he had gotten his clearance back, there were a few questions asked when he requested to see the prisoners. The unsuspecting and half-asleep guard didn't notice Franko nabbing the keys to the cell from him either. He entered the cellblock, the one he had just been held at as a prisoner, and requested that the guard on duty give him a moment to speak privately with the prisoners. The guard reluctantly agreed but didn't speak up when he noticed Franko's vest.

Franko approached Quinn and Bric's cells. They were both sleeping, so he rattled the bars to get their attention.

"Well, look who it is. The broken blade brigade," a groggy Quinn said with a bemused expression. "What in stars' light are you doing here?"

"I need your help," Franko replied flatly, looking over his shoulder to make sure nobody was listening in.

"No, I'm not helping you," snapped Bric.

"You either help me, or you stay here and find yourself on the wrong end of a rope, Bric." Franko bit back. "You don't have much choice, the way I see it."

"What could you possibly want our help for?" Quinn asked incredulously.

"I'm going to kill Lace and the Garelians. I need all the help I can get."

"Right," Quinn scoffed. "That's a death sentence, kid," he added as he turned his back to Franko and lay back down.

"Looks to me like it's a death sentence for you, no matter what, Quinn," Franko retorted. "This may be your only chance at freedom."

"Really?" Quinn said cynically. "And say we, by some miracle, are able to take those freaks down. Why would you let us just go free afterwards?"

"Because you understand how cruel the world can be to a broken blade," Franko replied as he looked Quinn in the eyes earnestly.

Quinn studied Franko for a moment before looking at Bric. "Okay," he said with a nod. "Let's do it."

Franko unlocked the door and led the two convicts out a back service entrance, grabbing some of the guards' swords from a storage locker on the way out. The newly formed team of three quietly snuck out of the capital under the cover of darkness with a mission to take down Lace and his followers.

***

"Where did you say their hideout was, Franko?" Quinn asked as they set up camp in a wooded area outside of the capital.

"It's some old Star Temple several days' travel to the north, deep in the northeast forest. But it will take us a good bit longer," Franko replied. "First of all, we'll have to move slowly and avoid any possibility of running into any people, guardsmen, rangers, or otherwise. And... we need to see someone else first."

"Who?" Bric asked as he took a bite of stale bread.

"An old friend," Franko said as he stared off into the distance.

Quinn looked wide-eyed at Bric, then back at Franko. "Oh, no," he sighed as he sagged his shoulders. "Don't tell me you're visiting the Forest Demon again."

"I need to talk to her before we do this," Franko responded.

"I'm not having anything to do with that demon," Bric interjected.

"I think I can get her to help us out. She'd be a valuable ally," said Franko.

"Franko, what exactly is it with you and that thing?" Quinn pressed.

Franko glared at Quinn, then anxiously rubbed the side of his face. "I don't want to say for sure until I know. But I will say this, *she* isn't a demon. She's a Sedowin woman."

"Sedowin?" Bric remarked in shock. "I heard they were wiped out years ago."

Franko shook his head. "Not all of them. Two survived. Lace and Ghost."

Quinn and Bric both looked at each other in disbelief. "This is unreal. You're saying the Forest Demon was human all along?" Quinn remarked as he quickly shook his head, as if to process the thought. "But what makes you think she'll help? Especially if it involves attacking Lace, one of her own people?"

Franko closed his eyes and drew a deep breath. "That's why I need to talk to her. *Alone*," he said adamantly. "Let's just say I may be even more *her people* than Lace."

The group gathered their belongings and set off deeper into the forest, first heading toward Quinn and Bric's old stomping grounds in the hopes of recruiting another member. And then, it was off to face the Garelians.

Chapter 39

In Two Hours

It had been weeks since Franko left. Gwendolyn had assumed that he was granted permission to go after the Garelians, so she thought nothing of it. Though she had told him that her plan was to go back home, she had decided instead to hang around the capital, hoping he'd come to his senses sooner than later.

Nobody told her the full story. That the scene among the Guard back in the Wyverly capital was a frenzy since Franko disappeared. She learned that he was believed to have gone AWOL, and on top of that, he helped two prisoners escape. Gwendolyn started hearing rumors that the Shattered Star Brigade was going to have a squad of rangers go after him. Her suspicion got the best of her, so she decided it was time to make her move.

She strapped a knife to her leg, put on her cloak, grabbed a small pack of rations, and headed out to speak with Jaron.

Once she reached the Star Cathedral, she walked right past Baxton, who was frantically trying to tell her that she couldn't just walk into his office, which is exactly what she did.

When she walked in, Jaron had been sitting at his desk, writing something on a sheet of parchment.

"I told master Baxton that I was not to be disturbed this morning," he said, not bothering to take his eyes off his writing. "I have no doubt that he tried to convey this information to you. You seem to have little concern for matters such as etiquette. I can see you and young master Franko are much alike in that regard."

"Save it, Jaron," Gwendolyn said sternly as she walked past his desk to stare out of his window. "If they send the Shattered Star Brigade after him, they'll kill him if he resists. Which he will."

"I am aware of that, young Gwendolyn," Jaron said as he folded up the paper he had been writing on and placed it in an envelope.

She quickly spun around to face him, still sitting at the desk, now writing something on the envelope. "How exactly are you involved in the guard, Jaron?" she asked accusingly. "What does a Star Priest have to do with the Wyverly Guard and the Shattered Star Brigade?"

Jaron finally turned in his seat to face her, hands folded and resting on his chest. She didn't know who he really was, and he had hoped to keep it that way, but now seemed like the right time to come clean. Jaron told Gwendolyn everything, about how he was really Sassporo, a founding member of the Shattered Star Brigade and an officially retired elite guard member, how he was still heavily involved and influential with the daily activities of the Wyverly military, especially the secretive Shattered Star missions.

"I knew there was something more to you, Sassporo," she said disdainfully. "I already know who he's with—he ran off with that woman. That witch, or demon, or whatever in stars' light she is. I'm sure of it. I want him back. So, will you help out or not?"

Sassporo tapped his thumbs together thoughtfully, arching his eyebrows as he was taken aback by her lack of formality and bluntness in addressing him. "I have been taking steps to mitigate this disaster that your husband has brought upon himself since the start."

Gwendolyn closed her eyes and bit her lip to fend off her agitation with his indirect response. "Just get to the point and tell me, Sassporo."

"I was working on it when you so rudely barged into my office, young lady," he said as he grabbed the envelope and waved it in front of him. "This is a mission update. The last mission young master Franko received was to scout activity near the northeastern border. He was never officially removed from the mission. So I have prepared a letter to update the ranking members of the Shattered Star that Franko is still on his assignment. Sometimes these assignments take weeks, or even months," he added with a shrug.

Gwendolyn jerked her head back in surprise. "I don't understand. They're saying he helped two criminals break out of jail. Mission or not, that's a problem."

Sassporo nodded knowingly, "Yes, it is. But I've accounted for that as well. I mention here that I spoke with the two convicts and made a deal with them that I would request a lighter sentence for them if they would assist, seeing as they were both familiar with the territory. They accepted, and I had Franko break them out because we could not wait for all the bureaucrats to approve such a request." He stood up and took a step toward Gwendolyn. "I hope you understand that I am using the full weight of my influence to get this matter settled as peacefully as possible."

She slowly exhaled, a bit of relief finally setting in. "I do, Sassporo. Thank you so much for this," she said, her tone softening. "But I'm going out to find him and bring him back."

Sassporo's eyes widened in concern. "I would advise against that. This is a matter for the Wyverly Guard to sort out. I am of the understanding that you resigned several weeks ago, so you are not authorized to interfere with Guard affairs."

"I don't care. I'm going to get my husband back. That's final."

Sassporo hesitated a moment before responding. "I see," he took a deep breath and stroked his salt-and-pepper beard thoughtfully. "Then I will be going with you."

She furrowed her brow as she considered his offer. "Do you really mean that? You'll go with me?"

He nodded slowly. "I will. And I think I have an idea that can allow you to go out there while still under our protection. I can write a request for a patrol mission on the border," he said as he went back to his desk and pulled out another piece of paper. "Since neither you nor I are in the guard anymore, we'll need to have a ranked officer and at least one guardsman with us. If we can do that, this will all be considered legitimate in the eyes of the guard and the crown."

"Sassporo, I truly appreciate everything that you're doing, but I just want to bring Franko back," Gwendolyn said as she stepped toward his desk. "I don't see the need to get the guard involved."

"Young Gwendolyn, please," Sassporo pleaded. "I've already violated a number of Guard policies and personal policies, for that matter, over this. Let's do at least one thing by the book. Besides, it will give us some backup. Which we can certainly use if things get... out of hand."

Gwendolyn began to nervously pace around his office. "Can I choose who comes? I don't want someone who doesn't know Franko."

"Of course," Sassporo said as he started writing a mission request letter. "Just let me know, and I'll add their names. However, I do suggest well-experienced guardsmen. Just in case young master Franko and his accomplices decide to escalate the matter."

Gwendolyn shook her head. "No. He won't resist. Not once I talk to him. I'll bring him back home. With or without help. I promise you that."

Sassporo gave her a sideways glance. "You are that confident in your ability to convince him?"

She turned to face him and stood still. "He'll come back once I talk to him. I promise," she said adamantly.

He paused for a moment as he studied her expression. "Of course," he said quietly as he continued his writing. "This would go quicker if you were to give me the names. Remember, we need at least one ranking officer and one guardsman."

"Deni and Jac," she said quickly. "The only problem is that they're not ranked officers," she said aloud as she started pacing the room again. "Who's an officer I know?" she asked as she rubbed her temple, trying to jog her memory. "The one who recruited him in Greencourt. What was his name?"

Sassporo sat still, looking at her expectantly.

"Aldo! That was his name. Captain Aldo," she blurted out.

Sassporo wrote down the names and placed the paper in an envelope. "Excellent. We have a squad now," he said as he rose from his chair. "I will have Baxton deliver this, and we can all plan on meeting there in four hours."

"I can go grab Jac and Deni myself," she said as she made her way to the door. "We'll be there in two hours."

Sassporo let out a short laugh at her tenacity. "Of course, young Gwendolyn. I will seek out Captain Aldo and meet you at the west gate—in *two hours*."

Chapter 40

I Know

In addition to the dreams Franko had of the forest village, he had also been having many troubling dreams about his father since that fateful day, but this one was different. He found himself dreaming of a familiar place. This wasn't just any dream; it was a memory.

He found himself looking upon a younger version of himself alongside his father.

I remember this, he thought as he studied his surroundings. They were in the middle of a market street in Velldale, one of the many towns of Wyverly. *The streets were empty because it was pouring rain and everyone had sought cover.*

This was my eighth birthday. We were in Velldale trying to sell some goods, he recalled. *Father and I, we found shelter under an abandoned street vendor stand nearby.*

Young Franko was tearing up, but trying desperately to hide it from his father.

I was so sad, he said to himself. *It was my birthday, and Father told me he would buy me something nice if we could sell a few items. He and I had whittled some branches we found into walking sticks a while back. Father also had found some abandoned leather jerkins that some wealthy noblemen had discarded and repurposed them into gloves, satchels, and other goods with the intent of selling them. But with the rain, nobody went to the market to shop, which meant I wouldn't be getting a gift for my birthday. I was heartbroken.*

"Are you okay, Franko?" Ringo had asked him tenderly. "Are you crying because you're sad about it raining on your birthday?"

"It's not tears, it's just rain on my face, Father," the boy said, his voice thick with emotion. But Ringo could tell he was lying.

"You don't have to hide the fact that you're sad, Franko," his father assured him. "I'm sad too. This is a special day."

"It's okay, Father," Franko replied, as he wiped his wet face with his sleeve. "Maybe the weather will clear up tomorrow."

Ringo stared ahead and nodded thoughtfully. "Perhaps," he said. "But tomorrow won't be your birthday."

"It's just another day, Father," Franko said with a sniffle.

"It is not just another day, Franko," Ringo replied as he put his arm around his son's shoulders. "I told you we would do something special, and that's just what we'll do."

He looked up at his father skeptically. "What can we possibly do?" he asked. "Everyone else is in their homes to get out of the rain. There's nobody we can sell to."

"Well, there may not be anybody to sell to, but that doesn't need to keep us from enjoying ourselves," Ringo said as he raised his eyebrows and looked at his son with playful expectancy.

"What are you talking about, Father?" Franko asked with a puzzled expression on his face.

"Well, Franko," Ringo said with a mischievous smirk. "It's been a while since you've put on your wings..."

Franko's head jerked back. "No, Father. In the pouring rain? Are you mad?" he asked in disbelief.

"Why not?" Ringo said with a shrug. "I think it's time you took flight."

"I don't want to get wet, Father. I hate the way my clothes feel when they're soaked."

"Ahh," Ringo replied with a dismissive wave of his hand. "You'll get used to it. It only feels unpleasant at first. Then, it's like a second skin."

Franko shook his head. "You can't be serious, Father. As hard as it's raining. We'll get—"

It was too late. Ringo grabbed his son and hoisted him up high in the air. And off they went.

"Put your wings on, Franko!" he hollered as he ran through the market street. They were both completely drenched within seconds.

"Father, what are you doing!?" Franko yelled back through the sound of pouring rain hitting the cobblestone streets. His body tensed up from the cold water soaking every square inch of his body.

"Hurry up and spread your wings, son!" Ringo shouted. "It's time to take flight!"

Taking flight was one of my favorite things in the whole world, Franko remarked fondly as he watched on. *Father was stronger than he looked. He could lift me up like it was nothing more than lifting an empty sack. It felt like I was soaring through the air like a bird.*

Young Franko quickly adapted to the feeling of wet clothes sticking to him, just as his father had told him. Before long, it seemed no different than taking a bath in the streams. He stretched out his body and held his arms out straight in the air, as if he were flying.

"I have my wings, Father!" the boy exclaimed, his face beaming in spite of the heavy downpour.

"We aren't stopping now, Franko," Ringo hollered. "We have much to see!"

Ringo ran through the streets with his son still held up high over his head, past the market and through the residential lanes. People looking on from their porches. Some shook their heads, others laughed along with the boy and his father, cheering young Franko on as he flew.

"It's his birthday today, everyone!" Ringo shouted for all to hear. "My boy is eight years old today!"

"Happy birthday!" the onlookers shouted with joy as they clapped at the sight of the father and son having the time of their lives.

A young woman ran out into the pouring rain and held out a bag of candy for the boy to grab. Ringo lowered his son in a swooping motion as he grabbed the small sack from the woman's hand. An older gentleman was standing on his porch. He stretched out his hand to give Franko a couple of copper coins.

Father, Franko remarked as he looked on, his eyes tearing up. *You always knew what to do to make me feel better. That was the best birthday gift I ever could have hoped for... Lace,* he thought spitefully, *he took this from me. And now it's time for him to pay.*

***

It had been several weeks since Franko, Quinn, and Bric had escaped. They had to venture deep into the woods and take long, winding paths in order to avoid any potential scouts to get to their destination, making sure to find good hiding spots and camp out for several days at a time before moving on.

"Are you sure you know what you're doing, Franko?" Quinn asked him as they approached the area of the forest he used to pick his prey.

"Yes. But like I said, I need to go alone," he whispered. "We can meet back here in two days."

"What makes you so sure we won't take this opportunity to run away?" Bric asked facetiously.

Franko looked at both of them and smiled. "Because I don't think you guys are like that. You're both men of honor, are you not?"

Quinn smiled back and nodded. "Two days, Franko. If you aren't here, we're gone. Got it?"

Franko nodded back in agreement before shaking both of their hands and heading off to meet the one who he knew as Ghost, the Forest Demon.

He came back to the spot where he had last seen her some months prior, after he took down Quinn and his men and before everything changed. He looked among the tree tops for her, his heart racing and his knees shaking.

"Ghost!" he hollered. "It's me, Franko. Again."

Franko stood still for a few minutes. Then he heard it. Tree branches creaking and leaves rustling. Before he knew it, there stood Ghost.

"Back so soon?" she asked as she landed on the ground just a few feet in front of him.

"Ghost..." he said, almost out of breath as he felt his heart pounding so hard that it was going to burst.

"Something wrong?" she said, her eerie voice sounding almost perturbed at his lack of any explanation for calling her.

His mouth felt dry as he began to have cold sweats. "I know," was all he could manage.

"*Know...* what?" she asked as she glared at him, her mouth open in a half-smile.

"I know... I know who you really are," he said as he swallowed.

"Oh, really?" she replied, her smile turning into a snarl. "And who am I?"

"You are Riva, Princess of the Sedowin," he said, his voice quivering.

Her snarl intensified, her sharp canines now showing. "Don't you ever call me by that name again, child. It means nothing to me anymore!"

He marched up to her, leaning toward her with his face just inches from hers. "Riiiiiivaaaaa," he rasped.

She lunged at him and grabbed him by the throat, pinning his back to a large tree. "You will do well to respect me in these forests, Franko!" she growled, brandishing a knife in front of his face for him to see. "Choose your next words wisely."

"It all makes much more sense now," he said, struggling to get his words out with her holding him by the throat. "The peculiar interest you showed in me from the start. The obsession with those letters. There's a reason you wanted that letter in Father's pendant. It's the same reason you wanted *my* letter... because *you* were in both of them, weren't you?"

"You... are speaking nonsense," she growled.

"Are you my mother?" he quickly blurted out.

Her eyes shot wide as she pressed him harder against the tree; he had almost forgotten how incredibly strong she was. “You!” she grunted. “You have been meddling with things that you ought not to.”

“Please,” he choked. “Please just tell me.”

“What did I tell you before, boy?” she asked him as he struggled to gasp for air. “It’s unbecoming for a man to beg.”

“Riva, please. I can’t breathe,” he said through his teeth.

“I told you never to call me by that name!” she shouted as she tossed him to the ground.

He lay on his hands and knees, gasping for air.

She leapt toward him, stomping her heel into the back of his knee to keep him planted on the ground. Then she grabbed him by the hair and yanked his head back, holding her knife to his throat. “Who have you been talking to?” she asked sternly.

“I read. That’s all,” he pleaded. “I read a book on the history of the Sedowin people. I know what happened to them—what happened to you.”

"You know nothing about me!" she shouted as she pulled his hair, causing him to groan in pain.

“You already know that my mother’s name was Riva,” he said as he grimaced. “That’s your name—or at least, it was. If I’m wrong, then just say it.”

She released him and then slapped him across the face as he turned to look at her. “You know nothing about me!” she repeated.

Franko slowly stood up, favoring his knee with one hand and the side of his face with the other. “But you are, aren’t you? You’re my mothe—”

She lunged at him again, this time grabbing him by the lapel of his cloak and pinning him once more to a tree. “Don’t you say it!”

“I deserve to know!” he snapped. “You owe me that much.”

“I owe you nothing!” she bit back.

Franko gently placed his hands on her arms, still holding his cloak. “It’s okay, Mother,” he said quietly as his tone softened. “It’s okay. I’m just glad you’re still alive.”

For the first time, he saw raw emotion on her face as her yellow eyes glistened and her lip quivered slightly. She looked less like a demon and more like the frightened little girl from his dream who lost her family.

“Please,” he said softly, his hands still on her arms. “Can you please tell me? I want to hear it from your mouth. Are you my mother?”

Her chest began to quiver as a tear rolled down her painted face. “Yes,” she whispered as she began to sob.

"Good," he replied softly. "I'm glad to hear you say that. It's nice to finally meet you, Mother. I'm your son, Franko. I love you very much." Franko pulled her close, embracing her for the first time as mother and son. Riva leaned against her son's chest, arms falling limply to her sides and eyes clenched shut as the world she had created for herself came crashing down around her.

Chapter 41

The Sound of Screams

Riva was doing her daily patrol of the forest one morning when she heard people talking in the distance. *More Forest Folk*, she thought with an exasperated sigh.

When she went to see who the intruders were, her heart began to race. A man she once knew with a trimmed beard was leading a wagon cart. *Is that... Ringo?* she said to herself from high atop the trees.

Along with Ringo was a young boy who looked to be about ten years old. "No!" she rasped. "It can't be... my son... Damn you, Ringo. Why did you bring him here?" She found her knees beginning to shake and her breathing ragged. Riva hadn't seen the boy since he was an infant.

She watched on, cautiously, being careful not to make a sound and alert them to her presence. *They can't see me like this,* she told herself frantically. *They can't see me at all. I will keep my distance until they leave... Franko... I can't believe it's really you.*

Riva kept an eye on them the entire time, all the way through the evening. She couldn't help but chuckle to herself when she heard the boy admit that he was scared of the demon that lurked in the forest.

Once they both fell asleep, she made her way down to their camp, circling them for hours. *Franko,* she thought. *You're such a handsome boy, just like your father,* she added as she looked longingly at Ringo.

The next morning, she tied some squirrel skin to a long string and made it rustle leaves not far from the boy in an attempt to rouse him awake. He eventually woke up and chased after what he thought was an easy breakfast.

"Ugh," she moaned. "He's got a lot to learn. I'll make sure to put some fear in him. That'll teach the child to wander off in the woods."

She began to move into position. "Besides," she added, "I've got a reputation as a bloodsucking demon that needs to be upheld."

She made sure to have a rag that had been soaked in slumber root oil in her satchel and made her move. Riva wasn't much for social graces, but she knew how to make an impression on someone. And she was about to make an impression the boy would never forget.

The following day, Riva noticed Quinn and his gang approaching Ringo and the boy as they were making their way through the forest. *Dammit, Quinn, you worthless thief. Stay away from them!*

She kept her distance, telling herself she would stay out of it as long as they didn't lay a finger on her son. As it turned out, Quinn's goons couldn't keep their hands to themselves.

Riva flinched when she saw Bric backhand Franko and then break his toy sword. A murderous rage filled her heart as she decided to take action.

After she quickly took down Quinn and Bric, she tossed the star pendant toward Franko. Riva remembered that pendant. She was with Ringo when he had won it in a card game the day they met many years ago.

Once Quinn and his thugs had left, she quickly hid herself so Ringo and Franko wouldn't see her, but she kept an eye on them from a distance. Riva continued to follow the two, unaware that they were being watched.

As the sun was beginning to set, she heard them talking about separating—Ringo was going to catch some fish for dinner while Franko went off on his own to get firewood.

Riva longed to speak to Ringo again, but was fearful of what he might say to her. She also couldn't pass up the opportunity to meet her son face-to-face for the first time. *This may be my only chance,* she thought.

She pursued the boy and waited for the opportune time to introduce herself, rubbing her hand with crushed slumber root to relax his nerves when she finally made her move.

***

It had been several days since Riva had seen Ringo and her son leave the forest. She had been patrolling the path regularly in hopes she would spot them on their way back. It was late one afternoon when she heard the sounds of battle in the distance.

"That's coming from the mountain pass near the Garelians' territory!" she gasped. "Please don't be Ringo and the boy!"

She sprinted toward the direction of the sounds, but it was too late. By the time she got close enough, she saw Lace and Rayla from a distance standing over the body of Ringo.

"Where did Franko go?!" she whispered frantically to herself.

She heard more sounds. *That's a child screaming for help! They must be chasing after him!*

She followed the sound of the screams, her heart racing and tears streaming down her face.

I will save you, Franko!

She spotted two Garelian guards chasing him through the woods. He was favoring his arm and crying desperately for help. One of the guards picked up a fist-sized stone near a stream and threw it at the boy, striking him in the head. Riva bolted after them as fast as she could—Franko lying dazed on the ground begging for his life. She threw a dagger and struck the first guard dead, swiftly killing the next one just in time to see Franko pass out.

Riva quickly grabbed her son and checked his wounds to make sure he was still breathing. She inspected his injured arm and could tell it was broken, so she quickly fashioned some sturdy tree limbs into a splint and tied his arm to it, then bound his arm to his body to make sure he didn't move it. She pulled out some wolfsbane and peppermint leaves and spread them around to deter any predators while she left Franko to check on Ringo.

When she arrived, Lace and the others had already gone; Ringo lay on the side of the mountain pass like discarded old garbage.

Ringo, she lamented, *you deserved so much better than this.*

She approached Ringo and went to grab his arm so she could take him to get a proper burial. But she noticed faint breathing. He was still alive, barely.

"Ringo?" she asked in astonishment. "Ringo, can you hear me?"

Ringo groaned, his eyes dim and his voice weak. "Is... Franko okay?" he wheezed.

"Yes, he'll be okay. I took him to a safe place," she replied.

"R—Riva?" he asked faintly. "You're still alive?"

"Yes, Ringo. It's me," she said gently as she held his hand. "It's been a long time."

"Is he still... mad at me?"

"No, Ringo. He loves you deeply," Riva said as she brushed the side of his face.

"I'm dying, Riva," he said. "Please, watch out for him. Tell him... I love him... Franko... he's a good boy... "

"I will, Ringo. I'm sorry for how things ended between us. I am here at your side now. You can go in peace," she said, a tear running down her cheek.

"Thank you, Riva," he said, his voice fading.

"Ringo," she sobbed. "Why did you ever involve yourself with me? If you had just stayed away from me, you would still be alive."

"You... were worth the risk, Riva."

Ringo breathed his last breath and passed away with Riva at his side. She wept over him for several minutes before carrying his body to a clear spot nearby and giving him a proper burial.

"Damn you, Ringo. Even in your last words, you charm me," she remarked as she mourned over his grave.

Chapter 42

Nothing to Say, Nothing to See

Riva sat leaning against a tree trunk, a defeated expression on her face as she stared blankly out into the distance. She was seated on the ground, one leg propped up, her arm resting on it, the other splayed off to the side. Franko couldn't help but notice how unbelievably human she looked sitting that way.

This is unreal, he thought as he studied her while he stood leaning against a tree a few paces away. *For so long, I thought she was some sort of demon or something. But she's just human. A woman. Not a very ladylike one, but a woman nonetheless.*

"What are you looking at?" she said derisively as she sneered at him.

Franko couldn't help but chuckle. "I just can't believe this," he said as he shook his head in pleasant astonishment. "But you're right, Father told me it's impolite to stare."

"It's fine," Riva sighed begrudgingly. "If anyone has that right, it's you."

He couldn't keep himself from smiling, learning that this strange creature he lived with for two years was really just his mother, set off a flurry of emotions in him.

Now feeling less bashful, he walked to another nearby tree and began to relieve himself.

Riva looked at him in a mixture of shock and disgust. "Were you raised by wolves?" she said incredulously as she watched him.

"You know, I would like to hear more about you and Father at some point," he said over his shoulder, the sound of a stream of urine splashing against the bark causing him to have to raise his voice.

"Ugh," she spat out. "I liked it better when you were afraid of me."

"And I would also like to see what you really look like," he added as he plopped down next to her.

"Do you have any idea what I would do to anybody else if they had behaved this way in front of me?" she asked spitefully as she glared at the urine-stained tree.

"But you won't do anything like that to me, will ya?" he teased as he playfully elbowed her in the side.

He began to chuckle as he thought back about his first meeting with her. *"The trees told me,"* he said mockingly. "The trees didn't tell you anything. You were eavesdropping."

He studied the horns on her head for a moment and then reached over and yanked one of them off.

"Ouch!" she hollered as she slapped him so hard across his chest that he coughed.

"I knew it!" he exclaimed. "Fake horns. You stuck these on your head with pitch. I should have known all along."

"You are getting on my last nerve, Franko," she grunted as she pulled off her other horn.

"What about those fangs in your mouth?" he asked as he began to reach toward her sharpened canines.

She swatted his hand away. "Those are real," she rasped. "And you're about to find out how real if you try to put your hands on me like that again."

"Oh, relax, Mother," Franko said with a teasing smile and a dismissive wave of his hand. "I'm not your protégé anymore. You wouldn't do anything of the sort to your own son."

She exhaled sharply and stared straight ahead. "So this is what teenagers are like, I see."

"So what do you say?" he asked as his expression changed to a more sullen one. "I'm going to fight Lace and the Garelians soon. I brought some friends along to help. This might be it for me. I may not make it out alive. I'd like it if I could at least see your real face and get to know my mother a little better."

She faced him and leaned in closer, the black and white paint on her cheeks smudged from her tears earlier. "There's nothing to say... and nothing to see," she whispered spitefully.

Franko looked down and shook his head. "Fine," he said with a sigh.

He stood up and gathered his gear. "I just wanted to see you one last time and ask you to come with us. Don't feel you have to." He started to walk away. "I'll be heading back to wait on them now. I told them to meet me in two days if you wanted to say goodbye. If not, it was good seeing you, Mother."

"Would you stop that?!" she snapped as she shot up to her feet. "You thought I wouldn't help you? That I wouldn't even say goodbye?"

"I didn't think you wanted anything to do with fighting them. That's what you got mad at me over before," he replied.

She hesitated for a moment. "It's true. I think this is a suicide mission. But you're my son, and you've made up your mind," she said as she walked up to him. "I'll go. If I die, it'll at least be by your side."

He stared at her excitedly. "Really?!" he replied. "That's good news. I'm glad!" He nodded as he hesitated to make his next request. "So... in that case... are we camping out here tonight?"

She looked at him with a quizzical expression. "Yes... Why do you ask?"

"Just wondering, that's all," he replied as he blew out a nervous breath.

Riva kept her eyes on him, her brows furrowed. "Is there... something else?" she asked.

He nervously bobbed his head while he worked up the nerve to speak again. “It’s just... what I was asking about before. I’d like to see what you look like without the paint, and I want to hear about you and father.”

“Ugh... this again,” she said as she let out an heavy sigh. “Let’s just get some food and set up for the evening.”

Franko shook his head in disappointment as they set up for the evening. He sat across the campfire from his mother. She was staring blankly at the fire, or perhaps through it. It made him think of the time when he had first stayed with her, when she had asked him about his mother.

“Can I say something?” he said, breaking the awkward silence.

Her face stayed fixed on the fire, but her eyes cut in his direction. “What now?” she said with a tinge of annoyance.

"You taunted me with your own name back then," he remarked. "Even to the point where I took a swing at you, my own mother. Unbelievable. You knew exactly what you were doing," he added as he shook his head.

She sagged her shoulders and let out an embarrassed groan. "I was so proud of you in that moment, Franko. It felt good to know that name still meant something to someone, you especially."

He leaned toward her. “And why did you ask me about my mother all those years ago, back when we were training together? You already knew I was your son.”

She closed her eyes as her jaw visibly tightened. “I was curious what your father had told you about me. That’s all,” she said slowly as she went back to staring at the flames.

Franko looked away and nodded.

“You can’t get your mind off it, can you?” she asked. “You want to hear some sort of romantic love story about us, don’t you?”

He dropped his head and shook it, hopelessly, “Can you blame me for wanting to know more about you, Mother?”

Riva sat silently for a moment, weighing his words. “I think it’s time to lie down for the evening. We need to start getting prepared. I will not discuss this any further tonight,” she said as she lay down with her back turned to Franko. “Goodnight, Franko,” she whispered.

Franko exhaled in frustration. “Fine,” he sighed. “Goodnight... Mother.”

Chapter 43

I Was Afraid

Franko awoke the next morning to see that he was alone; Riva was gone. His heart sank as he feared she might have abandoned him again.

Maybe she just went to get food, he told himself as he tried to shake away any despair. He started going through some of his belongings to grab his soap and wash in the stream. As he was getting ready, he heard footsteps approaching.

He turned to see a woman walking to the campsite and sat down on a log facing him just a few feet away. She was wearing dark brown pants with a tan-colored sleeveless shirt. He noticed her blood-red hair neatly braided and slung over the front of her shoulder. She had a coy smile, and she raised her eyebrows as her eyes met his, with an expectant expression on her face.

"Mother?" he said in disbelief, his mouth hung open.

She let out a muffled chuckle. "Franko," she replied with a slight nod.

He studied her face, now with no skull painted on it. She looked neither young nor old; her eyebrows were thick and deep red, matching her hair. He could tell by looking at her features, from her cheekbones to her jawline and nose, that her features were his as well. There was no mistake—this was his mother, without a doubt.

Riva raised her eyebrows even higher and leaned her face in, as if it were his turn to speak. "Cat got your tongue?" she teased. Her voice was no longer low and raspy, but sounded smooth, yet strong. It was like the voice of a noblewoman with a kind heart.

"I'm sorry... you're just..." His words failed him as he went silent.

She shrugged her shoulders and tried her best to hold back a smile. "Yes?"

"You're beautiful," he gasped.

Her head jerked back, and her yellow eyes shot wide. "You were expecting me to look unsightly?"

"Well, no... I..." he stammered.

"It's okay, Franko," she snickered.

"I guess... I always wondered what my mother looked like. Father never would tell me much."

"I don't blame him," she replied softly. "For anything Ringo did or didn't tell you about me. I'm just glad you don't hate me."

He caught himself still staring, and her eyes were shifting around uncomfortably. "I'm sorry," he said quickly. "I'm staring again."

"I already told you, Franko. It's okay," she said as she smiled, her cheeks dimpling. "If anyone has that right, it's you."

He laughed uncomfortably. "I wasn't sure what to expect. You're just so pretty, Mother."

She smiled and nodded as she looked off to the side. "Now you sound like your father," she sighed as she tilted her head and scratched the back of her neck.

"You know, those compliments won't get men anywhere with me," she said as she got up and sat beside him. "Well... most men," she added, patting him on his arm.

Franko sat silently for a moment. "Why didn't you say anything before, when we first met, back when I was with Father? I don't think he recognized you."

"I'm sure he didn't," Riva said as she rubbed her face anxiously. "He thought I was dead. Besides, it had been about ten years since I'd last seen him."

She let out a weary sigh and stared absently at the forest floor. "And to answer your question, I was afraid."

He turned to her, stunned. "Afraid of what?"

"I was afraid that you two would want me to come with you," she replied. "And I was even more afraid... that you wouldn't."

"Why?" he asked desperately.

"Is this the part where I tell you my life story?" she asked with a cynical laugh.

"You know I'd love to hear it, Mother," he responded with a shrug.

Riva wearily held her face in her hands. "Very well..." she sighed.

Chapter 44

The Last Prince of the Sedowin

Riva steadied herself with a heavy sigh and rubbed her face anxiously.

"I was born and raised in the Sedowin tribe. We lived not far from here, a little closer to the border. My parents were the king and queen of the tribe; they were amazing people. Lace is my older brother. He was always a bastard and a bully. He and Father would lock horns frequently. Lace felt he could be a better leader. Father ended up excommunicating him. He evidently came across the Garelians and joined their ranks, rising to the top."

"It was shortly after my twelfth birthday. I had just gotten my teeth sharpened, as was the custom for Sedowin girls that age. Lace came with a large group of followers, including his lover, Rayla, that witch," she said spitefully. "They demanded that we all join them. When Father refused,

Lace killed him and the others began slaughtering the tribe, my parents screamed for me to flee. I didn't want to just leave them to die, but I was terrified, so I ran. He didn't spare a soul. Except me, I narrowly escaped with my life."

"Mother, I'm sorry," Franko said as he listened intently. "That must have been terrifying."

"It was," Riva replied, staring blankly straight ahead. "I soon found myself surrounded by Rayla and several other Garelians. I tried to fight back, but I wasn't strong enough. I did manage to sink my teeth into Rayla's arm, making her shriek in pain, but I soon found myself on the ground, beaten within an inch of my life.

Lace soon caught up with them. He wanted to kill me right then and there.

"No," Rayla argued. "Let her die a slow death," she said. "Maybe she'll even get eaten by wolves overnight," she added as they walked off, no doubt believing I would bleed out and die before sunrise. But I somehow managed to survive."

Riva hunched over with her elbows on her knees. Franko patted her on the back, doing the best he could to comfort her.

"I'm sorry this happened to you, Mother," he said gently. "I didn't realize just how bad it was. You don't need to tell me all of this if you don't want to."

"It's fine, Franko," she replied, rubbing her face. "I think you should hear it... and maybe I need to hear it myself."

She continued. "I don't know how long it took me. But I crawled, inch by inch. Every movement was agonizingly painful. It was daybreak by the time I finally made it to a stream, but was too weak to even drink from it. That's when I first met him, Ringo, your father."

"He was about the same age as me and was traveling with a group of merchants. The others would have left me to die, but he brought me to their camp and nursed me back to health."

"It was that night that I watched him win a card game. When he won that ridiculous star pendant that he was so proud of. I ended up sneaking away one evening shortly after. I stole that pendant from Ringo as he slept, with the plan to sell it for some coin later on, but for some reason, I wasn't able to bring myself to do it. Perhaps it was guilt over stealing from the boy who saved my life," Riva remarked with a sigh, shaking her head in embarrassment as she thought about what she had done.

"I found myself orphaned and homeless, I sought refuge with the Forest Folk. They took me in for a while, but I could not adapt to their way of living, so I roamed the forests. As the years went by, I would periodically visit different towns, often stealing to survive. That's when I ran into your father again. I tried giving him back the pendant, but he refused to keep it," she paused for a moment, shaking her head once again. "That damned Ringo, he was as cocky and charming as he was handsome. I'd never met anyone like him before. So confident, so charismatic, yet earnest and kind." She turned to look at Franko once more. "Like a certain boy I know."

"I knew it!" Franko interrupted. "I knew Father was a ladies man when he was younger. You couldn't resist him, could ya?" he teased.

"Ughh," Riva groaned as she rolled her yellow eyes. "You really are just like him."

She went on. "I was young, barely a woman. As was your father young. It was a brief affair, never meant to last. At least, not to me. I soon realized that he was madly in love with me, so I used it to my advantage. I had a raging hate burning inside me, an unquenchable lust for revenge. I trained your father how to fight the Sedowin way, he took to it well enough, though he wasn't a killer—he was too gentle. I was foolish and bent on revenge. Again, like a certain boy I know," she said as she looked at him with a knowing grin.

"I convinced him to join me and take down Lace. The battle didn't go well, that's when that sword you have got broken. Ringo grabbed me and fled, saving me from certain death—though I didn't see it that way at the time. When we reached safety, I cursed your father. I said some things I deeply regret. I told him he was a coward. I said he was no different than that broken blade, useless and to be discarded. I told him I never wanted to see him again, and I left him by himself in the middle of these forests."

"Several weeks had gone by and I realized that I was with child. So I sought out Ringo, knowing he was the father. I guess I was hoping that this could somehow give you a better life. I finally found him, and you know what? The fool forgave me, he wanted me back and promised he'd take care of me and you. Your father wanted to civilize me, but I soon realized that I couldn't live that way—I was broken. So shortly after you were born, I fled... for good. One day, not long after, I ended up saving a courier in these woods who was being chased by some Garelians. As a way of paying me back for saving his life, I had him forge a letter to look like it came from the royal guard. It said that a scout had found me dying in a ditch. That my last words were to find a merchant named Ringo who was last seen in Greencourt and give him this letter, informing him that I was dead. I did this to keep him from ever coming looking for me."

"That's how I ended up here, as the Forest Demon. I wore face paint, put on some fake horns, and a cloak to hide myself so my brother and his followers would never recognize me. My presence kept them at bay, as it soon kept most travelers from using this route. The Garelians didn't know who or what I was, but they knew not to venture too deep in the forest. Any who did, never came back."

She then turned to her son. "When I first saw you that time, Franko, traveling with Ringo. I paced around your camp while the two of you slept that first night. My heart practically leapt out of my chest."

"Kind of like how my heart nearly leapt out of my chest when you jumped me the next morning and were about to suck my blood," he teased.

Riva couldn't help but chuckle at the memory. "I'm nothing if not a fan of theatrics, Franko. I wanted to make sure I left an impression."

"You certainly did that, Mother," he snickered. "It never occurred to me until later. But in all the time we spent together, you never once hunted down a human. I probably should have thought something was off about that part."

Riva nodded thoughtfully as her countenance dropped after a moment. "When I first saw you, I couldn't believe it, my own son had come to me. I know you were traveling, but I also knew we would meet some day, the Sedowin blood drew us together."

Franko stared at her, speechless, and held his hands to his head. "I had no idea. Why didn't Father tell me more of this? He told me you were killed after leaving to visit family."

"If that's what he told you, then he was being charitable. He said what he felt he had to, Franko," Riva said reassuringly. "Please don't hold anything against your father. He was a good man. The best I've ever known."

"I know," Franko sighed. "I just wish he had told me more at some point. Maybe he was planning to someday."

Riva reached in her pocket and pulled out an old-looking, folded piece of paper. "This is the letter your father had in the star pendant. I think you should read it," she said as she handed it over to him.

"You're not going to jump on me like you did last time, are you?" he asked facetiously.

"Just read the letter, child," Riva said with a stifled laugh.

He unfolded the letter and read aloud:

Ringo,

I know you think you're doing what's best, but I am not fit to live in your world. I am broken and nobody can fix me. I came back to you because I wanted to give Franko the best chance at a decent life. You are the finest man I've ever met, and I know you will give him the love he needs and deserves. He will be better off without me. Please don't let him follow me or my path. Tell him whatever you feel you need to. Make him hate me if you feel you must.

I am deeply sorry for the hurtful things I said to you before I left last time. Please know that you will forever be in my heart, and Franko will always be my shooting star.

Forever yours,

Riva

Franko teared up as he handed the letter back. “Thank you,” he said as he struggled to hold back from sobbing.

“Your father always held a special place in my heart, Franko. Maybe in another life, things could have worked out.”

“I wonder what that would have been like. Having a normal family,” he said with a pang of longing in his voice as his gaze drifted off into the distance.

Riva closed her eyes and nodded. “I’m sorry, Franko. You deserved a better mother and a better life.”

He reached out and put his arm around her. “So did you, Mother. You didn’t deserve what happened either.”

She leaned into him, tears flowing. “Thank you, Franko. You and Ringo are the only people who have ever said that to me.”

He looked at her face, reddened and eyes swollen with tears. “Is this part of the reason you wear face paint?” he asked playfully. “So people won’t see when you’ve been crying?”

Riva let out a quick laugh. “Maybe,” she said as she sniffled. “This is the last time you’ll ever see me this way, Franko. Do you understand?”

He looked at her, puzzled. “What do you mean? You’re not coming back with me after this?”

“I can’t, Franko,” she told him. “I’m not made to live out there. The forest is my home. You can come visit any time.”

He nodded in resignation. “I understand. Maybe I can start painting my face and live out here with you,” he teased.

“Please don’t, you belong out there,” Riva laughed. “And no paint," she added, "I like seeing your face.”

“I guess I don’t have a choice then,” he said as he rose to his feet. “Let’s get prepared, Mother. We meet up with Quinn and Bric tomorrow. Then, we make our move.”

***

Franko awoke the next morning, planning to get ready and meet Quinn and Bric later in the day. When he looked over, he saw his mother standing by the remnants of the campfire, looking down at it thoughtfully.

"You're awake," she said flatly, without shifting her focus away from the small pile of burnt-up wood.

"Yeah," he mumbled as he rubbed the sleep from his eyes.

As he focused on her, he saw that she had changed outfits yet again. She was wearing a white tunic that fell about halfway down her thighs. He noticed that her legs were muscular and toned. *I can see how getting kicked across the side of the head with one of those could knock a guy out cold,* he thought with a snicker.

She wore her hair in a crown braid, with strands of braided hair off to the side, wooden beads threaded throughout.

Franko studied his mother's appearance in bemusement. *She looks like she's all dressed up for a royal ceremony or something.*

She crouched down by the extinguished campfire they had used the previous evening and stuck her hand into the ash and soot. In her other hand she held some twigs and vines tied together into what looked like an ornate crown.

"Impressive handiwork, Mother," he chuckled.

She ignored his remark and shook off the excess ash from her hand.

"What are you doing, Mother?" Franko asked as he watched on.

"Come here, Franko," Riva said softly as she stood and faced her son.

"What's going on?"

"Just come to me."

His eyes darted back and forth as he cautiously approached her. "What is this about?"

"Stop talking, Franko," she replied calmly as he now stood in front of her.

He stood completely still as she took the hand she had just stuck into the campfire's remains and ran her fingers slowly across his face, leaving a trail of soot that looked like claw marks, similar to the tattoo he remembered that Lace bore on his own face. She raised the crown made of twigs and vines and placed it on his head. She studied his face for a moment, her eyes welling up, filled with admiration and pride.

Riva then lowered herself to one knee in front of him and bowed her head.

"Hail Franko, the last Prince of the Sedowin."

Chapter 45

First and Last Warning

"We've been searching for three days, soldier," Captain Aldo said with a tinge of irritation in his voice. "Are you sure he's out here, Gwendolyn?"

"I'm positive, and it's just Gwen now, Captain," she replied, still looking off into the distance, clutching her cloak to keep it wrapped over her body. "And I'm not a soldier anymore."

It was a cold and rainy afternoon in the northern forest. Gwen had been working with Captain Aldo and the others to track Franko down. She wouldn't tell anybody why it was exactly that she felt the need to do so, but either way, Franko was a highly respected and valuable member of the Wyverly Guard, and they wanted him back.

"It just seems like we would have found something by now, at least some trace of him somewhere out here," Aldo replied, shaking his head in frustration.

Gwen finally turned towards him, her jaw tightened. "He's—out here," she said adamantly.

"What makes you so sure of this?" he asked sternly. "He could have run off with that woman to stars' know where. You said so yourself, remember? We're on the border of Vodavi; we've got to be careful. Relations with the Northern Kingdom are better than they were, but still not—"

"I told you, he's out here!" she cut him off sharply.

Captain Aldo sighed and ran his fingers through his hair. "Okay, I guess we'll just keep looking," he replied in resignation as he turned to walk back toward camp to join the others.

Gwen closed her eyes and exhaled sharply. She was beginning to lose her patience; they all were. *Franko,* she thought to herself, *where in stars' light are you? I know you're here. It's time to come home. You... are coming with me.*

Unbeknownst to them, a hooded figure stood watching from the treetops.

***

As Riva shifted in place on the branch she was watching from, a pinecone fell to the ground. Gwen jerked her head and saw a figure moving in the corner of her eye.

“Franko?” she whispered.

Gwen began to follow the movement and looked behind to make sure Captain Aldo and the others didn’t spot her drifting away from the campsite, as she knew they would have under no circumstances allowed it.

She spotted the figure again. There was no mistake; someone was up there.

“Franko!” she hissed a little louder, hoping the mysterious figure had heard her.

Gwen found herself in a clearing, and yet she lost sight of the figure she had been chasing.

"Franko! If that's you, come down here," she said adamantly.

"So, little girl," an ominous voice rasped from the treetops. "You've come for Franko, have you? What is it you want from him?"

Gwen kept turning frantically, trying to place where the voice was coming from.

"That must be you," Gwen replied as she stiffened her jaw. "Whoever you are, this is none of your concern. I just want to see Franko. If you know where he is, take me to him."

"Nobody gives me orders in my forest, little girl," the voice replied. "And, as a matter of fact, it *is* my concern. I will ask you one last time. What do you want with Franko?"

"Who are you, witch?" Gwen responded defiantly. "What have you done with Franko?"

"Little girls should stay with their families where they belong," the voice replied.

"Franko *is* my family, witch. And stop calling me *little girl*," Gwen said tersely.

She heard the sound of leaves rustling and turned to see Riva perched on a tree branch several paces away, her face painted.

"I would leave now while you can," Riva said, her voice taunting.

"Where's Franko?" Gwen demanded.

"Don't take my threats as idle talk. You and your little party best stay away. Your lives could depend on it," Riva replied.

"Your little act won't scare me away," Gwen shot back. "You're no demon, you're a woman, just like me. An unusual one, but a woman of flesh and blood—nothing more."

"Oh, I'm like you, am I?" Riva mocked. "You're afraid. I can smell it from here."

"Maybe," Gwen replied as she straightened up. "You get afraid sometimes as well, I'm sure."

"Do I?" Riva replied with a mischievous smile.

"Everyone is afraid of something. Anybody who says they aren't is a liar," Gwen said as she inhaled nervously. "But that's where we differ."

"Oh, how so?"

"Because, witch, when I get afraid, I keep marching," Gwen sneered. "I don't paint my face and run into the woods to hide from my problems."

Riva lunged at Gwen so quickly that she never saw it coming. She grabbed Gwen by the chin from behind and held a knife to her throat.

"Do not speak of things you know nothing of, little girl," Riva growled as she pressed her knife into Gwen's neck. "You and your friends leave now, or next time... my blade will not stop. Understood?"

Gwen didn't respond; her breathing became ragged as she nervously gasped for air. The cold metal of Riva's blade stung her neck.

"This will be your first and last warning. Go... now," Riva hissed as she released Gwen and disappeared into the forest.

Gwen fell to her knees, holding her neck and trying to regain her composure. She felt a small drop of blood from where Riva had held the knife.

"I've got to get Franko back. Fast," she said to herself.

Chapter 46

Not Our Enemies

The rain had finally subsided, and the sun was about to set. Franko took shelter in a cave they had come across, along with Quinn and Bric. He stood at the mouth of the cave looking out toward the ancient Star Temple ruins in the distance. They weren't far from where he had his encounter with Ponzer and the Garelian guards.

Quinn looked around to make sure Riva wasn't in earshot. "Even if she is your mother, are you sure bringing that demon woman along was a good idea, Franko?" he asked as he took a puff of his pipe, the smell of the tobacco filling the air in the cave.

"That demon always gave me the creeps. Now we're supposed to go into a fight alongside her?" Bric added.

"Wouldn't you rather fight alongside her than against her?" Franko asked, without turning around to look at them.

Quinn and Bric both exchanged a glance, knowing he made a valid point. This did little to ease their mind, as neither of them slept well knowing that the Forest Demon was in camp with them.

"My ears are burning," came the raspy voice of Riva, the Forest Demon, as she neared the cave entrance.

"Did you find anything, Mother?' Franko asked as he turned to look at his two comrades and smiled as he saw the look of terror on their faces, knowing that she was listening in on them.

"We're being followed," she replied. "It looks like a small party was sent to retrieve you."

Franko sagged his shoulders and sighed. "Great, must be members of the Shattered Star Brigade. Those guys are dangerous. If they find us, it'll be a fight to the death."

"They didn't strike me as especially elite-level soldiers," Riva informed him. "Two young soldiers, not much older than you. They didn't look like much. There was one slightly older soldier who might be trouble, along with an old man in priestly garb and a young woman who seemed particularly interested in you."

Franko jerked his head over to look at his mother. "Gwendolyn? What's she doing with them?"

"Yes, I believe that was her name," Riva answered. "A mouthy little brat. I had to... persuade her a little."

Franko's eyes shot wide. "*Persuade her*? Mother, please tell me you didn't hurt her."

"Not too much," she replied. "But I did tell her that would be her one and only warning."

"I'll deal with her," Franko said sternly. "I don't know what she came out here for. I have nothing to say to her anymore."

"Either way, if you wish to avoid a... confrontation, we will need to move quickly. They aren't far from us."

"Who were the others with her? Did you get any names?" he asked.

"I believe the younger ones were named Deni and Jac. The older one was Aldo, of that I'm certain. Then the priest was named Jar—"

"Sassporo," Franko whispered.

Quinn, Bric, and Riva all exchanged a startled glance, then looked back at Franko.

"Did you say Sassporo?" Quinn asked incredulously. "No way. Uh uh, I'm not fighting some legendary warrior, Franko. I'll take my chances with the gallows."

"Same here," added Bric. "If that's Sassporo, I want nothing to do with him in a fight."

"Franko, the name I heard was Jaron, not Sassporo," Riva retorted. "I have heard of Sassporo before. I didn't know he was still alive."

"That's Sassporo. No doubt about it," Franko gasped. "What in the world is *he* doing out here with Gwendolyn?"

"If what you're saying is true, Franko, and Sassporo is among them, we need to tread carefully," Riva said. "A fight with him is certain death."

"It's almost evening," he remarked. "I say we stay here tonight, then move first thing in the morning."

"If that's what you want, Franko," Quinn said with a hint of skepticism. "But I'm serious. If Sassporo shows up, he'll be all yours."

"He'll have to go through me first," Riva said adamantly. "And if that happens, you run, Franko. Understood?"

"I'm not running anymore, Mother," Franko replied firmly. "We'll do everything we can to avoid a fight with them. They are not our enemies. But if it comes down to it, then so be it."

As they went to retire for the evening, Franko stood at the mouth of the cave overlooking the forest from on high, the Star Temple off in the distance.

Sassporo... Gwendolyn... what in stars' light are you up to?

Chapter 47

You're Coming With Me

Franko and the others were awakened just before sunrise by the shouts of Riva entering the cave.

"They're here, Franko!" she hollered. "I told you we should have kept moving last night!"

Franko jumped to his feet. "How's that possible!?" he grunted. "How could they have caught up to us?"

"They must have kept moving throughout the night," Quinn chimed in. "Like we should have."

"Dammit!" Franko shouted. "We should be able to outrun them."

"Franko!" the booming voice of Captain Aldo echoed through the cliffs outside. "It's over, Franko. We know you're there. Come out now peacefully, and there will be no conflict."

Franko emerged from the cave, Riva, Quinn, and Bric just behind him.

"This is none of your concern, Captain," Franko replied. "This is my business."

"Young master," Sassporo pleaded. "I strongly urge you to turn from this vengeance quest of yours. It will only end in much bloodshed."

"The same goes for you, Sassporo," Franko responded. "I say this with all due respect... butt out."

Gwendolyn emerged from the group, her jaw tight and determined. "No, Franko. It's over. You're coming back with me," she said sternly.

"Gwendolyn," Franko said in frustration. "Why did you come along with them. It's over between us. Go home."

"Not without you, Franko. You're done playing army. This whole ridiculous mission of yours ends now!" she snapped. "Say goodbye to your friends and that little witch that you've been shacking up with. You're coming back with me—and that's final."

Riva took a step toward them but was stopped when Franko blocked her with his arm. "I'll take care of this, Mother," he told her.

Gwendolyn looked back and forth between Franko and Riva, puzzled. "Did you just call that witch your mother?"

"Call me a witch one more time, little girl, and I'll finish what I started yesterday," Riva hissed.

"Sassporo, did you know about this?" Gwendolyn asked as she turned to the priest.

Sassporo sighed uncomfortably. "I had my suspicions, but I wasn't certain," he conceded.

"It doesn't matter, Gwendolyn. I told you, we're through," Franko interrupted.

"No, Franko," Gwendolyn replied. "We're not... I'm pregnant, Franko. And you're the father," she said as she pulled her cloak back, revealing her belly, visibly a few months along in pregnancy.

Franko stood wide-eyed as his knees began to wobble and his breathing became erratic. "Gwendolyn... why... why didn't you tell me?"

"Because I wasn't sure at the time you told me to leave," Gwendolyn replied derisively. "It doesn't matter anymore. Like I said, you're leaving this foolish quest, and you're coming home. The baby needs a father."

Franko began to heave; he leaned his hand against the cave wall. "Damn you, Gwendolyn," he gasped. "You should have said something before."

"Are you certain the child is yours, Franko?" Riva asked.

"Don't insult me, witch," Gwendolyn snapped. "Say something like that again, and this time *I'll* be the one who takes a knife to *your* throat."

Franko jerked his head toward Riva. "You held a knife to her throat?" he asked, his brows furrowed.

"I was only trying to scare her. That is all," Riva replied as she held her hands out in a placating gesture.

Franko turned back to Gwendolyn. "Gwendolyn, I—"

"It's just Gwen now, Franko," she interrupted. "It doesn't matter what that witch did anymore. I'm sure she would have handled herself differently if she knew I was bearing her grandchild. Now, as I was saying, you're coming home with—" her words stopped as she felt a cold steel blade press against her throat.

"Oh, my, my," a voice cut in. Lace appeared from out behind some trees, along with Rayla, Ponzer, and about a dozen armed guards, one of them holding Gwen while the rest had their weapons pointed at the others. "What do we have here? Invaders, it would seem. Trespassing on holy ground."

"No!" Franko shouted desperately as he reached toward Gwen.

"I wouldn't move an inch if I were you, child," Lace replied. "What should we do, Rayla? Should we kill them all, or give them a chance to bend their knees to Garel first?" he asked contemptuously as he then turned to Riva. "And Riva, here I thought you were dead. It's good to see you again, little sister," he said with a mischievous smile. "I had never gotten a good look at you before, but behold, the Forest Guardian was my loving little sister the whole time. I'm sorry, but you've already had your chance to join me; you don't get a second one."

"You dare call me your sister, Lace," she sneered. "You will not make it out of this alive. I will make sure of that."

"They no doubt came to kill us, Lord Lace," Rayla replied as she glared at Franko, then turned her gaze to Gwen.

"Giving any of them a choice to live would be a waste," Ponzer added. "Kill them all."

"Who should we start with?" the guard holding Gwen hostage asked. "Did I hear that this one is with child?" he said in a sinister tone as he lowered his blade to Gwen's stomach.

"Stop!" Franko cried out desperately.

Gwen's eyes began to light up with a furious amber glow. Both Sassporo and Lace gaped at her in astonishment; they knew what they were looking at.

"The Glare?" Lace gasped. "Impossible!"

Just then, Gwen grabbed the guard's arm bearing the knife and, in one swift motion, snapped it like a twig. The Garelian guard howled in pain as Gwen turned around and backhanded him so hard he flew backwards into a tree and fell to the ground dead.

"She has the Glare!" Lace shouted. "Kill her first, and the child inside of her!"

The guards that had been holding Aldo and the others in Gwen's group hostage lunged at her, blades drawn.

"Star shield!" Sassporo bellowed out as a protective, translucent white wall rose in front of Gwen, deflecting her attacker's advances.

"Dammit!" Rayla shouted. "They have a Star Mage! That group is the greater danger right now!" she said as she, Ponzer, and Lace all charged toward Sassporo and the others, while a group of guards faced off against Franko and the others.

Chapter 48

At Your Service

"I'm coming, Gwendolyn!" shouted Franko.

"You're not going anywhere!" hollered a Garelian guard as he swung his sword at Franko.

He effortlessly blocked the attack and was about to counter when Riva jumped in and killed the guard along with two others shortly after.

"Go, Franko!" she told him. "We'll hold them off."

Another guard who had been waiting in hiding charged at Franko, but was stopped by Bric, who kicked him so hard that he fell off the nearby cliff edge.

Franko nodded in thanks at Bric, who nodded in return, only for the large man to be stabbed from behind by another guard who had ambushed him, a blade protruding through his chest.

"Bric!" Quinn shouted desperately as he charged and cut through the guard who fatally stabbed his friend in one vicious swing. "Bric!" he cried out to his friend, who lay wounded on the ground. "Are you gonna be okay?"

Bric groaned and looked up at his old friend, blood pouring from his wound and his eyes fading. "I'm not gonna make it, buddy," he said softly as Quinn's hand was gripping his. "Tell my son... I'm sorry... for everything..." Bric breathed his last breath and died by his long-time comrade's side.

As Quinn sat weeping over his fallen friend, Franko patted him on the shoulder. "I'm sorry, Quinn," he told him softly. "I wish there were more we could do right now."

Quinn nodded, tears streaming down his cheeks. "Thanks, Franko," Quinn replied. "If you want to do something, take those bastards out," he said bitterly.

"We will, Quinn," Franko assured him. "You stay here and look out for any more that would ambush us. Mother and I will go after the rest."

***

“We must protect Gwen at all costs!” cried Sassporo. “Captain Aldo, you, Deni, and Jac get her out of here as quickly as possible!”

“Got it!” affirmed Aldo, and he and the others attempted to flee with Gwen.

“Not so fast!” Rayla shouted, clasping her hands together as she advanced on the group. “Yellow Fang!” she called out as a wave of yellow energy flew toward the group.

“Star Light!” Sassporo countered. A white flash of light flickered in the air, dissipating the yellow energy that had emitted from Rayla.

“Red Fang!” Ponzer yelled out as a wave of red energy came from him.

“Star Song!” Sassporo bellowed out, this time a cloud of white energy rose up and blocked Ponzer’s magic attack.

“You’re a crafty old bastard, aren’t you?” Lace growled.

“I will take care of him, Lord Lace,” Ponzer said as he scowled at Sassporo. “You and Rayla go on ahead. This won’t take long.”

Rayla and Lace continued to pursue Gwen, while Sassporo and Ponzer faced off.

"I see you know the proper counter spells to dark fang magic, old man," Ponzer said mockingly.

"Old man?" Sassporo laughed. "Look who's talking, you aren't exactly in the prime of your youth yourself."

"I'm still more than enough to take you down. I've got a trick that I promise you have never seen before," Ponzer said as he knelt and placed his palm on the ground. "Rage of the Haundo!" he shouted.

Sassporo looked upon his opponent, his eyes wide in astonishment. "*Rage of the Haundo*? What sort of dark magic is this?"

Ponzer began to glow red as he nearly doubled in size, his muscles bulging and tearing through his clothes. The Garelian's eyes turned a sinister yellow, and his teeth looked like fangs.

"Let's see how well your precious star magic holds up against this!" Ponzer shouted, his voice now sounding deep and guttural as he roared and lunged at Sassporo.

"Star Shield!" Sassporo cried out. The translucent white force field lit up before him.

Ponzer bashed against the protective wall, causing it to crack and eventually shatter after several blows.

"Fool!" he shouted. "I told you that you have no counter for this," he added as he grabbed Sassporo by the neck with one of his now massive hands and pinned him against a tree.

"I would love to take my time with you, but I must make sure that the woman is killed," he grunted as he squeezed Sassporo's neck. "You cannot defeat me, old man. My body is now quite literally an impenetrable weapon."

"Is... that... so?" Sassporo groaned with what little ability he had as he grabbed Ponzer's massive arm. "Shattered Star!" he rasped through his clenched teeth.

Lines of white light shot through Ponzer's arm as he released Sassporo, howling in pain. The light beams continued to spread throughout his body while Sassporo still maintained hold of the Garelian's arm.

"What... have you done to me?" Ponzer gasped as he knelt in pain, and his body turned back to normal. "How... did you do this?"

"A man your age should know better than to share too much information," Sassporo said confidently. "You said that your body was now a weapon. The Shattered Star spell is made to destroy weapons of war."

"How is this possible?!" Ponzer grunted through his teeth. "Who... are you? Who could possibly know this type of—" he stopped himself as the realization hit him. "Sassporo?" Ponzer rasped as he looked in terror at his opponent.

"At your service," Sassporo answered with a nod and a smile as he released Ponzer's arm. The Garelian's body then shattered like a glass hitting a stone floor.

Chapter 49

The Battle of the Princes

Sassporo breathed a sigh of relief and took a moment to collect himself. "So how long have you two been watching me?" he said over his shoulder to Franko and Riva in the distance as he tried to get his breath back.

"I see the stories about you are true, Sassporo," Riva said with a hint of admiration in her voice.

"We just arrived when you used that spell on that freak," Franko answered as he approached his old friend. "You did that when we were training together back then. I remember."

"What was that exactly?" Riva questioned.

"Just some star magic I picked up along the way, your majesty," Sassporo replied. "We must get moving and catch up. Your daughter-in-law is in danger."

The three chased after the others, Riva staying well ahead of them.

***

"They're catching up on us!" Jac hollered frantically.

"Slow them down as much as you can!" Aldo yelled back as he and Gwen continued through the forest as fast as they could.

"Got it!" Deni shouted. "This is it, Jac. This may be our last battle."

The two nodded at each other, standing their ground as Lace and Rayla approached.

"We don't have time to waste with these grunts!" Rayla yelled. "Yellow Fang!"

Yellow energy shot out from her, striking Deni and Jac blind, causing them to drop their weapons and cover their eyes.

"Let's keep going!" Lace shouted.

"Oh no, you don't!" Jac said as he wrapped his arms around Lace's ankles.

"Damn you!" he cursed. "Rayla, keep going. I'll take care of these two."

Lace lifted his axe to bring it down on Jac, but was stopped when Deni tackled him to the ground and started pummeling his sides.

Since Deni couldn't see, he couldn't block Lace's elbow across his jaw, which knocked him off and allowed Lace to get back up.

As Lace got back up to his feet, he swung his axe at Deni, but Jac took a wild swing and punched him in the side of his head. The blade still cut Deni badly across the side of his leg, but he was spared from certain death. Lace whipped around and slashed Jac across his side.

"I'm done wasting my time with you two!" he spat as he charged toward the direction of Gwen and the others.

"Yellow Fang!" Rayla bellowed out as she aimed her attack at Gwen.

"Run, Gwendolyn!" Aldo shouted as he shoved her out of the way at the last second and absorbed the blinding attack.

Rayla ignored Aldo and kept running toward Gwen. "You're next, little girl," she hissed as she tried to speed past the captain.

Aldo couldn't open his eyes, but he was able to hold Rayla back by reaching out and grabbing her cloak, holding her back.

"Let go!" she shouted as she pulled out her dagger and sliced him across his arm.

Rayla turned to run, but was tripped up by Aldo, who reached out and grabbed her by the leg. "You're not touching her!"

Lace charged in and swung his axe at Aldo. The captain blocked the attack with his sword, but had his weapon knocked out of his hand in the process. Aldo hadn't regained his sight yet, but still managed to deliver a vicious elbow to Lace's side, cracking one of his ribs.

Lace cried out in pain, and Rayla lunged at Aldo, stabbing him in his side with her dagger. Aldo hunched over from the attack, and Lace finished him off with a deadly swing of his axe to Aldo's back.

The captain collapsed to the ground and breathed his last breath.

"There are more coming," Rayla said as she heard Franko and the others in the distance.

"Forget them, we have to kill the girl," Lace said adamantly. "You keep going, I'll take care of them."

***

"I found something!" Riva hollered from the tree tops up ahead. "Franko, it's your friends. They are hurt."

They came upon Deni and Jac, lying wounded on the ground.

"Deni, Jac! What happened?" Franko asked as he inspected their injuries. They both had bad cuts on their arms and sides, but thankfully, not fatal.

"That woman cast her yellow fang magic, and it blinded us," Jac groaned.

"Then the man used that damned axe and cut us up pretty bad," Deni added. "He said something about not wasting any more time on us and going after Gwendolyn."

"I'm sorry, Franko. We stalled them as long as we could," Jac remarked.

"I appreciate you both," Franko told them as he patted Jac on the shoulder. "We'll take it from here."

The three continued their pursuit, with Riva leading the way, her being much quicker at navigating the forest than Sassporo or even Franko.

As they advanced, they heard the shouts and clanging steel of battle up ahead.

"Mother, can you see anything?" Franko hollered.

"It's Lace!" she cried out. "He's just up ahead!"

As Franko and Sassporo made their way to the battle, Riva stood facing Lace. He was breathing heavily and holding his bloodied axe. There on the ground before him lay the lifeless body of Captain Aldo.

"Dammit, Aldo," Franko groaned, "I'm sorry, "

"Your friend put up quite the fight. Even blinded by Rayla's attack," Lace sneered as he stood slightly hunched over from his battle with Aldo.

"It did little good," Lace added as he studied his opponents. "Rayla will catch up to that woman soon and end both her and her child's life," he scoffed.

"Mother, you're faster than any of us. Go catch up to Gwendolyn while Sassporo and I finish him off," Franko said, keeping his gaze fixed on Lace.

Riva nodded and sped off to find Gwen.

"So," Lace said with a confident grin on his face. "I see you took down all my guards, boy. And you, old man, you took out Ponzer? You must be quite the mage."

"We'll make quick work of you, Lace," Franko said with a scowl. "You're gonna pay for all the people you killed—for what you did to my father!"

"Ah," Lace said as he gave Franko a knowing look. "Now I remember you, the little coward who ran away," he mocked. "Afraid to fight, just like your father."

"I would watch how you talk, Lace," Franko replied. "Those may be your last words!" he said as he lunged toward the Garelian leader.

"You come at me with a broken blade expecting to win?" Lace mocked him as he blocked Franko's sword with his axe and countered with a vicious swing of his own, narrowly missing Franko's neck.

Franko jumped back and readied himself for another attack.

"Red Fang!" Lace shouted as a wave of red energy shot out toward Franko.

"Star Song!" Sassporo belted out as the red wave was blocked.

"Damn you, old man!" Lace growled as he lunged toward Franko with his axe.

"Star Shield!" Sassporo yelled as the force field covered Franko and blocked Lace's axe.

"Yellow Fang!" Lace quickly called as a yellow wave struck Franko before Sassporo could cast a counter spell, temporarily blinding him.

"Now your turn, old man," Lace shouted as he lunged toward Sassporo with his axe.

"Star Shield!" Sassporo bellowed out as the force field encapsulated him.

"Blade of the Shooting Star!" Lace yelled as the blade of his axe lit up with a white flame.

"What!?" Sassporo said in shock. "Star magic! Impossib—"

It was too late. Lace's axe cut through the Star Shield like paper, slicing Sassporo across the chest with deadly force.

"Sassporo!" a blinded Franko called out helplessly.

"Did you think Dark Fang magic was the only kind I know?" He asked mockingly. "King Garel does not need humans who know only dark magic; he knows it himself. Garel needs humans who can wield Star Magic as well," he said as he turned his focus to Franko. "Don't worry, boy," Lace said derisively. "You'll be joining him soon enough!"

His axe had lost its white flame, but he still lunged at Franko and took an overhead swing at his head. Franko rolled out of the way and hopped back to parry when Lace attempted a backswing.

"How are you able to dodge my attacks when you're blinded!?" Lace asked furiously.

He swung at Franko again, who leapt out of the way of his axe yet again.

"This is a waste of time," Lace spat. "I need to take care of Riva and your woman," he added as he sped off.

Franko knelt, panting for air as his vision slowly returned.

"Sassporo!" he cried out as he approached his fallen friend.

"Young... master," Sassporo answered faintly. "You are okay... That is good."

"Sassporo," Franko sobbed. "I'm so sorry."

"It is... not your fault, young master," Sassporo assured him. "I... did not anticipate that attack. His weapon, it is enchanted with Star Magic. That is how he is able to wield it. He has it... the last enchanted weapon. You... can use star magic too."

"What are you trying to tell me, Sassporo?" Franko pleaded as he knelt beside his friend and held his hand.

"What I'm saying, young master," Sassporo rasped as he struggled for air. "Is that you have Star Magic inside of you—remember the stars have called you, Franko. I knew this when we first met. You just need to call upon their power. You can defeat—"

Sassporo's words faltered as his hand went limp and his life slipped away.

"Sassporo? Sassporo!" Franko yelled desperately.

There was no response. Sassporo had perished.

"Damn you, Lace!" Franko sobbed. "You're going to pay for this."

Franko sprinted after Lace, quickly catching up with him. He saw the Garelian leader bolting toward Gwendolyn and the others. He threw his broken sword at Lace like a dagger, narrowly missing him as the blade sank into a tree just inches from Lace's head.

Lace turned around to face Franko, a sinister smile on his face. "So, I see you too have a death wish," he said mockingly as he brandished his axe.

"No, Lace," Franko replied. "This is the end for you."

"Oh really?" he asked derisively. "You saw the power I wield. What makes you think you can defeat me? You don't even have a weapon anymore," he taunted as he motioned his head toward Franko's sword, still stuck in the side of a nearby tree.

"I like to take risks," Franko rasped as he grabbed his forearm and charged toward Lace.

"Blade of the Shooting Star!" Lace shouted as the head of his axe lit up white again.

"Shattered Star!" Franko bellowed out as his forearm lit up with a white flame.

As the two lunged at each other, Franko's forearm met Lace's axe, and the blade shattered like glass as Lace was knocked to the ground.

“Impossible!” Lace shouted in disbelief as he lifted himself and looked upon his broken axe. “My enchanted axe! Damn you!”

Franko wasted no time in retrieving his sword from the tree trunk it was stuck in. He quickly was about to turn and attack Lace when his legs gave out on him and he dropped to one knee, his strength leaving him.

“Was that your first time using magic?” Lace laughed as he saw Franko struggling to lift himself up. “What a fool,” he laughed. “To use magic for the first time in a real battle.”

As Franko turned to face Lace, he felt the Garelian kick him on his side, kicking him so hard he fell on his back.

“Let’s see if the fake Sedowin fighter can take on a real one,” Lace taunted as he lifted his boot to stomp on Franko’s skull. “I’ll have to make this quick before your strength comes back to you.”

With what little energy he had, Franko quickly rolled to the side just in time to avoid the deadly blow. Lace’s foot landed on the forest floor so hard that the ground shook. Franko started to get back to his feet when he felt another kick to his side, bruising his ribs and causing him to smack into a nearby tree.

“Not so tough when you’re up against a real warrior, are you?” Lace scowled as he went to reach for Franko’s throat.

Franko swung his sword towards Lace’s arm, his strength slowly returning to him, causing the Garelian to pull back, avoiding a brutal cut by mere inches. He went to take another swipe at Lace, but he anticipated the attack and struck Franko’s arm with such force that his sword was knocked out of his hand.

“I’d like to say that it’s now a fair fight, but who are we kidding?” Lace scoffed. “You’re no match for the power of the Sedowin, even after all that training with Riva.”

"You dare call yourself a Sedowin after you betrayed and killed your own people," Franko replied spitefully, breathing heavily as he favored the hand that Lace had struck. "You wiped out the Sedowin, Lace. Now it's time to pay. The ghost of the Sedowin will not rest until you're taken down."

Lace lunged at Franko’s throat again, attempting to choke the life out of him. But Franko swiftly ducked under and performed a double-leg takedown on the Garelian, putting him on his back. He quickly followed up with a knee to Lace's groin and a vicious elbow across his mouth.

Lace grimaced in pain and spat out blood before pushing Franko off of him with his immense strength, causing him to land on the ground face-first several feet away.

As Lace collected himself, Franko noticed his broken blade lying atop some dead leaves next to him. He grabbed his sword and rose to his feet.

"Enough of this!" Lace snarled as he clasped his hands together. "This will let me put you down for good."

He drew a deep breath and began to call out a spell. "Black Fa—"

Lace's spell was cut short as Franko leapt towards him and arced his blade down on Lace's arm, severing one of the Garelian's hands.

Lace shrieked in pain as he dropped to his knees, his breath ragged. "You fool," he hissed through his clenched teeth. "You think this changes anything? If you had bent your knee to me the first chance you had, you and your loved ones might have had a chance to survive what is coming. That axe you destroyed, it possessed the only type of magic that could have possibly defeated Garel had he turned on me."

"I'm not concerned with your dead demon king, Lace," Franko replied coldly.

"You know nothing of the lore," Lace snapped back, his body going into shock. "According to Sedowin tradition, Garel can only be defeated by wielding a blade with the magic that was in that weapon. And he could only be defeated by a Sedowin Prince. I am the last Prince of the Sedowin, Franko. If you kill me now, you will doom your own kingdom." He paused for a moment to grimace in pain, his face twisted in bitterness and contempt. "Impossible!" he lamented. "How could this be? I was the chosen one. I am of royal blood, I had the enchanted blade. How? How can I be defeated!?"

"You're speaking nonsense, Lace," Franko replied evenly, wincing in pain and struggling to catch his breath. "Nobody believes in those old tales. And nobody thinks that demon Garel is coming back, except you monsters."

Lace let out a wicked laugh. "You think so?" he heaved. "You are broken like that blade of yours, Franko. I should have discarded you when you were a child. Don't you see?" he asked. "This land is cursed... *You* are cursed!"

"Your words mean nothing to me, Lace," Franko responded. "And one last thing before I end your miserable life. You said that *you* are the last Prince of the Sedowin. Did you not make the connection that Riva, Princess of the Sedowin, is my mother?"

Lace glared up at Franko. "Damn," he gasped, his eyes darting around as the realization had just struck him.

Franko loomed over the defeated Garelian priest. "That's right, *Uncle*. *You* are not the last Prince of the Sedowin," he said as he raised his blade in front of Lace, pointing it directly at the killer's face. "I am!" he shouted as he drew his arm back and plunged his blade into Lace's chest, causing him to convulse and collapse to the ground dead.

Franko dropped to one knee, his breathing ragged. "Father... Sassporo... You can rest in peace now. I have avenged you, along with all the Sedowin people," he sobbed.

He then rose back up to his feet and ran to search for Riva and Gwendolyn.

Chapter 50

I Saw Him

Gwen ran frantically, her back and abdomen aching as she instinctively held her hands over her pregnant belly. A throwing knife from Rayla grazed her shoulder.

"I've got you now, you helpless little tramp!" Rayla shouted as she caught up to Gwen, grabbing her arm and spinning her around as she took a swing with her long dagger.

Gwen pulled her knife out from the sheath on her leg and deflected the attack at the last second.

"Ah, I see you can fight a little," Rayla taunted her, her breath heavy. "I also see you can't seem to call upon the glare of your own free will. I'll have to dispatch you and the child inside of you before it flares up again."

Gwen stood, her chest heaving as she gasped for air. "Glare? I don't know what you're talking about, witch."

"You don't know your own power?" Rayla scoffed. "How pathetic. I won't risk awakening it with a prolonged battle. This ends now," she grunted as she clasped her hands together to cast a spell.

Rayla was interrupted by Riva lunging at her and jump-kicking her in the side, sending the Garelian sorceress to the ground.

"You'll have to get through me first, Rayla," Riva shouted.

The sorceress quickly recovered and got up on one knee. "No matter, Riva. I'll make quick work of you. Besides, I owe you one for this," she replied as she revealed the scar on her arm given to her by Riva when they hunted her down so many years ago. Rayla then clasped her hands together, "Yellow Fang!" A yellow wave of energy struck Riva, blinding her.

Rayla charged at Riva, dagger in hand, as she swiped at the Sedowin princess, only to have her attack blocked by Riva's own blade. Riva cut Rayla's arm and then spun and stabbed her in the gut with her knife.

"How?" Rayla gasped as blood sputtered from her mouth, and she fell to her knees. "You were blinded. I know... my spell worked."

"I have been training for this moment my whole life," Riva replied as she backed away from her opponent, her eyes clenched shut. "I made sure to hone all my senses to allow me to still fight."

Rayla looked at Riva defiantly, her chest quivering from the pain. "You may have defeated me. But you won't save the girl!" she screamed as she threw her dagger at Gwendolyn.

"No!" Riva shouted as she leapt in front of Gwen, Rayla's blade sinking into her chest.

"Riva!" Gwen shouted desperately as she saw her fall to the ground, limp.

"Dammit!" Rayla growled. "With my last bit of strength, I will take you down as well," she said as she slowly stood up and lumbered toward Gwen.

Gwen's eyes lit up again with an amber glow as she glared in fury at the Garelian sorceress.

"Ah, the Glare again," Rayla scoffed, wincing in pain from Riva's attack. "Let's see how strong it really is," she said as she clasped her hands together one last time. "Yellow Fang!"

Another wave of yellow energy shot out from Rayla, but Gwen jumped out of the way and lunged at her with blinding speed, striking the sorceress in the skull with a flying knee. A thunderous crack from the impact echoed through the forest as Rayla fell limp to the ground, her lifeless body sliding across the leaf-covered forest floor.

Gwen's eyes returned to normal as she stood panting for air, herself even unsure of how she was able to attack Rayla like that. She looked over to see Riva lying on the ground, barely breathing.

"Riva!" Gwen cried out as she sped to her side. "Riva. I'm so sorry," she sobbed.

"Gwendolyn!" Franko hollered as he approached, seeing Gwen sitting on the ground with Riva's head in her lap.

"Mother!" he cried as he sped toward them.

"Gwendolyn," he gasped. "Are you okay? Is the baby..."

"Yes, Franko. I'm fine," she replied softly. "But Riva..."

"Oh no, Mother!" he sobbed as he grabbed her hand. "I'm so sorry... I couldn't save you."

Riva's breath was faint, her eyes dim. "I saw him," she said weakly.

"What are you talking about, Mother?" Franko asked. "Who did you see?"

"Your son," she whispered. "I saw him. He looked so much like you, Franko."

"My... son?" Franko asked gently.

"He will be a mighty warrior someday, just like you," she said as her eyes welled up. "He will be just and kind. One day, the fate of the kingdom will rest on his blade. A blade that won't break. You must teach him, Franko... Don't let him follow the path of the broken blade. Teach him to love what is good, and to see what is beautiful. If you and Gwen show him the way, he will not falter," she said faintly.

"Mother, please try to save your energy," Franko pleaded as he held her hand.

"It's too late, Franko," she replied as her grip on his hand loosened. "Just promise me, you will lead him down the right path."

Franko and Gwen looked at each other and nodded, tears streaming down their faces. "We promise, Mother," he said as he looked back at her.

“Good,” she replied, her voice fading. “I’m so glad we got to be together again, Franko. I am sorry for how I treated you when you were staying with me. I let you walk out of my life without a fight that day. My heart broke every day after. You left because of how I was toward you back then."

"Mother, stop it," Franko pleaded through his tears. "You still took care of me. You mended my broken arm, you saved me from the Garelians. You were still good to me, Mother."

"You asked me a question one time, Franko," she replied softly. "I answered you harshly. I am so sorry for that. I have regretted it deeply ever since."

"Mother, I don't know what you're talking about," he responded. "What question?"

"It was when we found that little girl lost in the woods, the one we brought back to her family. When I saw you playing that game with her, holding her over your head and running so it felt like she was flying, you told her that Ringo used to do that with you." She paused to draw a ragged breath. "I was burning with jealousy when I heard you say that, how I had missed all those special moments with you. It was right after when you asked me if I would have given a dry blanket to you if you were cold and wet," she said, her voice quivering. "The answer is yes, Franko. Without a doubt. Yes. I would have given you every stitch of fabric on me if it meant I could keep you warm for just a... little... while," Riva rasped softly as her voice fell silent and her hand went limp. Her last breath escaped as she lay dead with Franko and Gwen at her side.

Franko buried his head in his hands and began to sob. Gwen reached out and put her arms around him.

“I’m sorry, Franko,” she said softly. “She really cared deeply for you. She sacrificed herself to save the baby and me.”

Franko held onto his wife. “Thank you, Gwendolyn,” he replied gently. “I think that was her way of telling me... that she loved me," he remarked through his tears.

"Gwendolyn, I’m sorry for all I put you through, and for going back on my word," he said as he turned his gaze toward her. "I hope you’ll forgive me someday.”

Gwen put her hand to his face. "You don't have to apologize, Franko. The Garelians were far more evil than I ever could have imagined. I'm glad you put an end to them. You're a hero, Franko."

Chapter 51

No Longer Broken

More Wyverly soldiers arrived several hours later. Deni and Jac were taken back to the capital to get their wounds treated. Franko would exchange letters with the two throughout the years, but life often got in the way, and they never saw each other again.

The bodies of Sassporo, Aldo, and Bric were all taken away to be honored as heroes and given a proper burial. Quinn helped Franko and Gwen take Riva's body to the mountain pass where his father had been buried. They laid her body to rest in a space right next to Ringo—two troubled souls whose lives briefly intersected and set off a chain of events that would eventually change the kingdom forever.

Quinn and Bric

Bric's only living heir, his young teenage son, Judd, was informed of his father's passing shortly after, leaving him now as an orphan. Quinn went searching for Judd to offer him a home, but found that he had joined a circus troupe and was traveling across the continent.

Quinn was granted a full pardon for his efforts. He got a job as a lumberjack, where he worked tirelessly to provide for his wife and two young daughters, Vickie and Renee.

Aldo

Aldo was given a hero's burial. After the funeral, Franko and Gwen reached out to his widowed wife and told her she was welcome to move to Greencourt, where they would treat her toddler son, Pearce, as if he were their own—an offer which was later accepted.

Franko and Gwen

Franko and Gwen moved back to Greencourt after he resigned from the Wyverly Guard. He walked away from his violent and troubled past, vowing to put all his focus on his family instead.

As the time came near for their child to be born, Franko visited Bruno in his blacksmith shop.

"Franko!" Bruno said excitedly as he went to give his brother-in-law a hug. "What brings you in today?"

"I was wondering if you could work on something for me," Franko replied as he pulled out the broken Star Pendant that he got from his father. He then took out the broken blade and set them both on a table. "Can you reforge this pendant for me using this blade?"

Bruno inspected the pendant and blade, his toddler daughter, Naomi, tugging at his pant leg. "It'll take some time. But for you, I'll gladly do it."

"Thank you, Bruno," Franko replied as he patted him on the shoulder. "Oh, and you can just call me Frank from now on. I'm proud of my time as a soldier, but I'm no longer that person anymore."

The two exchanged a handshake, and Frank tousled Naomi's hair before heading back to the cabin he and Gwen had been living in on the outskirts of town.

Father, Frank thought. *I no longer have a need for the broken blade. But I'm not discarding it—I'm giving it a new life. A new purpose.*

***

Gwen went into labor one evening shortly after. Frank waited anxiously on the front porch, bouncing Naomi on his knee.

He heard Gwen moaning in the pains of childbirth, followed by the cries of a newborn baby.

"Your wife and child are ready to see you now, Frank," announced a midwife nearby.

Frank set Naomi down, and the two walked into the bedroom to find an exhausted Gwen holding their newborn.

Gwen smiled when she saw him. "It's a boy, Frank," she said as she raised her eyebrows in excitement. "Just like your mother said it would be."

Tears streamed down Frank's face as he approached his wife and son, now having a new understanding of what people meant when they spoke of love at first sight. Gwen handed the baby over to him as Frank began to softly sob, meeting his son's gaze for the first time.

"Well, Frank?" Gwen asked expectantly. "What are you going to name him?"

Frank sniffled as he brushed the back of his hand across his son's cheek. "Rivo," he said gently as he looked deeply into the baby's eyes. "His name is Rivo."

"Rivo," Gwen repeated thoughtfully. "That's perfect, Frank."

Frank bent over to kiss his wife and then walked with the baby out to the front porch. He held his son before him, studying the boy in awe.

"Rivo..." he said softly as he lifted the baby and turned him to face the land that the boy would call home.

"One day, Rivo," he said as the tears flowed. "The fate of the kingdom will rest on your blade. A blade that will never break. Your mother and I—we will teach you. You will not follow my path," he went on. "You will see the beauty of this world and be uncorrupted by its darkness. You will have a love for this land and its people. You will love justice and live virtuously. You will face the darkness and not falter, Rivo."

He looked up at the night sky and saw a star shooting across the heavens. Frank closed his eyes and made a wish.

"My wish, Rivo," he whispered, "is that even if Gwen and I don't live long enough to see you grow up, that the lessons we teach you and the wisdom we share will always stay with you to help guide you through the storms of life."

He then turned the boy around to face him once more, gently pressing his forehead against his son's. "Because of your mother, and because of you, Rivo..."

"I am no longer broken."

The End

A Note From The Author

Read through it? Review it!

I thank you from the bottom of my heart for taking time out of your life to enjoy my work. Just like with Rivo's story, I poured my heart and soul into Franko's story as well. I hope you enjoyed reading it as much as I enjoyed writing it.

Self-published authors don't have the reach or the resources of a traditional publishing house. As such, we rely heavily on word-of-mouth referrals and reviews. If you read through this work, I humbly ask that you consider leaving an honest review on the storefront you purchased this from and/or your platforms of choice.

To discover more work from independent authors, you can check out some of the many writing groups on social media. One of my favorites is the Fellowship of the Indie Author (www.thefotia.com).

Thank you for supporting self-published authors!

-Matt

Acknowledgements

I'd like to thank my wife, Sheila, and our two kids for being so patient with me during the late nights I spent putting this story together (side note: my son's profile is the chapter art for the early chapters, as is my daughter's for chapter 3. My wife was also kind enough to let me use her profile for chapters 9 and 39). I'd also like to give a huge thank you to my editors, Daniel Riley with whimsyland.org. I cannot go without also thanking my endlessly patient cover artist, Jeff Dehut, my beta readers: Dennis Klatt as well as fellow authors TA Fehr, and Bob Perry (@RDP6455 on X) . I would also like to thank all the members of the online writing community who have given me invaluable feedback, guidance, and support throughout this process. And last, but not least, I thank God, from whom all good things come.

I certainly can't forget to mention the authors whose work inspired me: The works of C.S. Lewis, J.R.R. Tolkien, and David Eddings are certainly at the top of that list for me.

I'd like to also take a moment to acknowledge the stories, people, and events that inspire my own writing. I see the story of Franko, Rivo and their friends as a tribute of sorts to all of them and the special memories they made for me in my life. Memories of a more innocent and carefree time that I hold dear. Memories of the magic of childhood, a magic which can never be recaptured, but can still live on in stories.

I'll never forget the sense of wonder I felt as a child the first time I watched *The Princess Bride* and *The Neverending Story* and how they set my heart on fire for heroic and epic fantasy tales.

I remember the feeling of awe that filled me as a young boy the first time I laid eyes on the original *Legend of Zelda* on the NES with the gold cartridge, the cool music, and the adventure that followed while playing the game.

I remember my childhood friends, Nate and Bobby among others. Life got in the way and we lost touch over the years, but I'll never forget the time we spent as young boys venturing out to the woods behind my house to find the right sticks that would serve as our swords as we would go on to slay invisible monsters, hearts ablaze, with heroic fury in our eyes.

About the author

Matthew Linton was born in Syracuse, NY, and spent the bulk of his childhood in a small town called Chittenango (hometown of *The Wizard of Oz* creator, L. Frank Baum).

Matt has lived in four different states and has been calling South Carolina his home since 2000. He lives with his wife, Sheila, their two kids, Owen and Erin, their pet turtle, Sheldon, and their new addition, Oreo (adopted while writing this work).

When he's not writing, Matt enjoys reading, going for long walks, and spending time with his family and friends.

Matt's love of stories, and the fantasy genre in particular, was piqued at a young age. He grew up watching movies like *The Princess Bride* and *The Neverending Story* and playing video games like Zelda, Suikoden, Chrono Cross, and many more.

Other works by Matthew Linton:

Rivo: Blade of the Shooting Star. Available on Amazon and other storefronts.

The one that started it all. This is the story of Franko and Gwendolyn's son, Rivo.

For more information on Matt and his upcoming work, you can find links to his social media accounts and website at

linktr.ee/matthewlintonauthor

Also by

Rivo: Blade of the Shooting Star.

Available on Amazon and other storefronts.

https://books2read.com/Rivo

The story of Franko and Gwendolyn's son, Rivo.

"Rivo was like a shooting star; when it seemed the sun had set on the Kingdom and darkness came, he shone brightly. And like a shooting star, when the sun rose again and the darkness lifted, he was gone."

He falls in battle, only to be brought back to witness the rise of his own legend.

Drafted into the military from a small village on the outskirts of the kingdom, Rivo and his cousins are sent venturing across a land on the verge of collapse to confront a group of terrifying beasts called the Haundo, an unknown enemy with unnatural powers. His journey ends with his untimely death, a sacrifice to save a kingdom in peril.

He finds himself revived as a spirit and sent back to witness his own rise and fall again over the eventful final weeks of his life. Every battle fought, every mistake made, and every step that led to his tragic fall.

Rivo sees his final days played out again through new eyes: new friendships forged, family bonds strengthened, and a secret love he never realized was there all along.

Join Rivo as he takes part in the countdown to his final battle, a hero desperate to win back his life... and the heart of the one who loved him in silence.

www.ingramcontent.com/pod-product-compliance
Lightning Source LLC
La Vergne TN
LVHW090559110826
845146LV00001B/189

* 9 7 9 8 9 9 3 2 3 9 4 3 9 *